Praise for Mei Ng and *Eating Chinese Food Naked*

"Fortunately, Mei Ng has arrived to . . . delight readers with her excellent first novel. EATING CHINESE FOOD NAKED is terrific. Ng writes in an earthy, rhythmic prose that captivates the reader. She expertly captures the sadness and frustration of Franklin and Bell, immigrants toiling in a Queens, New York laundry; the alienation of Van, their rebellious son; the emptiness of Lily, the eldest daughter, and the confusion of Ruby, the prodigal and prodigious daughter, living at home with her parents after graduating from college. Ng can write at any level, expertly combining the explicit and sublime, humor and tragedy. . . . A marvelous book."
—*Booklist* (starred review)

"Ng's writing is full of energy. . . . EATING CHINESE FOOD NAKED succeeds as a well-drawn and sympathetic portrait of an intelligent young woman in contemporary urban America."
—*San Francisco Chronicle*

"Settings, people, and activities (especially the preparation of remarkable meals) play prominent roles and are vividly and lovingly evoked."
—*Kirkus Review*

"Clearly written. . . . Ng leads readers fluently through her heroine's travails. She handles the ingredients . . . with insight [and] adds some distinctly contemporary spice. . . ."
—*Publishers Weekly*

"Ng's compassionate, intimate, and honest portrayal of a young Chinese American woman's ambivalent homecoming is an eloquent exploration of the unshakable cultural burdens borne by family ties."
—*Ms.* magazine

EATING CHINESE FOOD NAKED

A NOVEL

MEI NG

WSP

WASHINGTON SQUARE PRESS
PUBLISHED BY POCKET BOOKS

New York   London   Toronto   Sydney   Singapore

This book is a work of fiction. Names, characters, places and incidents are either the product of the author's imagination or are used fictitiously. Any resemblance to actual events or locales or persons, living or dead, is entirely coincidental.

A Washington Square Press Publication of
POCKET BOOKS, a division of Simon & Schuster Inc.
1230 Avenue of the Americas, New York, NY 10020

Copyright © 1998 by Mei Ng
Originally published in hardcover in 1998 by Scribner

ISBN: 0-671-01145-6

First Washington Square Press trade paperback printing December 1998

10 9 8 7 6 5 4 3

WASHINGTON SQUARE PRESS and colophon are registered trademarks of Simon & Schuster Inc.

Cover design by Brigid Pearson
Front cover photo by Anastasia Gochnour

Printed in the U.S.A.

For my mom and my dad

Acknowledgments

Love to my family and to Stacy, Bethany, Don, Matt C., Matt E., Hillary, Ryan. Love to my Ronnie Mae. Thank you, Gloria. Also thanks to Leigh and Sandy. And to Cottages at Hedgebrook, Millay Colony and the Barbara Deming Fund. Where would I be without you all?

Eating Chinese Food Naked

Chapter 1

*F*ranklin was telling his wife, Bell, about the little boy who got his head caught in the power window of the family car, about the Chinese woman (a doctor) who was kidnapped from a Citibank, about the four people who were shot down outside a bowling alley, about all the people who got dead that day. Franklin likes the news.

He never have anything nice to talk. Why don't he be quiet and eat his dinner, Bell thought. He was talking and Bell was looking at his little brown teeth moving up and down. She pulled at the waistband of her pants; her stomach was getting nervous. The elastic was old and hardly made a sound when it snapped back around her. If not for her daughter, she would pick up her bowl and go down to the basement. Ruby had just moved back home and no one had told her yet that while she had been away, her mother fixed a plate for herself and went down to the basement while her father ate in the kitchen by himself.

Bell kept her face in her bowl, but every now and then her eyes opened wide as if she couldn't believe what she was hearing. What she really couldn't believe was that her baby had come back to her. And all dressed up in tight black clothes like she was going out to a party. Maybe it was her clothes that made her sit there so stiffly, as if afraid of her own family. Bell picked out a choice morsel of chicken and placed it in her daughter's bowl.

Ruby was so used to fending for herself that when the sweet white meat appeared in front of her, she nearly broke down and

cried right there at the table. It didn't matter that she liked dark meat better. Her mother was chewing on a chicken foot. "You eat," Ruby said and tried to put some meat in her mother's bowl.

Bell waved the foot in the air. "More sweet near the bone," she said.

Franklin talked louder. "So then, in the Bronx there was a big fire. Some young mother, one of those single mothers, go out and leave her babies alone. When she come home, the whole place is burning up. She run back in and try to save them, but she end up dead and the two kids too. One boy and one girl. The youngest one, a baby, all wrap up in a blanket, not even hurt. What good is it, all alone now, no father, no mother. Some luck, eh?" He talked quickly, then sat, chopsticks poised, not touching his food. He was used to Bell not answering him, but still, sometimes he hoped she would.

The night Ruby moved back home, she couldn't wait for her father to leave the table. Her mother was twisting her slipper on the floor as if she were smashing a roach; she hated bad news. Franklin pretended not to notice; he had news to tell and gosh darn it, he was going to tell it. Ruby felt his words sliding under her mother's skin, to rankle her long after he stopped talking, long after he put his bowl down, swished water around his mouth and left the table.

In the living room Franklin turned the volume up on the television and settled into his chair. Bell got up to close the door; she could smell his smoke already. "Your father and his cigars." She pushed a chair over to the sink, jumped up on it and opened the window. "Smoke, smoke, smoke. Every minute with that cigar in his mouth," Bell said. She held two fingers up to her mouth and blew imaginary smoke at her daughter.

"The minute I walk in, he tells me to buy cigars. I had to go to three stores," Ruby said. "Three stores. No one carries his stupid brand anymore."

"He told your sister to buy some, but you know her, take her time. He must be happy you're back." Bell got quiet.

"No, he doesn't like me anymore."

"He don't like no one." Perched on the edge of the sink, Bell turned her face toward the open window. Next to her, dried salted flounder hung on a string that stretched from cabinet to window. She touched them respectfully. "Remember you used to love salty fish? These are almost done. They have to get good and dry first."

"I still like it," Ruby said quickly. There was something in her mother's voice that she needed to defend herself against, as if her mother were accusing her of something that had nothing to do with fish.

"Nobody saying you don't like it. You need some pajamas?" Bell got down slowly from the sink, as if she had aged since climbing up there. She had no idea what her daughter wore to bed these days and her voice was gruffer than she had intended.

"How do you make salty fish?" Ruby knew she would never make salted fish in her life. Bell knew it too.

"On the farm I make salty duck. You open it up and make it flat with your hand so it's just like a cookie." Bell busied herself with the fish, although there was nothing she could really do with them.

"I had this duck one time. There was a sauce, with berries. And you know what? It wasn't even tough. You know how duck is. But this one, I don't know. It was real tender." Ruby talked slowly, as if it hurt her to remember that dinner; she had just thrown away all her pink clothes, cut her hair short and was ready to try kissing. But now, sitting in her mother's kitchen, she didn't think it seemed right that a duck should be that sweet and soft. "And the sauce. Oh, I told you. It had berries," she said. Her mother's hair was starting to thin on top. Ruby blinked and looked away. Just imagining that the sun might burn the top of her mother's head filled her with an angry rush of love and protectiveness.

"Berries, huh? At least it wasn't tough. Well, getting late. You better get some rest." It was only eight o'clock, but Bell didn't know what else to say. She wished she had never mentioned the fish, it seemed to upset her daughter so much. She put the kettle on and retied her apron. "Go ask your father if he want tea. Before he come in here with his smelly cigar."

Ruby was still thinking about the sun. It was May and starting to get hot. "Ma. Do you have a hat? A sun hat?"

"I walk in the shade when it gets hot."

"You've got freckles. Maybe you need a hat," Ruby said. Finding the right hat for her mother could occupy her for days. Shopping was a misery for her, but she was looking forward to it. She and her mother had always loved each other through sacrifice and worry, and ever since she could remember, her mother had been better at it. Look at their bowls. Ruby's bowl is piled high with all the good bits, and there in her mother's bowl, a heap of bones. But now that she's grown, for once in her life she would like to push away the full bowl and eat from the other, the one her mother guards with both hands.

For the four years that Ruby lived at school, she was haunted by a feeling of uneasiness, as if she had forgotten something, something important. But for the first time in her life she was having fun, so she ignored the feeling as best she could, hoping it would go away on its own. She bought new clothes that she thought disguised the fact that she was from Queens, wrote poems that were almost good, stayed up late talking with her new friends, who didn't think she was a geek at all; sometimes she drank and then she talked about how her mother had been seventeen when she was married off to a man she didn't know. But it bothered her to talk about that and after a while she didn't anymore. Late at night, she cooked. The first year there was no kitchen, so she bought a two-burner cooker and waited until the hall counselor went to sleep; then she opened the tiny rented refrigerator, which fit exactly two six-packs but which Ruby had filled with food she had bought that day at the markets on Broadway. Later, she walked down the hall to see who was still awake; she fed them. Her friends gave her cookbooks and told her she should be a cook since she wasn't going to be a journalist anymore. One morning her hair got in her way, so she cut it off. What was left stuck up all over her head. She took up with a boy she refused to sleep with for six months for fear of becoming a slut and after she became one she dated men who wanted to own her, giving her the pleasure of asserting that she wouldn't be owned (except in bed—damn that pleasure of giving in); she threw herself into her new life, but the nagging feeling wouldn't leave her. She pushed it away, but it came back stronger each time and finally, at the end of four years, she gave in, packed her things and came home again.

One summer, she told herself. One summer at home wouldn't kill her. But she would have to sleep in her mother's room again, as she had for eighteen years. Her brother and sister had slept in the same room too, but Lily had moved to the apartment upstairs and Van had moved away. Her father slept in his own room. It had been years since Ruby had slept in the same room with someone she wasn't fucking. It gave her a funny feeling. But right now she had no choice. She had $124 in her account. She would save money over the summer and then she would move out. She wasn't planning on staying forever. Not on her life would she stay forever. That's what she told herself as she packed up her things and headed back to Queens. She hadn't told her parents she was coming.

"What'd you think? We'd throw you out on the street?" her father said when she showed up and asked if she could move back for a while. He said it triumphantly, as if he had waited for years for her to ask him for something so he could say yes but begrudgingly, and there was her mother asking, "You're here for a while?" with fear and hope in her eyes. Ruby was fighting mad to be home again (she felt coerced, as if someone or something had twisted her arm behind her back) and she had answered grumpily, "I don't know how long." Her mother's face closed up again and then she disappeared into her room and when she came out again she was wearing a pale blue shirt with pleats and puffed sleeves that she had gotten on sale at JCPenneys. One side of her collar stuck up higher than the other; the buttons were done up wrong. Ruby put down her bags and it hit her right away that the blue shirt was for dress-up and that her mother had put it on for her sake. And then it was all over. The words "You win" popped into Ruby's head, although she hadn't been aware that there had been a fight going on. They didn't look at each other as she fixed up her mother's buttons. Her fingers were clumsy and damp; every little defense that Ruby had built up against her mother was stripped away. She wanted to throw herself around her mother's knees and cry out, "Don't leave me." It didn't matter that her mother wasn't going anywhere and that she herself would be the one to leave. The nagging feeling was stronger than ever (what was it she had forgotten?) and it was then that she realized that it was her mother she had forgotten; it was her mother she had left behind and had finally come back to get. Ruby buttoned the last button and took her hands reluctantly from her mother's shirt.

It is May and I am home once again in the rooms behind Lee's Hand Laundry, located in Springfield, Queens. It's not a place you would happen to end up in during your travels, you really have to want to find it. First you get on the R train and ride all the way out to the very last stop. Get off at Union Street. Go upstairs and take the bus, the Q44, the Q63, the Q29—or, if you're lucky, you can take the Q66 so you don't have to walk down from Main Street. But chances are you've come on the weekend; the 66 doesn't run on the weekends or holidays, like you should just stay home on those days. So take one of the other buses I told you about and walk down from Main. You can walk down Cedarhurst Boulevard if you want an ice-cream sandwich from the German deli, or you can walk down the side streets, where there is shade and rows and rows of single-family houses. You can tell who just got new aluminum siding. That was a good choice, nice color. But that one over there, the green one, just awful. In front are grassy plots with flowers and bushes trimmed on Saturdays by husbands in their undershirts. Among the bushes are statues of ducks and deer and the Seven Dwarfs and the Virgin Mary holding her arms out to you.

When you hit Hollis Avenue, you can see how things have changed. There are new bodegas that have the same yellow-and-red awnings and men sitting outside on crates. You can buy cold cuts, cold beer and big green bananas. There are homemade churches without stained glass, just cardboard signs: VISION OF VICTORY TEMPLE, HOUSE OF RECONCILIATION, LA PUERTA ABIERTA. Sometimes there isn't even a sign, just curtains across the storefront window, but you can hear the preaching and singing and clapping on Sundays and you can see the dressed-up people coming out afterward with light in their eyes. Some even wear hats.

Next to Shell Gas Station is the transmission place with the pack of rabid dogs that bark and jump and throw themselves against the fence when someone walks by. Better not to walk on that side.

The two bowling alleys are gone. The one on the corner, where we used to play handball, turned first into a karate school and then into a shooting gallery. Now you see people coming out of their cars carrying rifles in protective sheaths instead of bowling balls. Cardinal Lanes is now a nightclub. "Don't go near there," my father tells me. "People get shot."

In the middle of the block is Lee's Hand Laundry, where I grew up. The swinging sign that said LAUNDRY in big block letters no longer swings above the door since it fell down during a storm. My father was glad no one was walking by, or he would have gotten sued. The other sign, the one that's painted right onto the glass in red at the top of the window, LEE'S HAND LAUNDRY, is chipping off. You can barely make out the LEE'S.

The screen door slams behind you and you find you're no longer a visitor but a resident again. Visitors come for a few hours and leave when the sun goes down, before the sitcoms begin. The crumb cake or Danish ring you pick up at Hillsdale Bakery and swing back and forth as you walk down the hill is proof you are visiting. If you lived here, you wouldn't be swinging that cake like it was the sweetest thing you ever carried, the sweetest thing you were ever going to eat with a cup of tea that your mother will make for you when you get there, after she says *you shouldn't have gone to the trouble. If you lived here, you would be carrying an Entenmann's cake, like all-butter pound, or cheese buns. Now you're not swinging any kind of cake, but dragging your suitcase behind you.*

When Ruby was a kid, around the time when other little girls were being dandled on their daddy's knee, touching the stubble on his face and thinking about marrying him when they grew up, she was dreaming about marrying her mother and taking her away. She pictured a small house in the woods with a garden out back where her mother would grow vegetables. There would be no building next door blocking the sun, stunting her tomatoes and beans. In front, there would be a porch, not just a sidewalk in front of a store where people sat on lounge chairs and fanned themselves with magazines. In the evenings, she and her mother would sit on the swing bench, drink tea from a blue and white pot and talk until the night ran out.

Six years old and in love with her mother. After dinner, her mother would go out to the yard and water her garden. As she stood there with the hose in her hands, she would look past the neighbor's fence. Ruby watched her night after night before she figured out the look on her mother's face; it was a lonesome look. That was her father's fault, Ruby thought. He had gone to China and had taken her mother away from everyone she knew and brought her to a strange country, and then, to top it off, he wasn't kind to her.

The soil in the backyard was poor, there wasn't enough sun and squirrels picked the green tomatoes, took a few bites and left them on the ground. Ruby was six when she gathered the ruined tomatoes and decided it was up to her to look after her mother. Her mother was fiercely independent, though, and wasn't looking for anyone to take care of her, but slowly Ruby found little ways to help her mother and her mother came to lean on her.

Now Ruby was twenty-two and still wanted to take her mother away. It was past midnight on her first night back and she lay in bed too wired to sleep. The little house in the woods was gone and now she saw an apartment in the city—wood floors, lots of light. Sometimes it had one bedroom and sometimes two. Her mother had a lot of things. They would need hundreds of boxes and a big truck. Take a look at her kitchen counter, all cluttered with milk containers and bits of used foil and tons of jars, all the labels soaked off. Bell loved jars and ended up buying things she didn't particularly care for—stewed prunes, mint jelly, even pickled beets—just because they came in a nice jar. It made Ruby sad as hell that her mother ate all those things she didn't even like. Maybe she had made a mistake in coming back; her mother had always saved things and would go on saving things, and there was nothing Ruby could do about it. It wasn't just jars but paper bags and old zippers and bakery string and anything else she could put in a corner and forget about. Lately, Ruby had noticed that she had such tendencies herself, but she fought them by throwing everything away.

She liked her apartment bare. If her mother came to live with her, the place would get all cluttered. They would have to get a big place; her mother would have her own room and Ruby would have her own room and the two rooms wouldn't be right next to each other. You wouldn't hear every little thing the other person was doing in her room, but if you needed help and called out, she would hear you. Maybe they would live up the block from a bakery where they could get apple turnovers for dessert. Shoot, maybe they'd even get a ficus tree to put in the window. She latched on to the idea of the tree, maybe a braided one, but then again, maybe it hurt the tree to be all twisted up like that. The plain kind might be better, but a good tall one with lots of leaves. The tree helped to shake the feeling that she was fooling herself.

A two-bedroom in Manhattan. With lots of windows and wood floors. Keep dreaming, sister, she told herself. Don't be so negative, she told herself. How the hell are you going to get a house for your mother when you don't even have a house for yourself? I'll figure it out, give me a break. What are you going to do, play Lotto? Goddammit, maybe I will.

If she won Lotto, she would take her mother to Florida. Her mother had always wanted to go to Florida; she had heard that it was hot there, like her village in China. And then, a few years ago, her friends Louie and Sheila from around the corner had moved there. They used to stop by the laundry once a week with a box of Italian pastries, miniatures. Now they lived in Florida and called their old friends a couple of times a year to invite them down. They said to Bell: "When's the last time your old man took you on vacation? Tell that cheap bastard husband of yours to leave his cigar at home and come on down."

But Franklin would never go to Florida. The idea of her father getting on a plane with shorts and undershirts in his suitcase cracked her up. He didn't even walk to the corner to get his newspaper, cars made him dizzy and shoes hurt his feet. When he was in the army he had been stationed in different countries, and now he was satisfied to stay at home and resented it when anyone else went out except to run his errands. "I've already seen the world, why should I go out?" he said whenever anyone told him he should get some air.

Florida didn't cost so much; Ruby didn't have to win Lotto to take her mother on vacation. If she could put up with temping for a couple of months, they could go. A vacation, that's what they needed. Blow out of town, have some goddamned fun in life. They could visit Louie and Sheila. But Ruby didn't want to stay with them. She wanted to stay in a hotel where she could see the water as soon as she woke up in the morning.

The night she moved home, the room was too small, her hair smelled of cigars and her mother's bed was too close to hers. Her father was snoring in the room next door, making such a racket he might as well have been in the same room.

If only someone would touch her, maybe she would calm

down. Her hand played with the hem of the flowered granny gown that her mother had ironed for her and soon she was touching herself to ease the tightness. As her knees fell open, she wondered if her mother was really sleeping or whether she could hear the slippery wet sounds. Ruby waited, listened to her mother's breathing and then her hand started moving again until she was soft and open and soon she wanted to scream. She didn't because she knew that if she let out even the smallest, most harmless sound, all the rest would come rushing out and she wouldn't be able to stop. She wouldn't be able to stop all the noises she did not make in her parents' house. That no one made in her parents' house.

Now she lay in bed smelling her fingers. Christ, she smelled good. It was too bad Nick wasn't there; the smell drove him crazy. He was her boyfriend, although she didn't like that word. He wanted her to come and live with him, and when she was having a weak moment she wanted to. But then she thought about her mother sitting in the basement watching TV by herself and she got mad at him for harassing her, she called it. He'd look resigned and she'd wonder with fear in her heart how long he would wait.

He knew in his heart it was silly to think about marrying a girl like Ruby who wouldn't stop running around. But she loved him, she told him so. His friends who didn't know her thought she was a selfish bitch, the ones who knew her thought she loved him but was confused. Sometimes she cried when he fucked her, just as she was coming. That made him feel close to her and gave him hope that one day she would grow up and settle down.

Secretly, Ruby hoped she would too. At school she had wanted to sleep alone some nights, but when he knocked on her door at two or three in the morning, she only pretended to be mad. Now she wanted to call him. "Where are you?" he would say, even though he knew exactly where she was. He had never been there, but he had heard all about it for three years and had almost given up on seeing it for himself. When he first met

Ruby, he had taken her home to meet his parents, who lived in Boston. His father had given him the thumbs-up sign. His mother was a bossy lady who had decorated her house with country touches. Her extra-friendly manner was the only sign that she didn't like her son going out with a Chinese girl. Nick had pulled his mother aside and talked to her in his reasonable way and in the end she had let them sleep in the same room.

Now he was three trains and a bus ride away. Ruby got out of bed and went out to the laundry.

The store was dimly lit by the street lamp and passing cars that threw shadows across the walls. Two spray guns for spritzing clothes hung from the ceiling. Ruby remembered she hadn't been allowed to touch them or the ceiling would fall down, her father had said, but when he wasn't looking she would grab a sprayer and start a water fight with Helen Hong until he chased them outside, cursing in Chinese.

Although Franklin had never bought one plant, somehow the laundry was lush and green. Lemons and tiny sour oranges grew in the window. Aloe, good for iron burns, grew too big for their pots, crowding and pushing like too many children. Franklin hardly remembered to water them, but still they grew, defiantly, almost, not needing much from anybody.

The laundry was quiet except for the murmuring of the fish tank and occasional trains passing. Ruby sat cross-legged on the ironing table, meditating on the rows of laundry wrapped in brown paper with numbered tickets in front. There was no ironing, no starching, no heat. No Daddy's cigar puffing in her face, no Daddy telling her she'd get piles from sitting up there. No customers bowing and winking, "No tickee, no shirtee."

The last train on the Long Island Rail Road's Springfield line went by. People leaned their heads against the dark windows and had no idea that the storefront rattled and the whole house shook as they passed. After the train was gone, the only thing moving was the lonely sign at Shell Gas Station; it turned round and round with the patience of nuns, a big yellow seashell that split the night. It was hours before people would gather at the corner again, counting their change into open palms, waiting for the bus to bring them to the train to bring them to yet another day at work; hours before the first shopkeepers would arrive, unlocking the gates that covered their windows, waiting for the first sale of the day; hours before Ruby would put her shoes on, take a few coins from the register and go around the corner to Jack's Candy Store to get her father's newspaper so he could look for a story to tell his wife at dinner, a story that would make her look up from her plate and take notice of him once and for all.

In the darkened laundry she blinked her eyes, which were worse than ever. At college, with all the books she could pile on her back and carry home, soon she could only see things that were very near—words on a page, food on a plate. If it was near enough to touch, to taste, she could see it. That was it.

Graduation was over. On account of the rain, she hadn't even bothered to go, but she did put on the rented cap and gown, satiny blue, over her regular black clothes and Converse All Stars and walked around campus with her mother, who told her to stand by the blooming azalea bush, and then she took pictures to show her friends at the factory. ("Pretty, what a pretty daughter you have. Does she have a boyfriend? I have a son, same age. Good boy. Study hard, smart in school. Save money too, not like my other boy, spend all his money on clothes. Is she fussy about boys? She's kind of tall. How did she get so tall? Must be too much American food. Does she eat cheese?")

After they finished taking pictures Ruby and Bell went for tea and cake at Magda's. It was empty that day; everyone was standing in a muddy field, in their good shoes, no less, holding black umbrellas. Bell looked at the cakes. "What kind is that one? Is that nuts on top? What about that one? Oh, cranberry. Cranberry make my tongue feel funny. Do you come here a lot? What time does it close?" She did not say, "Is this where you are when I call you late at night and you're not home?"

Even though she hadn't lived so very far from the laundry, just one borough away, for God's sake, it was rare that she would visit. She told herself it was the subway ride she couldn't bear, and waiting on the platform for the train to take her closer and closer to Queens. Reading the same ads over and over gave her that closed-in feeling, and so she looked at the other people traveling to places they didn't want to go to either, driven by love or money or pain back to the places they would be happy never to see again.

Once again Ruby found herself in the four rooms she had grown up in and all she had to show for herself was a degree written in a language she couldn't even read, that hardly anyone could read. It did come with a translation, but she'd lost it the first day she got it. At first it seemed important that she find it, as if it could explain, of all the places in the world, what the hell she was doing behind the laundry again. It was only partly that she didn't have money or a job or a house of her own. There was something else, something she couldn't quite place that had pulled her away from mornings where she would reach out and touch the hair of the one sleeping next to her. This was how she figured which of her lovers would eat the plums that morning, drink the tea and slip her a dream, get on top and hold her down as if she were trying to get away.

And there were irises on the nightstand, for crying out loud. Day after day, croissants and omelettes and pancakes with cream on top. One day the butteriness was too much for her stomach. No one could hold her down long enough to keep her from running. When she stopped running, there she was, back where she had started from. She hated the entire borough of Queens and particularly the laundry and the people who lived behind it. Her hatred made the laundry and the people belong to her and her alone, and so her hatred was softened by a sense of ownership, like someone who kicks his dog and then gives it a biscuit because it is his dog to kick and to give a biscuit to. Even while she was hating it she couldn't take her eyes from the walls and the ceilings and the television, and out of the corner of her eye she could see her mother and father living in separate rooms. She put her hand to her chest and wondered how she had ever left the house that wasn't even a house but four rooms behind a laundry, how she had gone away to school and lived like a regular American girl.

Chapter 2

*I*t all started long before the day Ruby was born and Bell brought her home from Saint Claire's Hospital and moved out of her husband's room and into the kids' room so she could be closer to her baby in the night. The beginning might have been Bell's mother trying to give Bell away.

When Bell was born, her mother gave one last push and closed her eyes. When she opened them again, she saw her baby daughter and realized that she didn't have enough love for yet another baby, so she tried to give her away. Bell's older sister cried and swore up and down on her life that she would take care of her baby sister. And she did. But when Bell was ten, her mother gave her away to her neighbors, who had four sons and no daughters. A few days later, her mother came to take her back, but Bell kept her eyes on the dirt road all the way home and wouldn't speak to her mother for three days. The one time Bell's mother had tried to hold on to her baby was when the girl was seventeen and a man had come all the way across the ocean to marry her, but by then it was too late.

"My mother tried to give me away," Bell had answered when Ruby asked about her grandmother. Bell always looked triumphant when she told about all the times she had almost died when she was a little girl in China because her mother never warned her about anything. Bell thought that had been her mother's way of trying to get rid of her. "When I was little, I'm not scared of nothing. I almost got killed one time with quicksand. One leg got stuck and then the other leg got stuck. Lucky I grabbed on to a tree and pulled myself out. Another time I went fishing and a snake bit me. Right here on the leg," Bell said as she rolled up the cuff of her pants.

But maybe it all started even before Bell was born; maybe it had to do with Bell's mother being the first in her family to have big feet. Binding women's feet had fallen out of style by then. Bell's mother didn't breathe as she unraveled the stinking cloths that kept her mother's feet in their twisted little shapes. Just like holiday rice dumplings, she would kid her mother, all wrapped up tight in bamboo leaves and tied with string. When Bell was older, she took over the task of washing her grand-mother's cloths. Bell had started menstruating by then, and she hung her rags next to her grandmother's cloths in the back of the house, away from the rest of the family's laundry. The old woman leaned heavily on her as they walked once around the house, slowly and painfully, for exercise. For the rest of the day, Bell's grandmother would sit in the courtyard and tap her tiny foot. Bell's mother had inherited the same restlessness; maybe that's what made her want to give Bell away. Bell inherited it too and carried it with her all the way to America, along with her two dresses and the dishes her mother had picked out of her own kitchen to give to her as a wedding present.

Franklin came to marry Bell on account of a photograph. More than thirty years later, Ruby would find the picture in the basement as she was packing to leave for school. She held the black-and-white photograph in her hands, wanting to rip it, wanting to keep it forever. "Ma, can I take this with me?" Ruby had said.

"That old thing? What you want that for?" Bell had said.

In the picture, she stands stiffly by a vase of flowers, her hand resting on the table. The pagodas and trees behind her are made of paper. She wears the tight golden dress like a dragon wears its scales. Her stockings and shoes are spotless and her hair is hard and shiny and piled high on her head. She is not smiling but so very beautiful. If you look closely, you can see big creases in her dress.

"Are the flowers real, Ma?"

"Of course not. Everything's fake. The pagoda. The trees, the flowers, even the floor."

"Did you love him then, Ma?"

"I thought he was mean."

"Did you grow to love him? Ma, did you?"

"Love? Chinese people don't believe in love."

In the picture that made my father come all the way from America, across the ocean in a ship, to marry my mother, her face is smooth and white as a bowl. Her face isn't really that white; that's just powder.

On the day of the photograph, her father had said, "Put these on." He'd handed her a tight golden dress and high heels that belonged to her sister. "After school, you go to the beauty parlor and fix your hair curly. Then you go to the picture store and take a pretty picture."

"Everyone at school will laugh at me." She liked to wear long pants so she could run fast when it was time for gym. All the girls on one side of the yard and the boys on the other. When boys tried to talk to her after school, she'd run home. She wasn't interested in their talk, soft but with an edge that tickled her ears.

"You go put it on. Now. If you know what's good for you," he said. He walked out without looking at her. My mother took the dress and shoes and stuffed them into a bag. It sat next to her desk at school, tripping her when she got up from her seat. After school, she went to the beauty parlor, put on the dress and went to the picture store. She stood there in her sister's shoes, big and clunky. You can tell she was tired of standing still for so long.

When she got home, she ripped off the dress. She tore the stiffness from her hair, washed it in cold mountain water until it was soft again. She braided it back up, so it hung loosely down her back. Stepping from rock to rock, the sun on her body, her feet splashing in the water, she didn't think anymore about the creepy old picture taker. She looked in pools for a fish to bring to her mother. Not finding one, she picked a small bouquet of purple flowers that she would put in a bowl by the window. Her mother was happier when she brought a fish.

She found out she was getting married the day my father's ship landed and people from the village went down to the water to meet him. "Come and meet your new husband," they said to her. Her father hadn't mentioned a thing, but a month before, she had found a photograph in an envelope with American stamps in her father's desk. He wore a nice suit. His hair was shiny and black. He looked like a gangster.

My mother heard her parents fighting. "She has to go. He's a United States citizen now. He'll take her to the U.S. and she'll make him send us money. Everyone over there is rich," her father said.

"But can't you see she's so unhappy to marry him? She's still a baby. She can stay with us a little longer," her mother argued.

"She goes with him tomorrow," he said in his big-man voice, and she knew not to argue with him anymore.

My father walked into the small grocery store that smelled of thousand-year-old eggs and good tea. His legs were still shaky from the boat; his stomach still churning. Tried to save a few bucks and ended up sick as a dog. They'd have to take a plane back. In the store, he pointed to the melon that had lived in the refrigerator for a long time and plunked down his money as if it were nothing to him. The money that he had washed and starched and ironed for, the money that slipped from him so quickly in China to buy presents and parties. He invited all the family and all the villagers to feast and make merry. Whole chickens and slabs of roast pork and fancy pastries piled high on a table, everyone eating and saying how lucky my mother was to be marrying such a generous man.

My grandfather was impressed, and pleased with himself for choosing such a fine husband for his youngest daughter. My grandmother was not impressed with his honeydew and his soy-sauce chickens. She didn't like the way his money left him so easily and the way he smiled at her with too much teeth when she caught him looking at her daughter.

After a month, it was time for them to leave. My grandmother kissed her daughter and said good-bye, trying to memorize her face.

Then my mother was on a plane, flying with her new husband back to the United States, to her husband's bed in the back of the laundry, small but neatly turned down. Yellow-haired stewardesses passed around trays of cheese sandwiches, and for dessert, vanilla pudding. The thick orange slab between slices of white bread didn't smell so good. My mother looked out the window. "Don't they have rice in this country?" she said to my father.

He picked up his sandwich and pointed at it. "I bet you never ate this before. This is cheese and it's the best food in America. Everyone loves cheese there. They got it from the Italians. Wait till you try pizza." He bit into his sandwich and gestured for her to do the same. She shook her head and looked out the window at the clouds, big and white like loaves of bread split open, and no matter how hard she looked, the fluffy mountains of rice in her mother's bowls were gone.

When they finally got back to the United States, my father was surprised that all the money he had saved to open his own store was gone. Like the other Chinese people who wanted their own business, he could do two things: open a restaurant or a laundry, women's work.

Helen's parents had the restaurant two blocks away and I was jealous of the delicious food smells when all we had were strong sweaty smells and dust and lint. But Helen's mother said it was all the same, running from the hot kitchen filled with steaming black pots and sizzling woks back to the customers, who always wanted more soy sauce. "How much soy sauce can one person eat? Salty enough already."

My mother was surprised to see how dirty America was. Garbage all over the streets, even the people smelled different. The big boxes of powdered soap and the hottest water couldn't bring back the shiny picture she'd had before she came to New York.

It wasn't even Franklin's idea to marry; he was trying to please his father, who was a tough man to please. Franklin didn't meet his father until he was eighteen; his father was living in America, gambling away his money instead of sending it back to his wife in China. One day he got tired of working and sent for his son to join him. Franklin read his father's letter over and over;

he had always known that one day his father would send for him. He kissed his mother good-bye and told her that he would work hard and save money to buy her a ticket to come to America. She waited as long as she could, but in the end she died just before Franklin had saved enough to send for her.

The first question his father asked him was, "Do you know how to iron?" In the evenings after work, Franklin went to school to learn English. After one week, his father made him stop. His father wanted him to keep the store open late for any last-minute customers. Now that Franklin was there, his father had more time to chase women. Still, Franklin wouldn't say a word against him. He pretended he didn't see the women his father brought to the back of the laundry. He looked the other way and perfected his ironing, and when his father told him that he knew of a girl in China, Franklin went to marry her. For once his father was pleased with him, but unfortunately he was so pleased he tried to seduce his son's beautiful young wife. Bell told her husband and never got over the hurt when he raged at her. Somehow it was her fault; she had tempted the old guy.

Bell was seventeen when she got married and moved to America. As she changed the sheets and swept the floor and put fresh newspaper on the cabinet shelves, she thought about love. People said her husband was a handsome man; she looked at him and waited. They moved from his father's laundry in Chinatown to the farm in New Jersey and then to their own laundry in Queens, and still she waited.

Some men didn't like to look soft in public, like her father. He was a merchant. Once she had gone with him to the mountains to gather firewood. No one would respect him if he dirtied his hands carrying wood, so he had brought his daughter along. Bell walked slowly behind her father, the bundle on her back. It was heavy. Her father told her to walk faster and then he said, "Oh, let me do it." No one was there to see him. He swung the bundle onto his tall shoulders. Bell trotted beside her father and for once she wasn't afraid of the man who thundered in the house. Right before they got back to the village, they stopped and tied the bundle to her back again.

Bell was seventeen and married; her husband was stern and she tried hard to love him. She cooked the dishes he liked best, kept his house, and at night gave her body to him, but still he was stern. Sometimes he knew he was too harsh with her. Washing other people's dirt every day wore him down, and the only way he knew of boosting himself up again was to make his wife feel small, so he found fault with the way she salted the fish, the way she did her hair, the way she said good morning.

Bell waited for a sign. There was no one to ask how she could make love come. No one had talked to her about love before. She wished she had thought to ask her mother before she left China. It wasn't the sort of thing she could write in a letter. Bell thought about asking her husband but the look on his face stopped her. Bell's older sister was living in Chicago and Bell longed to talk to her, to ask if she had ever come to love her husband, who washed and folded towels with her at the Ramada Inn. It cost money to call Chicago, Franklin said. He was afraid she would get too chummy with her sister and then, before he knew it, she'd be getting on a plane and flying out there.

Bell looked around for someone else to talk to. Some of her neighbors were friendly. If she could talk to her neighbors, maybe they could tell her something. But she didn't know enough English yet. English was a funny language, but she was learning it as fast as she could.

Franklin had done the shopping for the first few weeks, but one morning he sent Bell to the store. She walked in the direction he had pointed her, but she didn't see any open markets where farmers sold live chickens that people bought and tucked into baskets or tied upside down to the handlebars of their bicycles. However, she did find a supermarket and in one aisle she found a can with a picture of a chicken on it and she thought, So that's how things work here in America. When she opened it up for dinner, she tasted the brown stuff that was gravy and not chicken at all. Over rice, it was tasty but not quite enough for two people who had worked all day.

The next day, she found the butcher. There, she pointed to the pork chops and held up two fingers. At the bakery, she stood in line behind a woman who asked for a quarter pound of cookies. Bell watched to see how many cookies that was. She needed twice that much as a present for the shoemaker's wife, who had brought over a dish of spaghetti when Bell first arrived. When it was her turn, Bell said, "Two quarter pound cookie." The woman behind the counter had eyes that were blue, of all the crazy colors. "Dearie, you want half a pound?" she asked. Bell got a little annoyed. "I want two quarter pound," she said. Everyone in the store laughed and she didn't know why until she came home and asked her husband.

He laughed at her too. He told her she didn't need to go to English school at night. In the pit of his stomach where his ulcer waited, he had a sinking feeling. At night school, there were plenty of men who thought nothing of seducing young wives away from their husbands. The men worked as waiters, their pockets were full of money, and some were good-looking to boot. When he thought that his wife might compare him to one of those dandies, he got so mad he wanted to hit her. The sinking feeling in his stomach told him to keep her at home. He didn't tell her about the feeling but said he would teach her everything as they ironed side by side in the laundry.

What is this? This is a shirt. What is this? This is an iron. What is this? This is a hanger. What is this? This is a dollar. What are we doing? We are talking. We are ironing. We are working hard. The baby is sleeping.

Who is that? That is the milkman. That is the mailman. That is the shoemaker, who lives next door. That is the customer, who brings his smelly clothes. This is the laundryman, who cleans the customer's smelly clothes. This is the laundryman's wife, who came all the way from China to marry the laundryman. That is the laundryman's baby, who will grow up and wear wrinkled clothes.

Where do you live? I live in the United States. I live in New York. I was born in China. My mother and father live in China. China is far away. A letter takes a long time to get there. I live in the United States now. My sister lives in Chicago. It costs money to call her. The baby is an American citizen. The baby is crying.

What time is it? It is eight o'clock. We eat breakfast at eight. What time is it? It is nine o'clock. We iron shirts at nine. It is ten o'clock. We iron more shirts at ten. It is eleven o'clock. We starch shirts at eleven. It is twelve o'clock. We eat lunch at twelve. We eat rice, chicken, bok choy.

But look. This here is American food. This is bread. American people eat a lot of bread. They eat it cold with butter. Or with cheese. Or, if you're really lucky, you eat it with ham. This is good food; here, taste it. This is Campbell's soup, and this is a cheese sandwich. The good thing about bread is you can make it into toast.

This is a car. No, you don't have to learn how to drive. This is a station wagon, a street, a stop sign. This is a hand, a leg, mouth, ears, nose. This is a marriage. This is America. This is American money. This is the life you didn't bargain for, this is the life you left China for. There are some words that are hard to say. Like three. Like thirty-three. Free. Firty-Free. No, put your tongue here, like this, between your teeth. Th. Th. Th. Thank you. Can't you even say thank you?

This is a kiss. A good-night kiss. This is lying in bed. This is for you. This is making babies. No, no, no, this is not duty, this is a good time.

He cut out newspaper articles and read them to her. See, you can find out about the whole country without ever going outside. He didn't like his wife going out by herself. Bell listened to his news stories. Every day, bad news. She went to the store and came right home. Franklin didn't mind taking her out on the weekend, as long as she held on to his arm. "Look. Here's Tad's Steak House." He ordered two big T-bones. "See how much meat you can eat here?"

He showed her this new country as if it were of his own making. Macy's, Coney Island, the Automat where you pushed a button and food went round and round. When you saw something you liked, you put in the silver token and voilà! the door opened and you got your ham and cheese sandwich, your custard pie, your Jell-O. He took her to the World's Fair in Flushing Meadows; a stranger took a picture of them standing by the Unisphere. Franklin was dapper in a short-sleeved white shirt and Bell looked almost Mexican with her round face, two thick braids, her full-flowered skirt. On the upper deck of the Staten Island Ferry, he undid her braids so he could see her hair fly in the wind.

After he had shown her everything he could, he stopped wanting to go out. He started getting carsick, train-sick, bus-sick. He sold his Chevrolet to his cousin in Chinatown. He wanted his wife to stay in with him, but she was young and wanted to see the city, see this big country of his.

It was nice of her husband to teach her English and maybe it would lead to love, she thought. Bell studied hard, but sometimes she forgot how to say a word and had to ask her husband again. "You're too dumb to learn anything," he'd say. Bell tried to be a good sport. She laughed too. But inside her, something closed up. She stopped asking him to say words in English. Instead she looked at the words painted on the side of trucks and tried to see what was inside. Maybe love wasn't so important after all. She would stop waiting for it if it wasn't going to come to her. It would be best to act as if nothing bothered her, she decided, and after a while, she believed that nothing did. She learned to do for herself and it wasn't until years later, after she had her babies, after she moved out of her husband's room, after she got sick and had to have what she called her woman's operation, that she realized she had been waiting all that time.

Chapter 3

Van was born on the farm in New Jersey. His father still had black hair and his mother still wore dresses. For eight years, Van was the only child. He played alone on the farm, and when they moved to the city, he still played alone. Bell didn't know what to do with her wild little boy. She tried scolding, pleading and reasoning with the child, but nothing worked. Franklin tried yelling, hitting and even a little coaxing, but that didn't work either.

Franklin didn't know the first thing about being a father but figured the important thing was to provide, not like his own father, who had left China before seeing his son born and then never sent a dime. When Van was born, Franklin had dreams for him. His son had his own ideas. Franklin tried to beat them out of him.

Seven years later they had Lily. Bell was afraid Van would hurt the baby and wouldn't let him touch her. But there was something about his little sister that brought out his gentle side, and soon Bell was happy to let him watch Lily while she cooked dinner. It wasn't until much later, when Lily got bigger, that he would punch her in the arm and trip her in the kitchen with his long legs. Bell told Lily to get away from him, but she wouldn't listen. She wanted to be as tough as her brother, who never cried, no matter how their father hit him.

Van loved rock and roll. He talked about starting his own Chinese rock band one day. He saved his money and bought a guitar and practiced in the basement. Franklin threw Van's guitar away and kicked him out. Van left home and came back with a new guitar. The next day he threw out all the ashtrays in the house (he knew his mother hated his father's cigars), and once again his father told him to get out. When he came back again, Bell tried to keep him out of his father's way, but the house was too small.

When Lily was eight and Van was fifteen, Bell felt a yearning she hadn't felt before. In department stores she fondled tiny bonnets, white socks trimmed in lace, soft little union suits with snaps up the side. On the street, she couldn't quiet the ache in her body when she saw women walking with their babies in their arms.

One boy and one girl was enough, Franklin said. Bell had to trick him into giving her one more. Bell left her husband's bed the day she brought Ruby back from Saint Claire's Hospital. She moved in with her kids, four beds crammed into one tiny room. Van had slept by the window, sectioned off from the girls by a white-paneled wall that didn't quite reach the ceiling. His side of the room was big enough for a single bed and a skinny night table where he kept his karate magazines and a Big Ben alarm clock. Above his pillow was a picture of Mick Jagger and next to Mick was a hand mirror nailed to the wall, where Van studied his hair every day until the day, tired of cutting it to suit his father's taste, he packed his many pairs of Converses and moved out once and for all.

Lily had kept her things locked up tight in her desk. The only other lock in the house was on the bathroom door. If she was in a good mood, Van would ask her to hold for safekeeping some small thing like a love letter or a condom. She carried the key in her hip pocket and reached for it during times of agitation. Closing her fingers around the small piece of metal helped to ease the panicky feeling in her heart so she could finish brushing her hair and pick out a pair of jeans to wear to the bowling alley, where her friends were waiting for her. "My dad's a dictator," she'd say to them. "Fathers are like that," they'd say.

There was just the one room. Ruby's brother and sister had already claimed all the good spots, so she attached herself to her mother's side and that became her place. "I really wanted you," Bell whispered to her baby as she put her to bed. Then she straightened and said, "I wanted your brother and sister too. But I was young."

Franklin hadn't wanted another baby. He was fifty by the time Ruby was born and just starting to realize somewhere in his softening belly that he could no longer rule by fear alone; he wanted his daughter to love him. He saw how she adored her mother and this made him want to break his wife more than ever. But the meaner he was to Ruby's mother, the more Ruby loved her. By the time she was five, she was carrying her mother's bags and bringing her flowers she had picked from the neighbor's yard. She was always touching her mother's things—her hairbrush, her scarf, her bobby pins, her scratched-up lipstick case. She picked them up and smelled them, put them in her pockets and carried them around.

Ruby was five when her mother found a job in the dress factory that had opened up across the street. Lonesome for her, Ruby would go out to the store and sit with her father. Customers made a fuss over her. Some thought she was cute and gave her change. She liked the change but hated being looked at and so when her father went to the kitchen to get his tea, she hid under the ironing table. She knew to be quiet, otherwise he would order her out of there. From under the table, she watched him sort the fifty-fifty poly/cotton shirts—pink, baby blue, white and striped. He grabbed each shirt by its collar and gave it a brisk shake, as if he would throttle the dirt from it. The screen door opened and closed and the pile of shirts on the floor grew higher. When he ran out of floor space, he tossed shirts under the table and they landed on his youngest daughter, but that was before she cared about dirt and germs.

That was in his heyday, when he washed five hundred shirts a week. The door slammed every five minutes with customers coming in and out. The regulars knew his name, called him Mr. Lee and said, "Thank you, see you next week." He didn't own a washing machine and every day he sent his kids to the coin launderette. After school, Lily and Ruby pulled their carts behind them all the way up to Hillsdale Launderette, armed with quarters and jam jars of soap. The clothes were sour from bodies that ate too much dairy, worried about every little thing, then tried to cover it up with perfume.

Then one day Sears had a sale on Maytags and Franklin bought the washing machine, which he put in the kitchen, of all places. What a joy not to go to the laundromat every day! But then the water bill got too high and Franklin started recycling water. First he did the whites and caught the water that gushed out in buckets. Then he washed the darks in the water that he had already used to wash the whites, grunting as he lifted the pails of water. Then he ran out to the store when the buzzer rang, which meant he had another customer.

From under the table, Ruby watched his legs walking back and forth, quick and purposeful. In the summer, he rolled his pants to the knees and she could see the dark veins popping out. On his feet were worn-out gladiator slippers made of genuine man-made leather. She could see his hands making change at the register, where she filched dimes and quarters to buy candy. She didn't have to steal; all she had to do was ask and he would take her to Jack's after the store was closed and tell her to get anything she wanted. Yet there was something irresistible about the cash drawer and about taking what she wanted without waiting for someone to give it to her.

That was before the neighborhood changed. It was Franklin who first said that the neighborhood was changing. The regulars said it too, and then they picked up and moved to Long Island so their kids didn't have to play in the street, hitting each other with weeds or throwing a ball into traffic just to watch it get crushed under the wheels of a car. The new people had new styles, wash-and-wear that didn't need ironing. Just take it out of the dryer and put it on your back. "People just don't give a damn about how they look," Franklin said, "they just go out wearing any old wrinkled thing."

The summer Ruby turned thirteen, she got her period and fretted about her father killing small things. He did it matter-of-factly, with neither pleasure nor distaste, much as he would starch or iron a shirt. Whenever she looked up from her books, there was his bare hand smashing roaches on the kitchen counter, twisting the necks of pigeons, pulling turtles from their shells. Her mother showed her how to use the pads with the belt and told her that seeing her own blood run out of her was making her too sensitive.

Franklin bought the building that summer and paid for it in cash, eighteen thousand dollars. He and Ruby had sat in the living room and counted out the hundreds. "It might be a dump," he said proudly, "but at least you kids always have a roof over your heads." Ruby counted out the last pile and pushed it toward her father. If he wanted to buy a dump, that was his business. She wasn't going to stick around for long anyway.

Franklin came back with the deed, waving it above his head. "How about a little celebration? How about some crabs?" He looked at Ruby. He was the only one who liked crabs. Bell hated cooking them, Lily was allergic to them, and Ruby hated buying them, hated walking up to Hillside to the fish store, where the men in bloody aprons told her to smile, that she'd be real pretty if only she lightened up.

The female crabs had more meat on them and eggs that cooked up bright orange. Franklin told Ruby to ask for all females, but it made her feel bad to get the girl ones, especially ones that were pregnant, so when a few boy crabs got slipped in with the others, she acted as if she didn't notice.

At home, Bell had her big pot ready. She dumped the crabs into the pot and poked them with a chopstick when they tried to climb out. The clacking of their bodies against the pot was terrible. Franklin put on his plastic apron, the one he wore when he starched shirts, and headed for the kitchen. He picked a crab from the pot, holding it from behind so its claws couldn't snap his fingers. Ruby watched the claws opening and closing, watched her father gather five legs in one hand and then push the shell away from the body. There was a cracking noise as the shell ripped away from the soft insides. The clear jelly heart still pulsed. He reached for the next crab. Bell chopped the crab into four pieces and still the heart pulsed. Ruby stirred garlic and scallion into the hot oil, then left the kitchen and practically ran around the corner to Jack's. She stood in front and ate a handful of Sno-Caps.

When she wouldn't eat the crabs smothered in black-bean sauce, their legs spilling over the plate, her father told her she didn't know good eating. As he cracked the hard underside between his teeth, Ruby wished she had been born into a family that didn't kill its own food and didn't live behind the laundry and where the father and mother talked to each other once in a while.

Lily, even after she grew up and got married, never got over being shunted aside for the baby sister she had prayed for on her knees in a corner of the kitchen even though she didn't believe in God. Once she got the sister she thought she wanted, she complained that the room was getting too crowded, that there was no room to grow. And so, to spite her mother, she stayed small and liked being coaxed to eat.

"Come on, eat some more. Send you back to China. People are happy to get something to eat. Four in a room, that's nothing. Send you back to China. Then you'll see what's crowded." When their kids were bad, Bell and Franklin threatened them with China—China and the bogeyman, so they became one and the same. "Be good or we'll tell the bogeyman come get you. Be good or we'll send you back to China."

Now Lily was thirty and felt all dried up; she lived in the apartment above the laundry, ate at her mother's table almost every night and paid rent to her father. She was getting married soon. When Lily first met Hector, he would go shopping with her. In the bright mirrored rooms, she would try on a dress and pat her hair into place before coming to stand in the doorway so he could tell her if she should buy it or not. He picked dresses for her that were just like the ones she already had. Lily smiled and hid her disappointment in a closetful of clothes that were serviceable and well-fitting. Secretly she wanted Hector to surprise her with a dress she would never have chosen for herself but that, when she put it on, would be perfect.

But Hector didn't give her pretty dresses; he liked her plain. They'd drive to the shopping center and talk about how it would be when they were married. He wouldn't have to leave at night after wiping her off with a towel and then himself. They would have whole nights together. The little apartment above the store would have to do for now, but one day they would have a house of their own. And so they shopped, strangely shy when browsing through the furniture department. It seemed impossible to pick a sofa that they would sit on and nap on and make love on for the rest of their lives. "Which one do you like, baby?" "Oh, I don't know. Which one do you like?"

Under the curved roof where the light was always the same, they ate soft pretzels and sometimes Hector talked about God. No pressure, but maybe she would like to come with him to church one Sunday. Lily had grown up without religion and had always coveted the plaid skirts and maroon socks of the Catholic girls, white knees exposed to all weather. Lily was not opposed to church, nor was she for it. Hector talked to her in his gentle way and she thought it wouldn't hurt to try it.

That was in the beginning, and that was seven years ago. Nowadays Hector would drive her to the mall but then stay in the car, listening to the radio while she shopped. He would park near the bakery and run in for coffee and a cookie, the frosted black and white cookies almost as good as the ones from Alicia's Bakery in the Bronx, where he grew up. At first Lily tried to persuade him to come in with her, but now she was used to it, maybe even relieved that he stayed in the car.

When they'd first met, she had been so certain. She wished he had asked her to marry him then. Now there was a great uncertainty in her that had nothing to do with marriage but more with not knowing what she was doing still teaching kindergarten and living above the laundry. But she fixated on marriage. As she went from store to store in search of a sweater, she'd ask herself if she should marry him. She had already said yes, but now she searched for signs that she had made the right decision. If she could find a nice sweater for under thirty dollars, then she should. If she couldn't, then maybe he wasn't the man for her after all.

But it was hard to find a sweater she could wear to work. She needed something that wasn't too delicate; the children were always touching her and she couldn't very well push them away. In college she had stood in line to file declaration-of-major cards. The line was moving along and she didn't know what to write down. Then she saw her friend Donna and she waved her hand and called her over. "Education is a good major. You like kids, don't you?" Donna had said. Lily did like children and so she wrote down "education," but she would never have guessed that, nine years later, she would be breaking pretzel rods in half and passing them around to a roomful of five-year-olds.

The classroom was quiet after the kids went home. Lily sat at her desk. The tiny chairs were turned upside down on the little desks, their legs sticking straight up in the air. The kids left the paintbrushes a little sticky, but Lily didn't mind washing them over again. As she straightened the dollhouse corner and put away the wooden blocks and trucks, she thought of her apartment. There was something cramped and stifling about it and she wondered how it would be to live there with another person. When Van and Jeannette had first gotten married, they lived in the apartment that Lily lived in now. From downstairs, Lily had heard the yelling and the thumping of their fights. Remembering the fights made Lily worry.

Jeannette Chen had worked in the card store. Van and Jeannette sneaked around and sometimes he slept at her house. One night Jeannette's mother caught them and made them get married. Bell blamed herself. She knew Van was lying when he told her he had slept on the subway all night, but she didn't know what she would do with the truth if she ever got it out of him.

It surprised everyone that Van rather liked the idea of getting married. The idea had always filled him with doom, but at some point he started feeling hopeful about it. He was teaching Jeannette guitar and she had a great voice. A girl singer was just what his band needed. But after they got married and had their first baby, Jeannette didn't want to sing anymore. She was often tired and grouchy and didn't like Van playing his guitar while the rug went without vacuuming and the clean laundry grew cold and wrinkled in the dryer. There was the time Jeannette cut Van's guitar strings in half because he was more in love with that damn guitar than he was with her, so she said. How they fought, knocking each other down. How they fucked afterward to make up for the terrible things they'd said to each other.

Lily wasn't worried that she and Hector would fight like that. She worried that Hector would start to feel cooped up in the little apartment. He had been born early and had spent the first two weeks of his life in an incubator. All closed up in that little box. When he felt that way now he liked to go out with the guys to bowl a few games. Lily didn't know if she would like to be left like that once they were married. She felt uneasy in the apartment by herself and would go downstairs and watch TV with her mother.

Van was still married and living in Ridgewood, Queens, ten minutes away. He worked at Reliance Federal Savings Bank, where he guarded the safe-deposit boxes. He wouldn't let anyone visit him in the basement of the bank and before he left work he pulled off the hated gray-and-maroon tie, changed out of the regulation chinos and shirt. He had been with the bank the longest time of any job he had ever had by far. He used to switch jobs all the time. One month he'd be driving a taxi and the next working refunds at Alexander's, and then he'd be selling pretzels on the street. But he had worked at the bank for almost ten years now. People there knew him as the guy who invited them to bars to listen to new bands after work. They didn't know much else about him.

They didn't know that on the weekend he chatted with old ladies in sandals and baseball caps on the bus to Atlantic City. He could have taken the car, but he liked sitting back in his seat and talking with the people on the bus about their losses from last week. The bus gave out chips, so the ride was practically free. Jeannette got mad at him every time he went. Before he was even out the door, she harangued the kids about what a no-good father they had, and by the time he came back, whether he had won or lost, his whole family was mad at him.

He didn't have illusions about winning big. He never gambled the rent money or the bill money, but he did gamble the little extra that Jeannette tried to put away for a new carpet or a new refrigerator. He liked playing the slot machines. His favorite part, though, was the bus ride. The other passengers talked about their families and their jobs, but Van never did. Sometimes they asked him and got answers like "Oh, here and there. Around. This and that." But he liked to listen and they liked to talk, so they didn't press him for details. He never mentioned growing up on the farm and then behind the laundry, nor did he mention that his parents had washed their hands of him. Van had washed his hands too, even before he left. The laundry house was dirty and he had tried to keep himself clean. After he took a shower, he would get a paper bag and put it on the chair before sitting down.

Now he lived in his own house with his own family and didn't visit his parents or his sisters. He used to come once a year at Christmas, his arms full of presents: oranges, a tin of mixed nuts and a box of almond cookies tied with red ribbon. He didn't stay for tea, never mind dinner. He said he was late for dinner at his wife's family's house. When Sylvie was born, he sent a card inviting everyone to the one-month celebration. How he doted on that little girl.

And then he stopped coming altogether. Years passed and his father and his mother and his sisters didn't call him and he didn't call them. It was embarrassing to call after all that time had passed, especially when no one was sure why they didn't speak or see each other.

His family didn't know it, but he thought about them. Sometimes he'd get in his car and get as close as Hillsdale Avenue. He thought he would stop at the bakery and pick up a cake to bring over, but when he went in he looked at all the cakes and couldn't pick one. He couldn't remember if he had ever seen his parents eat a cheesecake or a chocolate cake or a cherry pie. He'd buy a cookie for his daughter and drive home again. His sons were older and didn't light up at treats from their father anymore.

Chapter 4

The year Van bought his first guitar, Bell had her woman's operation. Her head was dizzy as she waited for her friends Louie and Sheila to bring her home. Saturday was her husband's busy day at the store and Bell didn't expect him to close the store and come to the hospital. He didn't, and when they got home, Louie said to him, "You better take care of your beautiful wife. Before she leaves you for someone who knows how to treat a lady."

Bell lay down and slept. When she woke up, she listened for her husband in the kitchen. He had been a head cook in the army, and if Bell had asked him, he would have marched into the kitchen and, in his showy way, made a tasty dinner. But she was too tired to go all the way out to the store and ask. It was almost seven in the evening. Bell waited in bed. Even if he had come into her room and asked how she was feeling, she might have been able to get out of bed and make dinner. Seven o'clock came and went and Franklin didn't come in.

That was it. She was alone and she would do it herself. Bell pulled herself from the bed and walked slowly to the kitchen, holding on to the wall with one hand, the other hand touching the place where her uterus used to be. When she got to the refrigerator, she found that she couldn't open it. She put both hands on the handle and pulled; she looked around for someone to help her. Her son was downstairs in the basement playing his new guitar; her older daughter was out riding, God only knew where, on her boyfriend's motorcycle; her husband was out in the store, listening to the horse races.

Ruby had just turned ten. Ten was such a nice round number that she was sure it meant she would have a good year, which made it even harder to understand why her mother had to have an operation. When she heard her mother in the kitchen, she came in from the yard, where she had been cutting out pieces of felt to glue onto the get-well card she was making.

Bell asked her to open the refrigerator and take out the chicken that was defrosting and while she was there to get the snow peas and the broccoli. "Climb up on a chair and get the dried lily buds, the tree ears, the mushrooms. Let them soak until they're nice and soft." And so Bell sat in a chair and taught Ruby how to cook. "Measure one glass of rice, wash it with cold water until it runs clear, add water up to your wrist. Start the rice first, then the chicken and last of all the vegetables so it's all done at the same time."

The next night, Bell thought Lily should learn to cook too. But Lily was older and had her own ideas. She followed the directions on the box for macaroni-and-tuna casserole. Her boyfriend came over and had seconds and thirds, but no one else appreciated the bright orange dish. Like her mother, Lily had her pride and stayed out of the kitchen after that.

It seemed stupid to force it on Lily, especially since Ruby had taken so to cooking. In the kitchen, Ruby had found a grace she didn't have with double Dutch or softball or flirting. Those things baffled her, but she had a way with ginger and black beans and garlic. She figured out the rice by watching her parents night after night. When the rice was too hard, her mother chewed slowly with only her front teeth. When it was too soft, her father jabbed at it as if he were trying to kill it. Eventually, Ruby learned to make a pot of rice that was soft enough for her mother and hard enough for her father, no small task.

Even after Bell felt better and went back to the factory, Ruby continued to make dinner, and when it was done, she would cover the dishes and run across the street to the factory to fetch her mother. Bell was so proud she thought she would burst. It didn't matter so much then that her husband didn't say hello when she came home; at least she had her little girl.

Then her little girl grew up and moved away to school. The house had been strangely quiet while Ruby was away; the phone didn't ring and people didn't stop by. Bell stayed later and later at the factory and went in earlier and earlier. Some mornings she was the first one there and had to wait outside for the boss to come and open the gate. Her friends at the factory remembered the girl who used to come and pick up her mother. They asked about her. Bell would say fine, she's fine, but the way she said it made them stop asking. The extra hours at the factory meant Bell took home a few extra dollars, which she put into a separate account without telling her husband.

Now her little girl was back. She had been back for one week and Bell still wasn't used to waking up and looking over at the other bed and seeing her. Sometimes Bell thought having her at home was worse than when she had been away. She had grown accustomed to the quiet house and to not talking except to tell her husband that dinner was ready or to ask Lily to pick up some snow peas or coconut buns in Chinatown. Ruby asked her about things that made Bell feel funny, things that had happened a long time ago in China. Just the other day Bell found herself telling Ruby about sleeping in the same bed with her brothers when she was a kid and how they wouldn't listen when she told them to stop touching her. Bell hadn't felt sad or angry when she said it and was surprised that it had made Ruby cry. It must be all those books she read that made her so sensitive. It wasn't good to be so soft in the world, Bell had wanted to tell her, but instead she pretended she didn't notice the tears that Ruby also pretended not to notice.

Now it was morning and Bell was sleeping. Ruby was awake and thinking about China. She had never been there, but she knew it would be better than sleeping in her mother's room again. Last night she had wandered out to the laundry again and had sat on the ironing table and watched the trains pass by. For eighteen years, she had slept in her mother's room, breathed the same restless air and dreamed the same dream of someday. Someday was a long way away, but it would be worth every waiting minute.

Ruby watched her mother as she slept. The room smelled of Jean Naté After Bath Splash. It smelled nice. As quietly as she could, Ruby called to her, "Hey, Ma. Let's go to Florida." There was no answer. Ruby tried again. "Let's go on vacation. You and me. A couple of weeks in Florida."

Bell lay perfectly still, thinking, Florida? Florida? What would the girl think of next? Bell had been careful not to mention to anyone that she thought about her old friends when she watched TV, watched with particular attention commercials for cheap flights to Florida. It looked hot there, like China. Bell thought that, in Florida, the chill that had entered her bones that winter over thirty-five years ago, when she stepped off the plane in New York, wearing nothing but a thin dress and a short little jacket, might finally leave her. Ruby used to bug her about going to China, but Bell didn't want to go back and see the empty stone house, with no one left to greet them with yells, no one to pull on their sleeves, no one to receive the tins of candy and thick bars of American soap.

But her friends were living in Florida, and they had a guest room. A couple of times a year Bell sent them dried foods from Chinatown—mushrooms, noodles, shrimp. She saw herself stepping off the plane, a package in her arms. "Special delivery," she would say. Bell had taught Sheila to make a few dishes when she lived around the corner. Louie would come around holding his stomach, and say in a loud whisper, "She feeds me poison. Her shrimp and noodles don't taste like yours, baby. I want yours." His teasing was affectionate; he loved his wife, and when he called Sheila's cooking "poison," it was his way of praising her. Louie liked all women and had enjoyed flirting with Bell. Bell liked Louie too, although she was a little afraid of him, of his fat fingers and his left eye that didn't look at you when he talked.

Florida. She needed time to think about it. The longer she waited, the harder it was to open her eyes and look into the waiting face of her daughter. If she said yes, what if Ruby changed her mind? One more disappointment would kill her. If she said no, Ruby would feel rejected, she might even cry. Then it was too late to answer and her hands closed tightly around her blanket and she waited for Ruby to stop looking at her and go back to sleep.

Ruby hesitated for just a moment before sliding out of bed. Her heart was beating fast as she stood above her mother's bed, then faster as she sat down on the edge. Gently, she smoothed the hair from her mother's round moon face and then kissed her lightly on the cheek. Her cheek was not as full as it once was; it was still firm but slightly lined, like a very ripe peach. Ruby straightened up and hurried back to her own bed. When they were awake they were awkward with such displays.

Startled, Bell's hand flew to her face. Her daughter's touch lingered there. Hippie. That was the only thing Bell could think of to explain her daughter's behavior; she had gone off to school and become one of those hippies. Her son had always been a hippie, with his long hair and his music and trying to talk to his father about peace and love. Bell thought hippies had gone out of style, but maybe they were making a comeback. Just imagine, kissing someone who wasn't even dying or moving to the other side of the world.

Back in her own bed, Ruby pretended to fall instantly into a deep sleep. Her mouth tingled and she felt embarrassed. They had never been like the Consaleses, who lived next door, always kissing and hugging and grabbing each other. When she was a kid, she would hide behind her friend Angela, but it didn't matter at all to them. They would go after her like some tasty little roll, fresh from the oven, so good to eat.

At Ruby's house, there was none of that. She had no memory

of her mother and father touching, never a kiss hello, a kiss good-bye. When her mother made her father tea, she wouldn't hand it to him but would place it beside him on the nightstand in the living room which held his *TV Guide,* a flashlight and an ashtray made from an old candy tin. Once he reached for the cup before she set it down. Instead of putting it into his hands, she held the tea just out of reach, then placed the cup firmly on the table.

At school, the first time Ruby left her room and went looking for someone to kiss, she blamed her family. All living behind the laundry and no one touching anyone else. For so long, no one had touched her except when she had a fever, and then it was the cool hand against her forehead as she lay still, afraid to move. Sweet sixteen came and went and still she had not been kissed. Once in a while a boy would say she had pretty hair or nice legs, but no one ever did anything about it. Seventeen came and went, and then she was eighteen and making bread on the weekend for her father. "What good bread," he'd say.

Then, at school, people kissed hello and good-bye and put their arms around each other. How hungry she was for that, to reach out and feel something solid against her. She pretended she had touched people all her life, but her lingering gave her away. First there were kisses on the cheek and then shoulder-to-shoulder hugs. She had never given much thought to her hips before. In the lounge on the seventh floor of John Jay Hall, she wanted more. The TV was on and she was sitting on the floor. Behind her, boys sat on the sofa. Slowly she leaned back against their legs. They touched her arms and her back, but soon they were touching her all over. How surprised she had been when this led to sex.

Her mother had tried to warn her. Wherever Bell turned, there were things that wanted to harm her daughter. She saw danger in eating fish sticks, in petting dogs, in drinking water straight from the tap, in using too much toothpaste, in wearing underwear that didn't fully cover your stomach, but most of all, in fooling around with guys. There was danger everywhere, but because Ruby was a girl, Bell fixated on sex and was keen on protecting her from it. Men thought they owned you once you opened your legs, and Bell didn't want her daughter stuck with the wrong man.

"Be careful of men, and boys too." In so many ways her mother would warn her. If Ruby hung her panties on the line in the backyard, her mother would snatch them back before they were even dry. "Don't hang these out there. People can see them. Do you want people to see your underwear? And why do you want to wear your skirts so short? Why do you look when a guy on the street tries to talk to you? You know if a guy asks you what time it is, he don't really care what time it is, he just wants to know what time you want to fool around. He has his own watch in his pocket. And that Charmaine, don't hang out with her, bad influence. I see her hanging out on the corner with those Carido brothers. Don't let Tito give you a ride on his motorcycle. Close the curtain when you change your clothes. And those jeans, don't buy those jeans. Everyone can see your whole heinie."

All these things she'd had to do on the sly. But now that she had moved back home, she couldn't hide a thing, especially with her boyfriend calling her up first thing in the morning. She took the phone into the bathroom and shut the door. "Ruby Lee. Sweetheart," he said. She wanted to touch him.

"I feel funny here," she said. "We had chicken for dinner last night, from the live market. It was alive in the morning with feathers, and then we ate it for dinner."

"You're not doing so good, are you?" he said.

"Oh, I don't know. What did you eat yesterday?"

"I ordered. Shrimp in black-bean sauce. Cold sesame. I ordered too much. There's leftovers—" He was asking her to come over.

The thought of the bus to the train and then more trains seemed too much to go through just to get a little comfort. "Soon," she said.

"I love you." He said it easily.

"Yeah, me too," Ruby said. "Listen. I want to take my mom to Florida."

He was quiet. He didn't quite understand Ruby and her mother. But no wonder, he had never met the woman. What he knew was that he would never go on vacation with his mother. "That sounds great," he said finally.

"You don't think so?"

"I'm just surprised, that's all." They had talked about going to San Francisco, but now she was going to Florida with her mother. "Hey, when am I going to meet her?"

She was trapped now. He was mad at her and she wasn't feeling as tough as she usually did. If he wasn't sweet to her, she might crumble. "Next week?" she said.

He perked up right away. "Next week? You love me?"

"Bonehead. Don't be silly."

When Ruby came out of the bathroom, Bell was making breakfast and could tell right away that someone special had called and she was frightened by the look on her daughter's face. It wasn't a good idea to care that much. People always said things and then they changed their minds. Look at Van. He used to say he was going to take care of her when he grew up, but then look what happened. He left and now she hardly saw him anymore.

Now Bell looked at Ruby and said, "Who was that?"

"A friend. Nick. Didn't I tell you about him?" Ruby answered in the quick cheerful way she had gotten from her mother. She had never said much about him. She had been waiting until she felt sure, but she had known him for years now and she still wasn't sure.

"A boy or a girl?" Bell said.

"A boy. He's nice," Ruby said.

"Everyone's nice when you first meet them," Bell said. They were both surprised by her vehemence. "What kind of people is he?"

"The regular kind." Ruby knew what her mother meant.

"You know—Chinese, white, Spanish, black?"

"What's it matter? He's a white boy. But Jewish."

"Oh. Jewish. Where do you know him?"

"You want me to bring him for dinner?"

"Maybe he don't eat Chinese food? Maybe he only likes potato and bread?"

"He eats everything. He loves Chinese food."

For no reason, Bell thought of how her mother had up and died on her before Bell had had a chance to go back and see her. She used to keep a box under the bed full of clothes and shampoo and coconut candy to bring back to her. A month after she got the letter that said her mother was gone, Bell opened up the box. The shampoo had spilled all over the neatly folded shirts and matching pants. Bell almost cried then but instead took all the clothes out and rinsed them in the tub. She rinsed them for a long time.

Now Bell stood in her kitchen, looking at her daughter's legs. They were the most solid part of her and Bell was glad that the girl could run or kick if she had to. She wanted to tell Ruby to be careful whom she gave her heart to, but that wasn't how they talked to each other. From the laundry, Bell heard her husband coming toward the kitchen. Her heart beat just a little faster.

Chapter 5

*F*ranklin stamped into the room. The two women stopped talking and he felt he was interrupting just by walking into his own kitchen. "Window open all the time. Let all the heat out. She think oil is free?" He glared at the open window. No one said anything. Bell went to the sink and started washing cups that she had washed earlier and left to dry. The water was on full force, splashing the walls and the tops of her feet. She could feel him pacing behind her and she fixed her eyes outside on the green shoots pushing up from the ground. She had planted tomatoes, four rows of beans and a couple of squash plants. As soon as the tomatoes came in, the squirrels would pull them off the vine and leave them half-eaten all over the yard. Bell thought of poison and traps to get rid of them once and for all, but had a feeling she would do what she always did, stamp her foot and shake a stick at them. As she looked out the window, her husband's smoke was in her throat like a tiny hand pressing her there.

Franklin suddenly remembered that it was spring and the heat had not been on for some time now. He was forgetting things now, was that it? This enraged him even more and when he spoke his voice had an air of forced amusement. "Look at your mother. What a slob. Undershirt hanging out, shirt buttoned wrong, pants wrinkle." He laughed and pointed with his cigar. Bell glanced at her outfit. Her undershirt *was* sticking out a little; it was an old one of her husband's. Pretending to brush some lint from her pants, she quickly pushed it out of sight.

"Her socks don't even match." Franklin looked his wife up and down. Ruby looked at her mother, then at her father and then she looked down at the floor, remembering the time she had laughed along with him. She was six years old then and hated the way her mother got quiet whenever her father came into the room. A dirty little piggy, he called her. A dum-dum of a wife. Slow like an ox, he'd say.

After he'd left the room, Ruby would whisper to her mother, "He's the dumb old ox. Tell him to shut up. Tell him to mind his own business, Ma." Bell would look at her little girl, at the somber eyes and the nose that was a bit on the flat side and the big wide mouth that was like her father's. She would be pretty when she grew up, Bell thought, and maybe smart enough not to marry the first guy who came along. "Takes two to fight," Bell had said. Then she said, "Pull your nose a little. You don't want a flat one like mine."

Ruby *had* wanted a flat one and not a witchy one like her father, so she only pretended to pull her nose. What she really wanted was muscle, and every morning she got a couple of cans of Del Monte cling peaches from the cabinet and pumped her arms over her head and then she did a hundred jumping jacks. "No, thanks, I'm in training," she said to her father one day when he asked her if she wanted to go to Jack's for candy. In the end she gave in and got Red Hot Dollars and Mary Janes.

The evening when Ruby had sided with her father he had lost at the races and felt the need to yell at someone. The water had boiled away and now the kettle was burned. He had put the kettle on, but his wife should have been watching. "You trying to burn the house down? Make you happy if the whole place burned down to the ground, wouldn't it?" he said. Bell tried to say something, but his smoke was in her throat again.

Ruby had waited for her mother to speak up, a sick feeling rising up in her. She listed all the things she would give up if only her mother would say something: the butterfly ring she had bought at Becker's Drugstore, the fairy-tale books that fit in one hand, the coins she had been saving for a bunny. She would dig a hole in the yard and bury all of it.

"Your mother's a real dum-dum," her father said. He smiled at Ruby, waited for her to smile back at him. If only she could have killed him dead on the spot. But she hadn't trained long enough, so she moved her mouth into a smile and then she laughed. A short, ugly laugh. The next moment she was weeping at her own treachery, at the satisfied look on her father's face, wept hardest of all at her mother's sudden busyness at the kitchen counter.

Afterward she put the incident out of her head. Now her betrayal came back swiftly and cleanly and compelled her toward her mother, who was still washing cups and trying not to pay any attention to her husband. Ruby took the cups from her and banged them on the counter. Bell held her hands in the air for one long second before dropping them to her sides.

"Dad. Leave her alone. Why don't you just leave her alone."

"What? She's a slob, that's all."

"Stop it. Stop laughing. It's not funny."

"Just look at her. She *is* funny."

"Stop it." Then all at once everyone was quiet and that was even worse.

"Can't you take a joke?" Franklin blew a big cloud of smoke before walking away, leaving them to make the tea. They stood at the counter, looking down at their hands. They opened packets of tea, measured out sugar and poured the milk. Her mother's arms were so pretty and round; Ruby wanted to touch her. There was a spoon on the counter and Ruby picked it up and gave the tea a good stir. "Ma. I'm sorry, Ma," Ruby said and it was hard to get the words out.

Bell softened. She hadn't felt like crying in a long time. "You better go give your father his tea now."

After Ruby went out to the laundry, Bell went to her room to get dressed for work. She pinned a clean cloth around her neck and another around her stomach. She liked those places covered up. At work it got hot with the machines and the irons going all day. When the fan hit her, her bones felt soft.

In her underwear drawer, she kept a small notebook that she wrote her few phone numbers in. She took it out and turned to the last page, where she had written, in large print, the number of her friends in Florida. In the basement, she dialed the number. Louie answered. He sounded pleased. He called her baby and said he would grill a fish for her and Ruby when they came down. "Leave your old man behind if he won't get off his duff," Louie said. Bell imagined Franklin at home by himself, cooking his own dinners and sitting in front of the TV, complaining to his customers that his stomach hurt because his wife left him to go on a damn vacation to Florida.

"If you don't hurry up and get on a plane, I'll have to drive back and kidnap you myself," Louie said.

Then Sheila got on the phone. "You're almost sixty years old and you've never had one vacation in your whole life."

After Bell hung up the phone, she wondered why on earth they were so nice to her. She felt twisted up inside and remembered suddenly that Ruby had just told her father to shut up, not that she had actually said "Shut up," but that's what she meant. Franklin had looked so surprised that Bell almost felt sorry for him. When he and Lily used to fight, he hadn't been at all surprised, but that was Lily. For eight years, Lily and Franklin hadn't said one word to each other. He picked on her for not cooking and not studying and for hanging out late. One night Lily blew up at him. Looking at her now, you would never guess she had said those things at the dinner table to make him so mad everyone had been afraid he would hit her. "Everyone has to do what you say? How come? Because Ma's a pushover? Because Ruby's got a sweet tooth? Because you hit Van so many times he won't talk back to you anymore? I'm sick of living under this dictatorship. You can't run my life forever." She left the table crying and started throwing clothes into a paper bag.

Bell had left the table and had talked to her quietly. "Where you think you going? There's no place to go. Here, give me that bag. You better go finish your dinner." Lily unpacked her bag but pushed Bell away when she tried to wash her face with a warm cloth. The fight had gone out of her and she looked very small.

Not leaving that night wasn't what broke her, but the years that followed. She didn't speak a word to her father, not one word. Franklin didn't speak to her either, but he had Ruby deliver his messages. "Tell your sister she better finish that ironing before she go anywhere. Tell your sister to pick up some cigars on the way home. Tell your sister it don't look very nice when she sit around in her pajamas all day."

Bell didn't like fighting. It made her stomach hurt. Calling her friends in Florida made her stomach hurt, as if in preparation.

Upstairs, Ruby had gotten out the Ajax and had started on the counter. She moved jars to get to the spilled sugar and rings of soy sauce. Bell came upstairs and stood there, wanting to tell her she had just called Louie and Sheila and that Louie would grill a fish for them. She watched Ruby cleaning and then she said, "You should wear gloves. Your hands will get rough."

Bell left for work. Ruby finished the counter. The stove looked even dirtier next to the clean counter, so she washed that too. Franklin came into the kitchen. He loved it when the house was clean. In his hand was a five-dollar bill. "Why don't you go around the corner and get some apple pies?" He meant Drake's, two to a pack.

"It's too sweet," she said and felt a pang of regret. She didn't know why it was so hard to say no to him. He was standing there, holding out the bill to her. "How come you're never like this with her?" Ruby said, almost choking.

"What? Like what?" he said but knew exactly what she meant. Then, in another tone, he said, "Sometimes I ask her what time dinner's ready and she looks at me like she don't even know me, her own husband."

"Maybe you should talk to her about it. Maybe you could cook dinner for her. You know, for a change."

"She don't like my cooking. She say it too salty. When I talk to her, she don't even answer. When I go near her, she walk away."

"Dad. You know she doesn't like your cigars. Why don't you stop smoking around her and then maybe she'll like you more."

"Just an excuse. I know. Come on, why don't you go around the corner and get some pies, maybe a couple of Twinkies?"

The bill was crumpled in his hand and he extended it to her. Reluctantly, she took it and went around the corner and bought the pies. On the way back she squeezed them to see if they were fresh. They were. She wanted to smash them in her hands and then smooth out the package so no one would know it was just one big mess on the inside. But knowing her father, he would send her right back to the store to get a new one.

She tossed the pies on the table. They looked especially tempting. If she stayed in the house, she would surely eat them. The package would make a nice rustling sound as she tore it open and her father would win yet again.

Before he could come into the kitchen and rip open the package for her, she threw on her clothes and left the house. Outside, she headed up the side street away from the main strip where she might see someone she used to know. She didn't want anyone to see her looking so downtrodden. It was past noon when she stopped to get a paper and have lunch at Dunkin' Donuts.

The Classified section promised beautiful apartments on every corner of the city, all empty and available immediately. As she read, she didn't feel as trapped as she had in the house, especially when she got out a pen and circled a few of the ads. Old people all around her were eating doughnuts and waiting for the library to open, and without knowing it, Ruby joined them in their wait. The ham and cheese croissant and minestrone soup were sitting there in her stomach, but she needed a doughnut to get her through the Help Wanted section.

At the counter, she gazed fondly at the neat rows of doughnuts, each kind resting in its own tray. She considered all her options before settling on a French cruller, the kind she always got. It was a comfort to her, but when she had finished reading about all the jobs she didn't want or that didn't want her, she was depressed again.

She lingered in the doughnut shop as long as she could, then followed the old people over to the library and took out all the Jane Austen books they had. It was a good time to catch up on her classics, she figured. The day stretched out before her and she didn't know how to occupy herself until evening. Then she remembered her mother's hat. In Florida, her mother would need a hat or her head would get burned. The only place she could walk to that sold hats was Woolworth's. That wasn't exactly what she had in mind, but she headed there anyway.

The hats were flimsy and loud, but that didn't stop her from trying them on. She would have to go to Manhattan for the right hat. She was looking forward to going to the city when she felt a sudden wave of panic. It was getting late. Her mother would be leaving work soon. Ruby became overwhelmed with the need to go to her mother's job and carry her bags for her.

On the bus, she knew she was acting silly but she was driven. Her mother brought dresses home to sew at night and some-times she picked up groceries along the way. When Ruby was little, as soon as she could, she had carried something for her mother, at first light things like bread or paper towels, but as she got older she insisted on carrying the heaviest bags even though her mother reproached her, but gently, "Your bones too soft to carry such heavy things. You want to grow up nice and tall or you want to have a crooked back?"

She had carried the bags but grew up nice and tall anyway. Now she got off the bus and waited outside the factory, a store-front with cloth draped across the windows.

Bell was flustered when she came out and saw Ruby. "What you doing here?"

"I came to walk you. Give me your bag."

"I can carry it," Bell said.

"Let me," Ruby said.

They tussled lightly over the bags and finally Bell handed her one. She reached into the other bag and took out a black dress with tiny white dots on it. "This was extra. I thought maybe you might like it. It's nice, a hundred percent cotton. And it's black. You wear black."

Ruby looked at the dress. It was ugly. But it *was* black and cotton, so she could see why her mother would think she might like it. There was something about the cut that made it a dress for an older woman, maybe someone who had worked in accounting for the last twenty-five years. "Maybe I'll wear it," Ruby said. "Maybe I can wear it to work."

"If you don't like it, that's okay," Bell said.

"I'll try it on. Maybe it'll look nice," Ruby said. The dress was in her hands. She looked slightly to the side of it. Luckily she couldn't imagine the day that would come in just a few months when she would be running late for work. Her closet would be full of the same old clothes she had worn all week, but toward the back she would spot the dress crushed between a cream-colored skirt with animals on it and a white blouse that was too short to tuck into the cream-colored skirt. The dress she had never considered wearing would look damn good to her.

Chapter 6

Ruby woke not to the sounds of loving from her friends who had lived across the hall at school, but to her sister walking, stamping around upstairs. Lily could walk quietly when she felt like it, so Ruby knew she was mad about something. It had never been easy between the two sisters. Ruby had a feeling that Lily wasn't pleased that she was home. She looked up at the squares on the ceiling and started to count. She used to think that if she could get an exact count, she would attain some sort of numeric enlightenment, but she could never get a definite number—57, 58, 59—before her mind would start to wander—60, 61, 62; did she count the partial tiles as wholes or as halves? She closed her eyes against the morning, determined and gray, that found her once again behind the laundry, and she counted squares on the ceiling after four years of lying under lovers, not knowing what the ceiling looked like when things were good and knowing every water stain and crumbling bit of plaster when they were bad—67, no, 65, 66, 67—if only she could concentrate. She counted the squares to 69; or was it 70?

A half hour later, she was still in bed. There were exactly 158 squares on the ceiling. Ruby was sure of it and she looked up at the ceiling for a sign. Of what, she didn't know. "Oh, Lord. Lord, help me. Help me, Lord," she said. Only one week back and she had taken to prayer. Her voice held just the right degree of anguish and entreaty. Of course she didn't believe, but she liked so much how the words sounded that she said them again.

"Oh, Lord. Lord, help me. Help me, Lord, please." The addition of "please" at the end gave her a humble feeling, that and her robe, which made her look a hundred years old.

The slippers her mother had given her were red with gold dragons. Ruby put them on and pointed her feet this way and that. They were bright and flashy in the way that Chinese people love; for two bucks, you felt like a millionaire. During the summer of third grade, the girls were wearing Chinese shoes, thin black cloth with flowers embroidered on top. Everyone was wearing them except Ruby. The other girls could play at being Chinese and she envied them, that they could put it on and take it off as easily as doing up the straps of their shoes in the morning and kicking them off after school. Even when she got older, people would get mad at her for trying to act black or white or Puerto Rican.

In the kitchen, her mother had left breakfast warming on the stove, chicken wings cooked in soy sauce, rice, and some leftover squash. Ruby had eaten bagels at school but had never quite gotten used to them. Now she hurried through her breakfast so she could get out of the house before her father got up. He was mad at her for messing up his schedule last night. At eleven thirty-five, she had been flossing in the bathroom. She was sick of his schedule. Every day, the same thing at the same time. He woke up at eight and put the kettle on and read the newspaper. Studied the racing sheet and drank tea and ate a hard-boiled egg at nine. At nine-thirty, he placed his two-dollar bets. After that, as if they were fine antiques, he feather-dusted the brown packages. There were washing days, starching days, and ironing days, but no matter what day it was, at four he had a cup of tea and a roll with a slice of cheese, and then he waited for dinner, no later than six. Even his bowel movements were precisely timed: 11:30 P.M., and everyone knew to clear out of the bathroom by eleven-fifteen to be on the safe side. Last night, he had pounded on the door. "Get the hell out of there. Now."

After he kicked her out of the bathroom, he told her to pick up some cigars tomorrow. Going to the cigar store would ruin her day. He wasn't the only one with a schedule. For the past week, after breakfast she had left the house and gone to Dunkin' Donuts, zipped through the Help Wanted ads and lingered over the apartment listings. When she thought about moving out, her chest got all tight. Her mother would be alone again. To make herself feel better, Ruby imagined fixing up her apartment so her mother would feel at home there.

Day after day, Ruby sat in Dunkin' Donuts and thought about the hard bed she would buy for her mother. After she finished her French cruller, she would walk up and down the streets and think about going to Manhattan, although she hadn't made it there yet. When she came home, she threw herself into her cleaning. If the house were clean, maybe she could think. Whenever she thought about calling her temp agency to get some work, her hands were soapy and wet. And then it was time to make dinner. At dinner, she and her mother listened to her father's news and afterward they told each other about the small victories and defeats of their day. After dinner, it was too late to call her agency, so Ruby watched as much TV as she could and then she turned it off and read, but she stayed on the same page night after night. Right before bedtime, she took the phone into the bathroom and called Nick. When they got to talking about all the things they wanted to do to each other, she talked in a whisper and listened for footsteps in the hallway. It didn't seem right to talk that way with her father right there in the living room watching TV and her mother in the kitchen, making room in the cabinet for the two five-pound packages of sugar she had bought on sale at Key Food that day.

The morning she took to prayer, she rushed through her breakfast. In the laundry, the day's ironing, damp and wrapped in plastic, lay like small blind animals caught in the morning's light. The irons stood at cool attention, awaiting Franklin's hand. Bell stood by the window, sweeping. Mornings were quiet in the store except for a few customers who knocked at the door, pretending not to see the sign that said "Open at Eight." They rapped their knuckles against the glass, then got out coins and keys. Franklin spoiled them; he let them in anytime of day or night, joking the whole time about how they were disturbing his beauty rest. His customers laughed and said he was the nicest man they had ever done business with.

He knew how to be charming when he felt like it, thought Bell. On the floor behind her were neat piles of dust. It was useless to sweep; in a few hours Franklin would only shake loose more dust from his customers' clothes. Last night, Ruby was sitting on her bed, talking to her so gently and quietly about Florida that Bell almost forgave her for staying away so long.

Bell hadn't told her friends at the factory that Ruby was back. Her friends would feel sorry for her if she told them Ruby was back and then the next day told them she had gone again. Ruby had told her that she would be leaving at the end of the summer, so Bell didn't want to get too used to having her around. If they went away to Florida together, it would be even harder to say good-bye again. So far, Bell hadn't said yes or no. Franklin would have a fit. Even now, when she went to the supermarket for a few hours, he told everyone who walked into the store that his wife had abandoned him.

As Bell swept she felt her shoulders caving in as they did when she sat too long at her sewing machine. With great determination, she stopped them from curving and stood up straight. Her shoulders were tight and she reached back and pounded them with her fists. In the early years of her marriage, Franklin would ask her to pummel his back in the evenings when he finished work. Her hands seemed small against his back, but she pounded and pounded until his eyes fluttered closed.

Now she put down the broom and stepped out of her slippers. She stretched her fingers to the floor and then toward the ceiling. Her morning exercise show wasn't on anymore and she missed it. In the narrow aisle between the packages and the ironing table, she twisted from side to side and then stretched her legs, kicking the air. In her big wide pants, she looked like she was doing kung fu.

She finished her exercises and sat down at her sewing machine. Nestled under the dresses she had brought home from the factory were some scraps of fabric she had been saving. The rustling of the bag seemed loud and she was afraid she would wake up the whole house. She laid the cloth on the ironing table. The softness of the cotton and the pale blue color made it perfect for a baby. She started cutting the fabric into pieces that would fit together into a little dress. The skirt would be a full circle and maybe she would trim the hem in lace.

She had finished cutting the collar when she heard someone coming from the back. In one desperate gesture, she swooped all the pieces back into the bag, at the same time admitting to herself that her granddaughter Sylvie would never wear the pretty blue dress Bell was making for her, or any of the other dresses Bell had made.

Bell grabbed her broom and started sweeping again, just as Ruby came out. "Oh, it's you." Bell put down her broom.

On the ironing table was a book Bell had gotten from the library. She picked it up and opened it. "You see this book? It's about the stomach." She traced her finger along the human digestive tract. "See. Chinese people have trouble with the stomach because too nervous. Like your father. He get mad at every little thing." Bell lifted her shirt slightly and poked her stomach, soft and lined after three children—four, really, if you counted the one that had died.

Ruby wanted to tell her mother that she had been looking at ads for apartments and that her mother could come and stay in the apartment with the ficus tree in the window and the spare bed anytime she wanted. "Hey, Ma?" she said but then stopped. It seemed silly to invite her mother to visit an apartment she didn't even have yet.

"Yeah?" said Bell. It was quiet then.

Ruby jumped up and swept all the little piles of dust into the trash can. She stood up and said, "Guess what? I called about tickets yesterday. They're cheap. Did you talk to Louie and Sheila?"

"They said to come," Bell said flatly. When she spoke again, the flatness was gone. "How much is it?"

"Two hundred. But you don't have to worry. My treat."

"I have money."

"I know. But I want to."

"We'll see. Remember we used to go to Coney Island?" Bell said, full of forgiveness.

"You used to make chicken and we had iced tea and grapes and cookies." Ruby was eager to remember their picnics fondly, although at the time she would get mad at her mother for staying up so late, frying chicken and packing the basket full of food the night before when all Ruby wanted was a Nathan's hot dog and some french fries.

Franklin came out to the laundry, dressed for work. In his dress pants with the perfect crease and his white shirt buttoned to the top, he looked more like a retired doctor than a laundryman. He went over to his cigars and counted them, then looked up as if just noticing his wife and daughter. "You going to get those cigars?" he said.

"I'm going," Ruby snapped. She watched her mother searching for her slippers, her feet curled up and small. Bell left the store, her slippers slapping against the floor in just the way she knew her husband couldn't stand. He made a face and lit a cigar.

In the bedroom, Bell laced her shoes tightly. They were wide and flat like nurses' shoes. She loved to walk, but sometimes her feet gave her trouble. Ruby came in. "He wants more cigars. Didn't I just buy some? I just bought some and now he wants more."

"Smoke, smoke, smoke," Bell said but her heart wasn't in it. After Ruby left, Bell rummaged in her sock drawer for her bank passbook. She took it out and looked at it. That was her money, she had worked for it.

That afternoon, Ruby sat in the last row on the bus and looked out at the stores passing by on Hollis Avenue. Above the stores were open windows and leaning out of the windows were people who lived above the stores: a woman in a housedress and a scarf over her head was drinking a beer, old people petted their cats, a man undid the buttons of his shirt but didn't take it off. Out on the sidewalk, kids waved at the bus and then shot at it with their water guns. They watched the street and anything that moved; they waited day after day for something to happen. Ruby knew that kind of waiting.

When she was growing up, she had waited behind the laundry, waited for little things like the mailman and Christmas. That was when she didn't know it was strange to live behind the laundry. Angela Consales had lived next door, behind the shoemaker's. They would play shoe repair, nailing bits of leather to customers' shoes until the customers complained. Then the two girls stole taps and shuffled and kicked their way around the block, arms flying. They didn't look at the other kids who stuck bottle caps to the bottoms of their sneakers and tried to dance too.

Then there was Helen Hong, who lived above Yang Kee Kitchen. At night, after the restaurant was closed, Ruby sat at the booth by the window and ordered won ton soup and lo mein. Helen, dressed in a red waiter's jacket, burst through the swinging doors and tossed the order on the table. Then they switched. Helen always ordered the most expensive things on the menu. She complained about the service and sent the food back.

It was when Ruby went to Sandra Costello's house that she realized that not everyone lived in stores. Sandra had a house with front steps that led right into the living room, where there was wood furniture instead of laundry. The house was neat and clean and there was no television because her parents were teachers and didn't believe in it. Her parents slept in the same room in the same bed. Ruby knew Americans did things differently, but she still thought it was strange.

There was no air-conditioning on the bus and Ruby hung her

arm out the window for air. Sitting in the seat across from hers was a man in a cheap blue suit. He was staring at her. "Shut up," she said to him. He looked away and she went back to thinking about her father's store. Nowadays, his washing machine sat quietly except for a few loads on Saturday. There were fewer customers, but more laundry piled up in the store, so much that it spilled into the living room. People brought their clothes in but often didn't come back for them. Bell told her husband to get a deposit, make them pay first. But Franklin wouldn't take money for a job before it was done, so he set up another rack in the living room. He took his time over the ironing, and when that was done he watched television, getting up only for a new cigar. He seemed to like watching TV surrounded by all his laundry.

Thinking about her father at home watching TV in the middle of the day made her forget what a tyrant he could be. She felt gentle toward him and worried that he would be lonesome if she and her mother went away to Florida.

A man on the bus, not the one in the blue suit, sensed that she was not as cross as she had been a moment ago and took the opportunity to stare at her breasts. He liked perky ones.

Ruby looked up abruptly, her charity gone. "Jesus. Will you just shut up?" she said. The man got a hurt look on his face and pretended to look out the window. Ruby got off the bus.

At Courtesy Drug Store, she bought the six boxes of Muriel Coronas on the shelf and waited while the stock boy ambled down to the basement to see if there were any more. While she waited, she studied the candy bars. She reached into her pocket for money. Her father would have liked her to spend his change on a little something for herself, but she didn't want to owe him. When she came home with the six boxes of cigars, he said, "That's all you got?"

That evening Bell tapped on the heat pipe with a spoon. Lily tapped back and came down a few minutes later, wearing tight jeans and a red T-shirt. It was the first night she had come down to dinner since Ruby had moved home.

"Lily," Bell said, "set the table." Lily tore paper towels in two and placed each half under a pair of chopsticks. She smoothed the paper towels as if they were fine linen.

"It's Bounty, for Christ's sake," Ruby said. Lily finished the table and leaned back in her chair. There was a mark on her little white sneakers which she rubbed with her finger after spitting delicately on it. Ruby thought of how Lily used to tease her about her size-nine feet. "Can I borrow one of your boats?" she'd say. Ruby had run crying to her mother, who yelled at her, "You want little feet like my grandma? You want little stinky feet you can't walk on? Big feet are good. Walk far. Go places."

But still, Ruby had wanted to follow her big sister. On Saturdays, Lily would rush through her ironing. Her friends, dressed in their brightest bell-bottoms and their tallest platforms, waited by the counter, fiddling with the water sprayer. They showed off their new breasts in tight midriffs. Finally, Lily folded her last shirt, slammed the iron down and headed for the door. Ruby ran after her. Lily held her back with one hand. "Where do you think you're going?"

"I won't bother you. Look, I have money. I'll buy you a soda," Ruby said.

"When you're bigger you can come," Lily said and dashed for the door. Ruby tried to follow and Lily yelled for their mother. "Ma, come get her. She's trying to bite me."

Bell came out to the store. "Come on. You stay here and keep me company, okay? Look what I have for you." She held out a box of raisins or a new pair of barrettes. After a while Ruby stopped trying to follow her sister and pretended she was an only child.

Lily still had the tiny white scar on her hand. She touched it now, sitting at the table. Franklin came in, excited. "Did you see this?" he said to Lily, pointing to a page he had torn from the newspaper. "Macy's has a sale on all TVs. Zenith, twenty-five percent off. I think the old one just about had it." He patted Lily on the arm before handing her the paper. Ruby stared at the two of them and it became clear: Lily had stolen her father's heart. While Ruby had been away, Lily had bought his *Sports Eye*, his cigars and his Entenmann's cakes until he loved her again, and now Ruby was the one knocking at the store window with a penny, looking in at the two of them.

It was hard to believe that Lily and Franklin hadn't spoken to each other for eight years. Now their heads were nearly touching as they looked at the newspaper ad. Ruby got up and looked outside at the yard. The plants were almost twice as tall as they'd been last week. Suddenly she said, "Was that the right kind of cigars?"

"Cigars?" Franklin looked at her as if she were crazy.

"You know. The ones I got today," Ruby said.

"Sure. It was all right," Franklin said, then went back to talking with Lily about the televisions.

"You don't need a new TV. What's wrong with the old one?" Ruby said.

"He wants a new one, let him buy a new one," Lily said.

"Lord," Ruby said. She looked around for someone to help her.

Chapter 7

The phone rang and rang in the house as it used to. Ruby's friends called her and invited her out for coffee and roof parties. They warned her to leave that god-awful borough before something happened to her. Like what? Ruby thought. Like maybe she would revert to wearing pastels, matching her socks to her shirts and curling her hair into two heavy wings on either side of her head. "Oh, it's not so bad here," she said and wondered why she felt the need to defend the place.

She wanted to go to Manhattan to see her friends, but she also wanted to clean the house. She wanted to see her boyfriend, who was starting to think she didn't love him anymore. It had been two weeks since she moved back home. She had her schedule. Her walks were getting longer and longer and one day she found herself at the subway station. Her friends were right. It was about time she got out of Queens. As she waited on the platform, she looked down at her outfit, a pair of blue running shorts (part of her high school gym uniform) and a faded March of Dimes T-shirt and her flip-flops. God, was it time to do laundry. A few trains came and went but she didn't get on. People were fashionable in the city. Five or six trains passed before she walked back up the steps. As she walked home, she thought about the basement.

The basement was one big mess. When they had divvied up the house, Franklin got the laundry and Bell got the basement, which she promptly started filling up with things that would come in handy one day. She especially liked soft things, so the basement became padded like a nest. No one bothered her in the basement; you had to pick your way through bags and boxes filled with thread, baby clothes, shirts with no buttons, leftover fabric from the factory, in order to get to her. You had to squeeze between the falling-down Ping-Pong table and the bikes with flat tires, and most likely you would dirty your clothes.

Sometimes, while she was walking on Hollis Avenue or emptying her father's ashtray or lying awake in the bed next to her mother's, Ruby thought about the day she had moved back. Her father had eyed her belongings on the sidewalk and joked about throwing her out on the street. She got mad every time she thought about it. She didn't really think he would kick her out like he had kicked Van out, although she had to admit she liked the idea of her mother sneaking her back into the house and hiding her in the basement like she had hid Van, sneaking food down to her until Franklin cooled off.

Ever since Ruby went away to school, there had been this bad feeling between her and her father. When she came back on the weekends, he hardly looked at her. He didn't like the way she dressed. He thought that some days she looked like a loose woman, on other days like a dirty old bum. She was lonesome when she came home, so she brought friends with her, but her father didn't like them. They came empty-handed to his house, not even a loaf cake to pay their respects.

He still seemed mad at her sometimes. The day she walked all the way to the train station, she had sat in the kitchen, wondering what she had done to make him so mad, when he came in. He put water on the stove. The sugar bowl was almost empty. He sighed and opened the cabinet. Inside, there were five or six bags of sugar. "God*damn* your mother. Why she have to buy something every time she go out? It's a sickness." He looked like he wanted to spit.

"It's just *sugar*. You think she buys that for herself? She doesn't even use sugar," Ruby said.

"I'm just saying." He didn't sound at all arrogant but almost forlorn. Ruby nearly kicked herself when she started to feel sorry for him. He reached for a bag of sugar and started to whistle some Mozart. "Well, your old dad won't be around for long. Maybe a couple more years, if I'm lucky," he said and laughed. "Looks like I'm just a bother to everyone around here anyway."

It was a thing he had said to her a hundred times, and when she was a child her eyes would instantly fill with tears and she was sorry for whatever it was that she had done to upset him. Now she could see what a ploy it was, but she couldn't help noticing that he had wrapped cloth around the top of his slippers, as if his feet were getting even more tender in his old age. After all, he was more than seventy years old. How long did people live nowadays? she wondered and tried to remember how old her uncles and Nick's father and Helen Hong's grandmother had been when they died.

"Chinese people live a long time," Ruby said. "I have to clean now." She trudged downstairs, mad that she could never stay mad at him for long. The basement was damp and cool and cluttered. Somehow, if things were stacked in boxes with labels on them, she could think better. In her dreams at school, she went back to the basement night after night and sometimes she had no shoes on and had to watch out for bugs and sharp things. For days now, she had been thinking about the basement. For all her feeling of urgency, she had done nothing.

The boxes she had brought back from school were piled up on the Ping-Pong table so they wouldn't get flooded when it rained. Her mother had tried to cajole her into unpacking. "Oh, come on, what you trying to tell me? You don't want to stay here in this nice dump? With a paint job, it wouldn't look half bad." Her mother was in the kitchen and had opened her arms wide to encompass the sad green walls, the TV, the smoky rooms and maybe even the separateness that lay like a rock between her and her husband.

"What, don't you like it here?" Bell had said and they

laughed about it, but later that night, Ruby unpacked one of her suitcases and stuffed her clothes into the drawer her mother had emptied for her. She refused to unpack the rest of her things, just to pack everything up again in a few months. When she needed something from her boxes, she went downstairs and looked around until she found it. It made her feel funny to see her things lying in boxes, the fragile things wrapped up in sweaters and towels.

Bell had saved a crazy amount of things over the years. Before, her saving had been tempered by Ruby's cleaning, but now the piles were bigger than ever. Ruby was careful to throw away only the smallest scraps, and gadgets that were so broken they could never be fixed. As her trash bag filled up, she wondered what would become of her.

At first it was easy to figure out what scraps to save and what to throw away. But as she went through more boxes, she became uncertain and didn't know what someone might need someday. Maybe one day someone would take up quilting and would need all those scraps. She couldn't see Lily quilting, but maybe when her mother was old she might start. Or maybe a young couple just starting out in the world would move into the apartment upstairs and might need the extra set of dishes the Consaleses had left behind when they moved to Italy. As a rule, she threw away anything polyester, but then she wondered if she could really judge. Alarmed, she went through her trash bag, fished out a few things and put them back where she had found them.

She kicked her trash bag aside and admitted to herself that she would have to start temping soon. The thought of putting on some ugly old dress and beige panty hose was devastating. And her pointy temp flats with the run-down heels. No wonder her parents had wanted her to study something practical. Too late for that, she thought and jumped up and went upstairs for a bucket of water. She chose an old cloth and was filled with a sense of thrift that was close to righteousness—if she used up all the rags in the basement, then somehow it would make up for her life at school, where she had spent five dollars on a little slice of cake and a lukewarm cup of tea without thinking about it.

The dust had sure piled up. She washed the stairs and the cement floor. Her wash water turned black in one rinse, but she kept using it. She wondered how her mother could sit down here. Bell would sit in her old armchair and watch TV, and once in a while she would push the stuffing back into the worn-out places. Old as the chair was, there was still something dignified about it; perhaps it was the curve of its wide back or maybe its dear little legs.

Draped over the back of the chair was some brown corduroy left over from the jacket her mother had made for herself. As soon as Ruby saw the fabric, she knew her mother had planned to fix the chair before it fell apart even more, but she had never gotten around to it. Suddenly, Ruby pictured the chair redone, maybe in a dark green or maybe even the same loyal brown. She got excited thinking of how her mother would love her new chair. There was an upholstery shop on Hillsdale that Ruby had passed thousands of times in her life and now she found their number in the phone book and called them.

The furniture lady asked all kinds of questions about the chair. Ruby told her, "It's a brown chair, pretty big. Kind of old, not an antique or anything like that." The lady said she would have to see it, but most likely she couldn't do it for less than six hundred. "Six hundred? I'll think about it," Ruby said. She hung up the phone and then she ripped the number of the furniture store into little pieces. Six hundred dollars for a tattered old chair!

She would do it herself. How hard could it be to fix a chair? More inspired than she had been in weeks, Ruby went upstairs for scissors and thread. "Make sure you put the scissors back where you found it," her father yelled.

Downstairs, she spread the cloth out on her lap and cut pieces to cover the shabbier places in the chair. Then she tried to sew a square of corduroy onto the arm. It was hard to hold the square in place, keep the stuffing from popping out, as well as sew with a needle that seemed too small. She sewed for a long time and couldn't believe she had only finished one arm. It was dark in the basement and hard to see what she was doing. She started on the next arm, which was no easier than the first. Finally both arms were done and her fingers were sore. She wanted to stop, but now the chair looked worse than it had before and so she kept on, doggedly patching here and there.

It was close to dinnertime. Ruby was still in the basement when Bell came home. "What you doing down here?" Bell said.

"Look. I fixed your chair." Ruby stepped away from the chair and they both looked at it. Then Bell laughed. Her laughing wasn't mean and had more to do with her uneasiness at taking than with anything else, but still Ruby's feelings were hurt and she wished she had never ventured down to the basement.

Bell stopped laughing as soon as she saw Ruby's face. "Oh, honey. It's a good job," Bell said and sat down. She patted the covered arms of the chair like she wanted to pat Ruby. She sat back and looked directly at her daughter, and all at once Ruby knew that her mother was happy that she had tried to fix the old chair, even though it hadn't turned out the way she had hoped it would.

"Who else would fix my chair?" Bell said.

Ruby knew no one else had noticed that Bell's chair was falling apart and it filled her with a big lonesome feeling. It wouldn't do to let her mother see her crying. "I've been cleaning," she said, suddenly businesslike. She reached for the trash bag. "You don't need this, do you?" Ruby held up the sleeve of a sweater. Her voice was brittle with effort.

Bell reached for it. "I need this." She put the sleeve in her pocket. "I use it for a leg warmer. What's that?" She pointed to something that had fallen from the trash bag and wondered what it would be like not to hold on to every little scrap that crossed her path.

Ruby pulled out the crumpled shoulder pad and put it on her shoulder, for a joke, although she didn't feel jolly. "I need that," Bell said, folded it up and put it in her other pocket.

"What for?" Ruby was really asking why Bell had filled up the whole basement with junk.

"I use it to wash dishes."

"Don't you like sponges?" Ruby said. She didn't know quite why it was so important that her mother use sponges with one soft side and one scrubby side instead of using a shoulder pad from an old blazer.

"Nothing wrong with this," Bell said.

"I'll buy you some," Ruby said.

"I don't need sponges. I better go cook dinner now. Don't stay down here too long. Make you sneeze." Bell went upstairs, her hands in her pocket touching her retrieved items. Ruby watched her go, then plopped down in the armchair. In a way, Ruby was relieved that her mother had caught her before she put the bag out on the street.

The cushion beneath her felt crooked and she wondered how she could fix that. She lifted the cushion and under it, in the hollowed-out part of the chair, was a bag tied with bakery string. Inside the bag were children's clothes. Five handmade outfits, each slightly bigger than the last. It took Ruby a minute to realize that her mother had made the clothes for Sylvie.

The outfits had clearly taken a long time to make. The buttons and trim weren't from Bell's stash in the basement, but had been chosen carefully at the fabric store. Ruby unfolded each little dress and wondered what else her mother did that no one knew about. She started to put the bag away and then stopped.

Upstairs, Bell was rolling her stockings down to her ankles. On the floor next to her was a pair of pants Franklin wanted her to hem. As soon as she'd walked through the door, he had shoved the pants at her. No hello, how're you feeling today. The pants smelled like dog.

"Ma, what's all this baby stuff?" Ruby held up the littlest

outfit, a red and white striped one-piece with flower buttons up the front.

Bell left her stockings where they were and reached for the jumper. "How come you never leave my stuff alone? Put that back."

"This is for Sylvie, isn't it?"

"So? I like to sew baby clothes. Babies supposed to wear cotton." Bell sat down and smoothed the jumper in her lap, holding it there in a way that made Ruby feel tight all over.

Bell buttoned the jumper all the way to the top before folding it back up. "Isn't this a nice one." She held up a blue dress with lace on the hem and sleeves. "You know what your brother say when I tell him I want to see the baby? He say he too busy to clean the house. The house too messy for people to come over. I tell him who cares about the house. He say when he have time, he bring her here. You think he ever have time?" Bell said. Ruby touched her mother on the back. She didn't know if she should pat her or just leave her hand in one place.

"That's enough cleaning for today." Bell turned her face from her daughter, then folded each little outfit, tucked them back into the bag and pushed the whole thing under the bed.

After dinner, Ruby stood at the top of the stairs, wanting to go down and sit with her mother. She tried to bend her legs, but they felt stuck. Maybe her mother wanted to be alone. She hadn't even finished eating but had left her bowl on the stove with a lid on top. After she left the table, Ruby went over to the stove and lifted the cover. What was left in the bowl really wasn't enough to save. She felt strange looking at those few grains of rice, as if she were intruding.

Usually in the evenings, Bell watched TV in the basement and Franklin watched in the living room. That night, Ruby stood at the top of the landing listening for her mother's TV, but the only sound she could make out was the hum of the furnace. Thinking of her mother sitting in the basement not doing anything at all loosened up her legs and she started down the stairs.

Halfway down she stopped and leaned far over the banister. If she leaned far enough, she could see her mother in the back of the basement, looking around as if she was trying to find a new place to hide Sylvie's clothes. At first Bell looked sheepish, as if she knew it was silly to look for a new place now that Ruby had found the clothes, but then a brazen look came over her face, as if she suddenly wanted to make hundreds of little dresses and bundle them up and get on the bus and take them over to Van's house, push the package into his arms. "This is for Sylvie from Grandma," she would say and then turn around and leave before he could say a word.

Ruby watched her go over to the pile of sticks Bell had been saving for her garden. A few weeks ago, Bell had pounded a few sticks into the ground, then wove lattices of string between them so her bean plants would have something to climb up. Whenever she went out walking, she was on the lookout for sticks. People threw away perfectly good brooms and mops. When she found one, she unscrewed the stick part and walked home with it over her shoulder. Once she had admitted to Ruby that she had more sticks than she could use, but when she came upon a good one, she couldn't help herself.

Still leaning over the banister, Ruby watched her mother carefully wedge the package behind her stick pile. Ruby thought she heard her mother say in a low voice, "Grandma," but she couldn't be sure because just then, her mother turned on the TV. She flipped from station to station. It was hard to find something to watch, everything was shooting.

Ruby plopped down on a step in the middle of the stairway. The volume was turned up high. She thought she heard her mother laughing along with the TV. Her heart contracted. She hated to see her mother sad. When she was sad she laughed at TV. The worst part was that her mother would smile as soon as Ruby came down those stairs, and if she did that, Ruby would fall to the floor. Then she would get up and pull the pink vanity chair over to her mother's chair and the two of them would sit there in front of the TV every night for the rest of their lives. It was musty in the basement and her mother's chair was all lop-sided. The cardboard ceiling was crumbling in places and there were roaches.

Deeply ashamed, Ruby turned and started slowly back up, placing each foot carefully on the step before lifting the other. She stepped lightly but the old wooden steps were full of creaks. By the time she got to the top, she thought what a great relief it would be to let go of the banister and tumble down the stairs, landing in a tangled heap at the bottom. When she woke up, her parents would be bending over her and then somehow they would carry her upstairs and put her to bed. She would sleep in her childhood bed and when she woke up she wouldn't open her eyes so the cool hand against her forehead would not be taken away. She would lie there with the hand resting gently on her head and she would try to figure out if it was her mother's hand or her father's hand, but she was so tired that soon she would stop wondering and open her eyes.

Chapter 8

But of course she didn't let herself fall down the steps. She held on to the banister with two hands until the feeling passed and then she walked back up the stairs. In the living room, Franklin was watching a special on the hermit crab. Strangely, these crabs lived in the forest and made their homes in trees. Thousands were scuttling out of the forest, across roads and highways, even, in their yearly exodus to the sea. Ruby plopped down on the chair next to her father's. At one time it had been a soft chair, but someone had stuck a board under it, and now it was as hard as a park bench. She looked at the TV, but really she was dying for a café where she might find some halfway decent person to go home with. That's what she needed to feel alive again. She could get on the subway and go into the city, but it seemed such a long way to go just to get laid. Franklin pointed at the screen. "Look at those crabs. I bet they're good eating." The crabs swarmed over a front lawn and a woman in high heels stepped over them.

"There's not much meat on them," Ruby answered.

"But I bet they're sweet." Now the crabs had reached the sea and were clambering on top of each other. Franklin and Ruby watched without saying anything. Then Franklin said, "Doesn't look like you have any work lined up yet." The crabs had finished copulating and the females were doing a funny dance in the waves, shaking their claws in the air. Franklin's tone had changed and Ruby knew she had disappointed him. He no longer expected anything from Van. Franklin had worn out his arm trying to beat some sense into him, but still Van wouldn't do what his father wanted. And Lily had never shown much of an interest in anything except hanging out, although Franklin had to admit she had turned out better than he had thought she would. But Ruby had been his last hope.

"Remember that commercial, the one with the customer asking the laundryman guy how he gets his shirts so white and there's this gong and the laundry guy says, 'Ancient Chinese secret'? I hated that commercial," Ruby said.

"You don't even study a normal subject. What's wrong with medicine or computers? Even journalism. Isn't that what you went there for? You study some funny thing that nobody ever hear about. What is it again, something about ladies?"

"Women, Dad. Not ladies. It's Women's Studies."

"You study some crazy subject, get crazy ideas. You even got your mother acting crazy. The other day I ask her to hem some pants and she give me a look like I'm trying to kill her."

"A dirty look? She gave you a dirty look?" Ruby said.

"That makes you happy?" Franklin said.

"You give her dirty looks all day long," Ruby said. Franklin blew a stream of smoke above their heads. Ruby didn't breathe until the smoke had drifted to the ceiling. "I'm going to temp for a while. Until I decide what to do."

"Temp work? That kind of job is fine for summer vacation but not for permanent. No security." He shook his head and went into the kitchen. He got the Entenmann's box from the top of the refrigerator. Walnut Danish. Ruby waited to see if he would offer her a little slice. He didn't and she told herself she didn't care.

While Franklin and Ruby watched TV in the living room, Bell sat in her patched-up chair in the basement. She kept looking at her pile of sticks. The package of baby clothes was tucked away at the bottom of the pile, but she still felt worried. She turned back to the television. Without taking her eyes from the screen, she reached into the drawer of the nightstand and took out her little notebook of telephone numbers. Van had had the same number for fifteen years now, but she still didn't know it by heart. Bell coughed a few times while the phone rang in her son's house.

"Hi, Jeannette? This is Van's ma," Bell said before she realized she was talking to the answering machine. Jeannette's voice on the machine sounded irritated. Bell started over, "Hello, Van? This is Ma. I think next week is your birthday. End of May, right? You want to come over for dinner? Come over and I make you a birthday dinner. Bring Jeannette and the kids. Okay, bye." After Bell hung up the phone she wondered if Van had been sitting at home, listening to her message. Maybe he was even crazier than he used to be. Bell got up and went over to the pile of sticks. She put her hand into the pile and felt around until she found the package of clothes. Sylvie was five now, must be in kindergarten already. Bell didn't know what Sylvie liked to eat, maybe noodles; all kids loved noodles. Van had always loved seafood. Bell thought she might go down to Chinatown and get a couple of lobsters, a pound of shrimp. Maybe Van was out at a concert. Those rock-and-roll people liked to stay out late. Bell didn't expect that he would call her back tonight.

After everyone was in bed, Ruby walked around the dark house and thought again of going into the city. If only she could meet someone and go home with him. It wasn't enough to do it herself anymore, she needed to push against something besides her own hand. She needed the clean feeling and then the going out afterward to look for food. Diners with murals of the Acropolis splayed across their walls appealed to her in the early-morning hours, diners that served up great big turkey clubs where she found herself sitting across from someone she might never have talked to if she hadn't fucked him. These days she found that she looked at telephone repairmen and train conductors and they looked back at her. "Hey, baby," they'd say and sometimes she liked it. She was tired of skinny college boys who thought the harder they fucked her, the more manly they were. Those boys only got one chance.

Nick looked wispy, but he was stronger than he looked. And, more important, he had finesse. She didn't know what was wrong with her, she had a perfectly good lover and she still wanted others. She felt like she was waiting. She looked at women and waited too long and missed her chance. Women were dangerous. Ruby knew a woman could break her heart just by looking at her. Men felt safer, maybe because her mother had warned her every day of her life about them, so she knew to keep a part of herself hidden away where they could never touch her.

On the street, Ruby would stare at old couples walking arm in arm, still finding things to talk about after all those years. They went by and she would stare after them until she realized everyone could see the longing in her. On nights when she and Nick made dinner at home and talked about their crazy families and the books they were reading and what kind of hats they would get for winter, she could see herself twenty years from now, living happily ever after. That gave her a queer trapped feeling that wouldn't go away until she went out and fucked someone else, but even then, sometimes she felt even more trapped afterward.

If she weren't in such a bad mood, she really would go into the city. Get some iced tea, buy some books, find a hat for her mother. Iced tea and books and hats were all well and good, but that night what she really wanted was to meet someone and go back to his bed. Maybe they would sit on the sofa first and have a beer (she hated beer but liked having something in her hands). He might ask her what music she liked or maybe he would just pick something out himself. After the music stopped and they were sitting there talking quietly, her head would start to move slowly toward his shoulder until it was resting there. Hopefully, his shoulder wouldn't be too bony but nice and round, like a pillow under her head.

Relieved, he would shift his leg so it was touching hers and then he would put his arm around her. Then the kiss. Some guys kissed her on the top of her head first. That made her feel like a baby. She liked it better when they went for her mouth.

If only she hadn't stopped in the middle of the stairs but had walked right down to the basement and then straight to the back where her mother was waiting for her. No, she couldn't fix it, but she could have held her mother's hand or patted her back.

Now all she could think about was running away to the city. You could walk for hours, stopping into one place after another, and you wouldn't see one person who knew you, who knew that you lived in a house where people watched TV in different rooms, knew that you were touchy about smoke on account of your father, knew that your mother has the most beautiful smile in the world but that it drives you crazy, especially after a friend noticed that you are inclined to smile when you don't really mean it. You could walk for miles and not meet one person who knew what your favorite part of the chicken was. The wing. Ruby likes the wing. But if it's turkey, then it's the neck. That would come as no surprise to you if you had been there every Thanksgiving, where she and her best buddy Helen would crouch in a corner, sharing the neck every year, until the year they felt too old for that, so they sat at the table with everyone else and ate some white meat instead.

That was why Ruby didn't like sleeping in her mother's room. Her mother knew too many things about her, so that even though Ruby wore the flowered nightie to bed, she still felt naked.

Ruby took the phone into the bathroom and dialed Nick's number. "Hey, sweetie. You asleep?" she said.

"Who's this?"

"Oh, stop."

"Is this the woman who used to be my girlfriend? The woman who never wants to see me anymore? Was it something I said?"

"Cut it out. I tried to come over today, but I didn't make it. Just couldn't get on the train."

"It's not good for you there. You're getting strange. Why don't you stay here awhile?" His tone was serious now.

"You know what my mom did today? She washed out all my panties and socks. By hand. And every day she makes me this huge breakfast. It's waiting on the stove when I wake up. It's driving me nuts."

"How come no one makes me breakfast every morning?"

"You know I don't like to eat in the morning. Never mind. What'd you do today?"

"Frozen drinks. Want a margarita? I'll make you one. You want cookies? I got cookies, chocolate-chip macadamia nut. My mom's coming for a visit. I have to get pretzels."

"When?"

"A couple of weeks. It'll be fine," he said. "What'd you do today?"

"The usual. Went to Dunkin' Donuts, ate a cruller, read the Want Ads. My dad's mad at me—no, disappointed. I fixed my mom's chair. Kind of. I don't know what got into me."

"I need to see you," he said.

She cringed. She hated it when he needed her. "You might have to come here."

"Haven't I wanted to come there for years?"

"No, not *here*. I'll meet you somewhere. At the station. We'll have tea."

"Tea? I don't want tea. I want you to lie on top of me."

"I'll meet you at the diner by the train station. Take the number one to Fifty-ninth, then switch to the D, and then the R. Last stop."

"What time?" He was tired of giving in to her. He wondered why he had to go fall in love with a crazy Chinese girl. Maybe his mother was right about finding himself a nice Jewish girl who wanted to settle down and have kids. "I love you," he said.

"Me too," she said. She hung up the phone. Everyone in the house was sleeping by now. Ruby thought of the day she had moved away. Her mother and Lily had walked around her dorm room in John Jay Hall. After they had tested the springs of the bed and looked into the closet and opened and closed the drawers of the desk, her mother said it was time to go. In the elevator, the three women looked straight ahead. At the gate, her mother waved her away and said, "You better go unpack now." Ruby and Lily embraced stiffly. Lily felt so small that Ruby felt some affection for her. "Take care of Ma, okay?" Ruby said. Then she went toward her mother. Her mother was crying and struggling not to. She put her arms tight around Ruby, then shoved her away and ran to the car. Ruby watched her go, waving at the car until it turned the corner, then she walked back to her room, and while everyone else was unpacking and wandering into one another's rooms to say hello, she was crying into the bare mattress and each time she tried to stop she heard the sob that had come out of her mother right after she pushed her away. She had never seen her mother cry before.

After that, she couldn't face her mother anymore. On the rare weekend that she went home to visit, her mother kept saying how late it was getting and how the subways weren't safe at night and that Ruby better get going soon. It didn't matter if it was only one o'clock in the afternoon, her mother still said it was getting late. Ruby had a feeling her mother wanted her to stay overnight in her old bed, but her mother was pushing her so hard out the door that she went.

But most weekends, Ruby didn't go back. Sometimes she told her mother she was coming over, but at the last minute she called and said she had to study, but next week for sure. After Bell hung up the phone, she checked on the ribs or the steak she had left to defrost. If the meat was still frozen, she would put it back in the freezer for next week. Lily and Franklin weren't big eaters. Then she went out to the yard and touched her plants. She was checking for bugs, but she liked handling the leaves and the vines and the green tomatoes that were warm in her hand. If there were extra flowers on her squash vines, she picked them and gave them to her neighbor Theresa, who fried them up in dough. In the afternoons, Lily might call Bell to go to the mall at Roosevelt Field. Bell didn't need anything at the mall, but she went along for the ride. Sometimes she bought undershirts for her husband if they were on sale. If Hector went, Bell stayed at home. Young people liked to be alone. So Bell went to the supermarket and filled up her cart with food and then she came home and put her groceries away. When the cabinets got too full, she took to hiding food all over the house. Whenever Franklin found the boxes of tea or the saltine crackers in the living room, he yelled at her.

Even Bell knew she was saving too much, but the house was so empty after Ruby left that Bell couldn't help piling up more and more things. The night Ruby decided to move down to the basement, she walked around the house and touched the things her mother had piled up in the house. She didn't want to sleep in the little room with her mother anymore. A grown woman should have her own room. Ruby went out to the laundry, where her father stored the spare bedding, and picked out a set of sheets, digging around in the pile until she found the ones with butterflies on them. In the basement she fixed up the old sofa, and when she woke in the morning, her mother was standing there looking at her.

Chapter 9

*F*ranklin and Bell found themselves talking about their daughter again, just as they had years ago when they would exchange a few words, lying on Franklin's bed together just after his orgasm. Those were moments of generosity before Bell straightened her clothes and went to her own room. They'd talked about the day-to-day things like dentist appointments and shoes and school pictures. They didn't mention the bigger things, such as Franklin losing his temper again and hauling Van off to the bathroom for another whipping while his sisters stood outside the door, screaming and crying until Bell whisked them away and then she went back and pounded on the door, yelling at her husband to stop before he killed her son. During those moments he was more her son than at any other time, even though he shot past her waiting arms as soon as the bathroom door opened.

They didn't talk about Franklin carrying a grudge a little too far by not speaking to Lily year after year. At first he had thought that shutting her out would teach her a lesson. What he hadn't known was that Lily, the middle child, already felt shut out. No matter how she tried, she would never be as much trouble as her brother or as smart as her sister, so she chose disappearance (but aggressively)—not eating, not talking—and she was just as stubborn as her father.

Just as Franklin and Bell hadn't talked about his temper or his grudge against Lily, they didn't talk about Bell's dream either. In the dream she's in Woolworth's with Ruby, who's five years old again. Ruby wraps dresses around her body and then crawls inside the clothes rack. She jumps out to scare her mother. They laugh. Bell is looking at fall jackets as she waits for Ruby to jump out and yell "Boo." She waits and waits. Then she gets down on her hands and knees and crawls from one clothes rack to another, but no Ruby. Bell gets up and runs (pitifully slow) to the toy section. There are children there but Ruby isn't among them, nor is she picking out school supplies or sampling the by-the-pound candies she loves so well. Bell rides up and down the escalator, calling for her.

When Ruby was in her last year at Pinecrest High, Franklin and Bell talked about whether she should go away to school and it was Bell who thought she shouldn't, that she should stay at home and go to Queens College like Betty Wu. After all, Betty had graduated last year and she already had a job at the bank, where she met a smart boy and now they were engaged. In fact, Bell had a great fear about Ruby going away to school. She didn't know exactly what would happen, but she had a feeling that no good would come of it. Queens College would be better.

But Franklin had said if she wants to go to the good one, let her go. He had the same feeling as Bell, but he'd fought it and thought it best not to mention it. His wife was afraid of things, so jumpy all the time. He didn't want his daughter to end up the same way. Ruby was smart; she didn't have to be a nobody. He hadn't washed and starched and ironed all those years to send his daughter to a second-rate school. Journalism. That's what she wanted to study. One day he'd be reading the paper and he'd turn the page and suddenly he'd see it, her name right there in black and white. He'd be so excited he would hardly be able to hold the scissors as he cut out the article. He'd nail it to the wall and point to it and say to his customers, "That's my daughter."

Since Franklin said Ruby could go, she went. After she was gone, Franklin and Bell found less and less to talk about. He tried to tell her what was going on in the world, but she acted as if she didn't hear him. Then he tried to tell her about some aches and pains he had in his hands and his shoulders, but she didn't seem interested. Just once, she wished he had something nice to tell her. Sometimes she wanted to tell him about some small thing that had happened during the day, like taking a gypsy cab home instead of the bus and how that had made her feel just a little bit daring. When her factory was making alligator shirts, she wanted to ask if he wanted one. She would ask her boss if there were any extra. But Franklin never asked her anything, so she figured he didn't want to know. The only thing he ever asked her was, "Where are you going?" But the way he said it made her feel like a child and so she kept her answers vague.

But now that Ruby was back they had her to talk about, like why she wanted to live in the basement. No one had questioned Van when he had moved downstairs. They'd figured he felt funny living in a room full of females. Or maybe he was sick of washing his feet. When he came back late at night from wherever it was he went, he liked to sleep with his feet hanging off the end of his bed so he wouldn't dirty his sheets. His sisters woke up to his stink-foot smell and they would elbow him until he got up to wash.

Van's room in the basement had a groovy purple shower curtain around his bed. He drew pictures and taped them to the walls, pictures of people with their thoughts in plain view. The things people think about, you wouldn't believe. He brought his hippie girlfriends home, kissed them a little, then left them in the basement and went to ask Lily for a condom. She kept them locked up for him so their parents couldn't prove he was having sex in the basement. Lily didn't look at him as she unlocked her desk and made sure not to touch his hand when she gave him the square packet. She wondered if he would think she was puritanical if she said she didn't want to keep them for him anymore. Having them in her desk made her feel tempted to try one with her boyfriend.

In the basement, Van would turn up the music so his parents wouldn't hear the girl moaning beneath him. He liked girls with long hair. After his girls went home, he would play his electric guitar and purse his lips like Mick Jagger. He was good at that. He had the lips too. Franklin would come running down to the basement. His white shirt and pressed pants looked even more out of place there than in his laundry. "Turn that goddamn thing down," he'd yell.

"Cool out, Dad. You just got to get into it." Van would sing a few bars of "Satisfaction."

"Maybe you want to get out of this house. Then you can get into it all you want." Franklin would pull the plug from the wall and Van would go on playing even though all you could hear were his fingers plucking against the strings.

Now Franklin and Bell spoke in Chinese about their youngest daughter, who was no longer the daughter who stayed home on the weekends and baked bread. All kinds she used to make: raisin rolls, cinnamon swirl, the one she braided up like hair and brushed with egg on top to make it brown and shiny. But now there was a tiredness about her, even in the mornings. Bell didn't mention that she and Ruby wanted to go to Florida. Instead, she pointed to Ruby's library books piled up overdue in a corner. Franklin grumbled that she was out all day and when she came back she wouldn't say where she had been. When the phone rang, she jumped up to get it and then she took the phone into the bathroom and shut the door behind her. Her clothes were wrinkled and her hair looked like a boy's.

Her parents whispered in Chinese and Ruby tried to make out what they were saying. She didn't know why they bothered to whisper since she couldn't understand the words. Her parents hadn't wanted her to end up like her cousin who grew up in Chinatown and didn't speak English. Her cousin sat in the back row at school and sucked on her pen. One day the pen burst and there was blue all over her mouth. She wouldn't answer the teacher and she wouldn't stick her tongue out. That was rude.

Franklin and Bell didn't want that to happen to their kids, so they taught them English, then called them stupid when they asked for English menus in Chinese restaurants, called them stupid when they couldn't talk to their uncles and aunties who lived in Chinatown, called them stupid American kids who didn't know where they came from.

Ruby didn't understand the words, but she knew what they were saying. They were disturbed by her need for privacy. They thought she must be doing something wrong, something she had to hide. Clearly she was ruined. Bell didn't say anything about how none of this would have happened if Ruby had gone to Queens College.

At first Ruby thought that moving to the basement would be as easy as laying sheets on the old sofa. But a few hours later she was upstairs again, gathering the things she had unpacked in her mother's room. At first she and her mother had been careful to confine their clothes to their own drawers, but after a while her mother's undershirts ended up on top of Ruby's jeans, Ruby's thrift-store shirts were mixed in with her mother's homemade pants, and the sock drawer was a tangle of panty hose and sweat socks. The day Ruby moved her things to the basement, her mother sat on the bed, shaking a plastic bag at her. "Here, take this. Make it easier."

Her mother was so sensible. But Ruby didn't want to do it the easy way. She wanted to carry everything in her arms. Her mother walked behind her, picking up the things that fell to the floor. "Why don't you use this bag?" her mother said.

It was just a lousy shopping bag from Key Food, but Ruby couldn't take one more thing from her mother. "That's okay," Ruby said.

In the basement she emptied out the dresser that used to be in the living room. The handles had fallen off years ago, but you could get the drawers open without breaking your nails if you knew how. Bell watched Ruby struggling with the drawers and had to restrain herself from going over and opening the drawers herself. Ruby had that look on her face that said "Don't. If you help me I will die of frustration and weakness, both."

The cellar door was open and Bell stood under it and looked up at her garden. The tomato plants were growing tall and were starting to droop to the side. With great care, Bell picked out a few sticks from her pile. "I think those tomato plants need a little help." She leaned on one stick and threw the others over her shoulder. The one she leaned on was bright orange and she walked slowly, leaning into it as she made her way across the basement. The shopping bag hung deflated from her pocket.

Ruby watched her mother walk up the stairs. Her stick landed sharply on each step like a reprimand and then it was quiet and Ruby was alone in the basement. It was dusty and cluttered, but at least her parents couldn't watch her every move. She didn't mind if they saw her *doing* things like cleaning or cooking or reading or even watching TV. It was when she just sat there doing nothing that she felt furtive. That was all she felt like doing, now that she was in the basement. Then she remembered her date with Nick at the diner. It was too bright outside. Now that she had moved to the basement, she thought the sun would hurt her somehow. If only it were a gloomy day, she could hide under her umbrella and then she could meet him. She tried to think of an excuse, but in the end she called him and told him it was too sunny for her and that she would come over real soon.

From the backyard, Ruby heard her mother pounding sticks into the ground. Then it was quiet, which meant her mother was squatting close to the ground so she could get at the weeds. Then the backyard door opened and Lily stepped into the yard. It was past noon on Saturday and she had just gotten up. She had always loved summer, and after she became a teacher she waited for it all year. On school days she'd wake up muttering, hop into the stingy shower that left her feeling soapy, iron one shirt and one pair of pants, fill up her thermos with tea, get on the Grand Central all the way to Chinatown, where she'd buy a coconut bun from the bakery on the corner. The buns were too big to finish before the kids came. But now it was summer and she stayed in bed all morning, then got up and toasted an English muffin. She ate it while she watched cooking shows.

The weekend Ruby moved down to the basement, Lily stood in the yard in her felt slippers. She was feeling good; last night Hector had come over and they had talked about going to Puerto Rico for their honeymoon. Lily was afraid of flying and the original plan was to go someplace they could drive to, like Virginia or Woodstock. But last night Hector had listened to every one of her plane-crash stories and although he hadn't said much, afterward she felt relieved.

Lily watched her mother weeding her yard. "Me and Hector are going to Puerto Rico," Lily said, just to hear how it sounded. It sounded like a reasonable thing for a young couple to do.

"Good, good. You don't have to be scared of the plane," Bell said.

Lily felt vaguely disappointed; she had expected her mother to argue with her and had been looking forward to convincing her that she would really get on that plane and fly away. But her mother didn't seem to need convincing. Lily looked at the growing pile of weeds and then at her mother's face as she grabbed another weed and wrenched it from the ground. Her mother looked almost ferocious. Lily didn't remember ever seeing that look on her mother's face before, and without meaning to, Lily drew back and made herself smaller.

As she watched her mother weeding, Lily wondered if she should see a doctor about her anxiety. Lately, when she was in a crowd, her heart beat so fast she thought she would pass out. Her mother looked up then and said, "Me and Ruby thinking about going to Florida."

Lily blinked a few times and then said in a deadly calm tone, "Lots of planes crash on their way to Florida. I don't know why, maybe there's too much traffic. And there's alligators. Spiders too." She knew she was being mean, but she couldn't stop herself. Someone had to stay at home; she didn't know why it always had to be her. First Van left, and then Ruby, and now even her mother wanted to go. Then it occurred to her that the older she got (she was almost thirty-one now), the more timid she felt, while her mother seemed to be getting tougher. Last week, Lily had walked in on her mother telling Ruby about how terribly she had missed her sister when she was first married and living in Chinatown, but how Franklin wouldn't let her call. Lily had walked in while her mother was in the middle of her story and was shaken by the sudden rage that had flashed across her mother's face. Lily had said something about calling Hector and hurried back to her apartment, where she snatched up her darling rabbit Fluffy from his cage, stroked him behind his ears until his eyes closed and he settled deeper into her lap.

"Who's scared of planes? Not me. And spiders, there's spiders here too. And if I see an alligator, I make a soup. Did you ever eat alligator soup? It's sweet." Bell didn't know why she had made that up about the soup. It was true that you could make a soup out of almost anything, although she had never personally tried to cook an alligator. She had heard people talking, though, so it wasn't really a lie; Lily got on her nerves sometimes.

"Maybe we won't go to Puerto Rico. Maybe we'll drive to Canada instead. See the falls," said Lily. She waited for her mother to retract what she had said about Florida. When her mother didn't even look up from her weeding, Lily said, "What about Dad? What's he going to do?"

"He can take care of himself. He's no baby," said Bell. The mention of her husband sobered her and she said sadly, "I hear there's hurricanes in Florida."

"Maybe you should go. You can visit Louie and Sheila. They always invite you," said Lily.

"First you tell me not to go, now you tell me to go," said Bell.

"Florida's hot. Lots of people get sunstroke."

Ruby had inched closer and closer to the basement door, until she was right under it. She had gotten excited when her mother had started talking about Florida. She didn't even know her mother had been thinking about it. Ruby wished Lily would shut up about the alligators and spiders, but she also felt kind of sorry for her sister.

Through the screens across the cellar door, Ruby could see her mother gather up her weeds and stuff them into a bag. She couldn't see Lily, but she knew she was leaning against the wall in one of her neat little outfits, always ironed. It seemed a long time before Lily left. Ruby called to her mother from the basement.

Bell walked over to the basement door. "What you doing down there?" She peered down at Ruby.

"Cleaning. Did Lily scare you?" She stood on the basement steps and talked to her mother through the screens.

"Nah, I'm not scared. Something's wrong with her, she scared of every little thing. She don't want to go nowhere, she don't want no one else to go nowhere. Just like your father," said Bell. Then her face lit up. "When I was little, I'm not scared of nothing. You know how we used to get honey? I catch bees and inside there's one little drop of honey. I didn't know I could get stung. My mother never told me. Well, I better cook lunch now." Maybe it was because she was standing in the yard and Ruby was down in the basement, but before she went into the kitchen, Bell gave a little wave, as if she were standing on a ship that was moving slowly away from the dock.

Ruby found herself waving back. The way they were waving at each other made Ruby feel she would never see her mother again. Ruby couldn't imagine how she would ever move out when she got choked up watching her mother waving in her garden, which was really just a run-down plot of dirt with a few tomato plants, beans and squash vines stretching their skinny arms toward the sun, watery and pale.

Chapter 10

*R*uby had moved to the basement and she still didn't know what to do with herself. Three weeks at home and she had given up on prayer. She stared at the faded pictures her mother had torn from a calendar and taped to the walls years ago. It was her mother's one attempt at decorating, and it happened the year they had the meat calendar. If only it had happened another year, then they would have had waterfalls or Hong Kong girls or even historic sites of Queens instead of the grainy pictures of ham fettuccine and beef roll-ups.

Later, Ruby would say that the meat pictures drove her to call her agency. Even a dumb temp job seemed better than staring at pictures of meat all day. The real reason might have been Lily trying to scare her mother about Florida, which made Ruby more determined than ever to take her mother away and show her a good time. So she called her agency looking for work. The agency liked her. She was a no-bullshit, kick-ass typist. Some clients complained that she wasn't very friendly, but they still asked for her again.

Ruby wakes up in her father's house. A laundryman's daughter with a college degree. I am here temporarily, she tells herself. At work, she tells herself the same thing. *I am not a secretary. I am a temp.* She gets called in when secretaries have slipped disks and torn ligaments. When their mothers and fathers and grandfathers have died. When they're sipping tropical drinks by the pool, writing postcards to the folks at the office, who will pin them up around their desks next to pictures of their loved ones. She gets called in when they're having babies. When they get fired for attitude: couldn't/wouldn't get the coffee right, skirts too short, skirts too long.

The high point of the day is the visit to the candy machine, filled with rows of Oreos, Fig Newtons, Ring Dings and everything else you loved as a kid. They taste exactly the same but somehow not as good. She types other people's letters, deciphers handwriting, kisses her eyes good-bye. They don't even try to write neatly. She answers other people's phones. Lies for them. *They're all in meetings. No one is available. They're all in one megameeting that will never end.*

There's something unclean about it all, kind of like washing other people's laundry. It's getting too close to their dirt. As if you want to know about their smells and who was nervous today and who wears perfume to cover it up. They don't even know enough to be embarrassed. All they know is their shirts come back clean and pressed, perfect, as if done by a machine.

"Do you take dictation?" they ask her. "Why, are you a dictator?" she wants to answer. She is a girl. The women who have worked for fifty years are girls. Some days she sits and sits. They pay her for sitting. Other days, she is loaded down with paperwork like a little pack donkey. She sleeps on the train and wakes up when the conductor says, "Union Street. Last stop."

At work she tries to feel lucky, like her mother tells her. She sits at her desk thinking about her mother at the factory. Rows of women sit hunched over, feeding yards and yards of fabric into their machines. Overhead lights play up the garish patterns and the lint that settles so neatly into the creases in the women's faces. The steam from the irons and pressing machines heat the room, so that by the end of the day the women strip down to their undershirts.

They shout above the roar of the machines and fans. They

talk about which children are good (good school, good job, hardworking Chinese husband or wife with good little children of their own) and which are bad. They talk of husbands, how this one is a picky eater, how that one looks at young girls too much, how this one knows how to cook pretty good. They talk of ailments and herbal remedies for them. They talk of the work, how hard the new style is, how the bumpy fabric itches their skin and how the color comes right off on their fingers. They talk about how cheap the boss is.

Her mother does piecework, where you get paid according to how many dresses you make. You get a bundle of dresses with all the parts cut out already, like a puzzle. First you sew all the sleeves, then all the belts, then all the bow ties, and so on. Then you sew all the pieces together, until you have your bundle of dresses. Then you go get another bundle.

Ruby sits at a desk lit with overhead lights. She feels the ridges in her nails, wishing she had a nail file. She is Evelyn Garcia for the day. She studies Evelyn's photographs. A dark smiling man is flanked by two women in matching shiny blue dresses. They have the same lipstick on and the same big hair. The one on the right is prettier, and both women know it. The man smiles cockily, like he's hung.

She looks at her skin under the white light. In high school, she found out her skin was olive-colored. The article described how to correct this sallow look and she walked around for months thinking she was green. It wasn't easy. She looks at the clock and it's three minutes later than when she looked before. She thinks of her mother doing piecework and her doing time.

The next morning, Ruby stood in front of her closet. She had a sinking feeling she would end up wearing a T-shirt, her long black skirt with the baggy waistband, and the beige cardigan she got for $1.50 at the Goodwill on Amsterdam. She was in the bathroom when the phone rang. Her mother picked up and yelled for her, "It's that boy. Mick."

Ruby finished brushing her teeth and touched her hair before she picked up the phone. "Three weeks. A guy gets lonely, you know," Nick said.

"I almost made it yesterday. I was on the bus. But then I got off at Dunkin' Donuts."

"What about me? I could go for a nice glazed doughnut."

"I get crullers, French crullers. They're fluffy. Hey, did I tell you I moved to the basement? It's dark, but I don't mind too much," she said.

"Wasn't I supposed to come for dinner two weeks ago?"

She pictured his face getting all red. "I'm ugly," she said.

"What's the matter, baby? Your period coming soon?" His tone was softer now.

She felt tired suddenly. "I don't know, maybe. My hair's flat and he never says one nice thing to her and I've got this dumb outfit on and I'm late."

"Who? Your dad? He never says anything nice to your mom?" He was getting mad again.

"I saw this dress the other day. There's this thrift store on the avenue. It had a little jacket with a velvet collar, maybe forties. But I didn't have any money."

"I can get it for you."

"That's not what I was saying."

"Can't I buy my girlfriend a fucking dress?"

"I'll buy it myself. When I get my check."

"*If you can do it yourself, do it yourself.* You turning into your mother now?"

"Shut up. Don't talk about my mother," she said, without a trace of viciousness.

"I love you."

"I love you too."

After she hung up, she had perked up enough to put earrings on. There. That was better. Bell came out of her room. "What he want?" she said.

"Nick? Just calling to say hi," Ruby said.

"So early in the morning?"

"He was lonely," Ruby said.

"*Lonely?*" Bell said and almost shuddered. She went back to her room and wondered at these young people who talked so easily about things better kept to oneself.

As Ruby was leaving the house, her father looked up from his newspaper. He took off his reading glasses. "You going to work like that? That won't make a very nice impression. Why don't you iron it?"

It was one thing to admit to herself that she had on a terrible outfit, but he didn't have to rub it in. Even if she had on a brand-new Ann Taylor suit, he still wouldn't be satisfied. No matter what she did, it wasn't good enough. She felt hot suddenly, remembering the grueling weeks in high school she spent studying for the math regents. When she burst into her father's laundry with her grade report of 98 clutched in her hand, he had said, "Who got the other two points?" After that, she vowed never to do another thing to please him. Whenever he asked for her report card, she shrugged and said she had lost it.

Remembering the math regents, she tugged at her shirt and said, "I did iron it." She walked quickly to the bus stop, trying not to think about him. He wasn't going to ruin her life too. As she crossed the street, she realized she had on the narrow skirt that made her walk as if her laces were tied together. Damn. She tried to stretch it out by taking extra big steps but only succeeded in ripping the seam. By the time she got to the train station, she had convinced herself that she didn't even know how to temp anymore. They would take one look at her and send her home. On the train, she looked down at her legs and thought they looked very bare next to all the women in their panty hose. At Rockefeller Center she got off the train, went straight to Duane Reade and bought a pair of knee-highs, which she pulled on in a doorway. At Speedy Deli, she got a sesame bagel with cream cheese, her first bagel in weeks.

When she walked into the offices of Marshall & Potter, she was glad she had stopped for the knee-highs and only hoped her skirt was long enough to cover them. The receptionist was a snotty English biddy, a bad sign.

Ruby spent the morning typing last will and testaments. Some people left a lot of things behind. Typing fast helped to ease the restlessness she always felt in low-ceilinged offices with windows nailed shut and mouse-colored dividers between the desks.

The secretary next to her had worked there for two years, but she was really a singer in a band. Right now, they did weddings, but they were getting close to a record contract. "Is that cream cheese? You're so lucky. I hate you. You're skinny. You can eat," she said to Ruby.

"You can eat too," Ruby said. Dieters made her edgy. "You want some?"

"Oh God, no. I'd just blow up. But you, you're so thin. Do you work out?"

"I hate exercise." Ruby didn't really, she just felt like saying that.

"I do jazzercise. He runs. Ten miles a day," the singer-secretary said, pointing to the closed door of Ruby's boss. He was fifty-five years old and ran ten miles every morning and was damn proud of his ten miles and his firm body that made love to his wife twice a week.

Ruby went back to typing. Some guy who lived in New Jersey was leaving his sports car to his son. Typing wasn't so bad. In fact, Ruby kind of liked it.

Piece of cake, she was thinking, right before things took a bad turn; her boss handed her a chart to revise. She didn't know much about charts and thought about asking Sara Ryan, the secretary next to her, for help. Sara had worked there for over ten years and had had a harassed look on her face all morning. Ruby couldn't tell if Sara was having a bad day or if she always looked like that. Ruby decided not to bother her.

Five minutes later, the chart was unrecognizable—numbers from one row had jumped over to the next, the last column had completely disappeared and nothing lined up straight anymore. She knew that pressing random keys wasn't helping any, but she couldn't stop herself. Suddenly she saw herself in ten, twenty, fifty years—at the same desk, caring desperately about some chart that she couldn't care less about. She'd be stuck there with the dieters and the lukewarm tea with powdered cream and she'd be wearing the same funny work outfit.

"Sara?" Ruby finally said.

Sara looked up. She was wearing frosted eye shadow. Ruby hadn't known that you could still buy frosted eye shadow. Sara came right over to Ruby's desk. A few keystrokes later, the chart was fixed. "There," Sara said. Ruby was so grateful she could've cried.

Then Sara's phone rang and she went to answer it. It was her husband. The harassed look left her face and suddenly she looked radiant. "Did you see the newspaper yet? Our stocks are up!" They were new to the market and every day they checked the newspaper and then called each other, excited over every tiny rise and fall. Sara touched her hair as she talked. After she hung up, she noticed that Ruby was staring at her. "My husband," Sara said. "We just started playing the market."

"How's it going?"

"We've got some winners."

"You been married long?"

"Twenty-two years."

"Twenty-two years!"

"We've known each other for twenty-five, though."

"Were you high school sweethearts or something?"

"We met in high school. Got married after graduation. He's an artist," Sara said, full of pride. "Are you married?"

"Me? Nah, I'm wishy-washy." Ruby paused. Then she said, "Did you always know you would get married to him, your husband?"

"As soon as I saw him. Love at first sight, I guess."

The two women went back to their work, but whenever there

was a lull, Ruby asked Sara questions about her marriage. She had never been so interested in marriage before, but she loved to watch Sara's face get dreamy when she said her husband's name. Usually, Sara didn't talk much about her private life at work, but she figured Ruby was a temp, so what the hell. Ruby didn't know why she felt so sad about Sara's marriage; all she knew was that the woman still lit up after twenty-five years.

It was hot in the office. The sun poured through the windows and the air-conditioning wasn't on yet. She wanted to take off her sweater, but that was the part of her outfit that made it a work outfit. And she didn't have a bra on. They were funny about that stuff at work. Her restlessness was growing. The trouble with typing fast was she was done too soon. Under the desk, she found a Victoria's Secret catalog, a few paperbacks and a pile of shoes. She tried on a pair of strappy sandals she could never walk in, but she liked the way they made her feet arch; she didn't know why. It made her want to call up and order some outrageous getup to wear in the middle of the day under her temp clothes. Nick would fall to his knees.

As she slipped Linda's shoes back into the box, she felt a sudden longing for the nights when she and Nick would sit in bed, leaning in close over the latest catalog. Nick would be wearing his rumpled shorts and she would have on her terry robe and the light in the room was soft and yellow. Once in a while they might order something—a shirt, a sweater, maybe a hat. The room expanded to let in the girl on the phone, her voice creamy as butter, so they felt like buying more just to keep her on the phone. It wasn't so much the shirt or sweater or hat they wanted but the sweet closing after they hung up and were alone again.

At night, the longing was still there as she watched her mother rummage through her "I Love New York" shopping bag. Her mother looked at her over her sewing glasses. "I have some collars left over. You want to turn them?" The collars were all joined together like link sausages. Ruby clipped them apart and used a chopstick to turn them inside out—really right side out because they're sewn inside out to begin with.

She stacked the collars, then took one and wrapped it around her neck. "You think you could get me one of these to wear to work?"

"You want one?" Bell said, then saw that Ruby was kidding and felt strangely let down. "You don't wear things like that."

Ruby took off the collar and laid it with the rest. She lingered over the work. "What's the matter, Ma?"

"Nothing. What?"

"You're quiet today."

"I don't know. How was work today?"

"You know. Terrible. But it was okay."

Bell touched the thin cushion tied to Ruby's chair. "Remember how your brother put a paper bag on the chair before he sit down. He don't want to get dirty," she said gently.

"God, remember how he used to wash bananas with soap?"

"I call him the other day. His birthday's coming up."

"You called Van?"

"He don't answer my message. I guess I better go finish these." Bell picked up the collars.

"Maybe he never got the message."

"He got it," Bell said and headed out to the laundry. Her trusty green Singer machine hummed late into the night.

Franklin was finishing off his cake in front of his television. He was in position for the night in his recliner. Ruby and her brother and sister had bought it for him, thinking he would like it since he would always put his feet up on a milk crate with a flattened pillow on top. He did try the recliner a few times, but he said it hurt his bum leg, so he tied the footrest to the chair so it wouldn't recline anymore and put his feet right back up on the milk crate. He wouldn't move until after the eleven-o'clock news.

Ruby went down to the basement. It was too dark to sleep. There were no windows and the air was very still. She could feel water bugs watching her in the dark. She turned on the light and confronted a monster one. She tried to run past it, but it ran in the same direction. It was big. It would splatter if she crushed it. Brown guts and crunchy shell. She wouldn't even try to step on it.

She couldn't believe she was spending another night in the basement flipping channels on the TV. Tonight she ended up at the Home Shopping Channel, tempted to buy a cubic zirconia ring. A long time ago, her family had watched TV together. They would sit on the couch and eat Planters peanuts or Jiffy Pop popcorn. Franklin would supervise: "Keep shaking it. In circles. Better turn the gas down low or it'll get burned. Hear that? It's almost finished."

But then Van grew up and moved out and Lily started going out at night and coming home late, after the news was over. Then Bell started getting more and more bothered by Franklin's cigar and went right to her room after dinner. He only watched scary shows and nature shows anyway. Ruby was the last one to stay and watch with him. Sometimes she even sat next to him on the sofa and if his smoke bothered her, she blew at it and he would wave his hands around, pushing it away from her. It was like a game the two of them played. Once in a while, his ash would get so long it would fall on her. Then he'd jump up and brush the ash vigorously off her, and stop smoking for about fifteen minutes. One time he burned a hole the size of a nickel in her favorite faded blue miniskirt. In the end, Bell sewed a daisy patch over the hole and it was better than before.

The night she came home after a long day of temping, she felt compelled to leave the house. But now that she had changed out of her work clothes and into her pajamas, she felt stuck there. Put on your jeans you like to wear when you have your period and the dark green shirt that your mother ironed so neatly you don't recognize it anymore and your boots, she said to herself. She forced herself to do it, hating her outfit, ill-fitting and ugly as her mood. There was no place to go unless she went to Manhattan. All the places in the neighborhood were closed, not that she wanted to go there anyway. The bowling alley, the pizzeria, Dunkin' Donuts, all closed. She used to love those places.

She decided to take a little walk on the avenue. Nearly all the stores on the block had gates now. The laundry and the barbershop were the only ones without them. Franklin talked about getting a gate. She walked up Hollis as far as the nudie theater and then she turned back. A realtor's window was lit up and she stood in front and priced apartments, not that she would live in Queens, but just to get an idea.

Someone called her name. It was Helen Hong. She looked as pretty as ever. Her hair was curled and a thick line of dark pencil made her eyes look even bigger. "Girl, is that you?" Helen said and then she hugged her childhood friend fiercely with the top of her body.

"Shoot. Look at you," Ruby said and took in the sadness beneath the loud cheer. Now Helen was affectionately slapping her arm.

"How the hell are you? You visiting?" Helen said.

Ruby was tempted to say yes, that she was just visiting for the weekend. "I wish. I'm back home." They were both quiet, then Ruby said, "My mom said you were working at Macy's."

"Hats and gloves. Another fucking-shit job." Helen grabbed Ruby's hand and inspected it. "You're not married?"

"Me? Nah." Ruby shook her head and made a face. "Are you?"

Helen showed her left hand, ringless. "I was seeing this cop for a while." They both looked down and then Ruby felt Helen looking at her clothes. They had been best friends for fifteen years and now they stood on Hollis Avenue and didn't know what to say. Helen said suddenly, "Hey, do you play pool?"

"Pool? Not much. The balls won't stay on the table."

"There's this place in the city. All these hot guys." Helen fanned herself to show how hot. "We should go sometime."

"Sure. I'll call you." At that moment Ruby believed she would actually call and that they would go out together like old times.

"Call me. Same number." They hugged again and then Helen walked quickly up the street. Ruby stood for a moment until her face settled into her regular walking-on-the-street face, which some people took for snotty. She waited for Helen to get a block ahead of her, then started walking again. It gave her an odd feeling to see her old friend. She walked slowly back home and for no reason found herself thinking of all the boxes of macaroni and cheese they used to eat. Every day after school, they would make a box, stirring in the cheese powder and milk and lots of margarine so it was nice and creamy. Then Helen would rush off to ballet class at Miss Elaine's, her stomach round in her leotard.

At the laundry, Ruby reached her hand through the hole in the screen door and undid the spring lock. Bell was sitting at her sewing machine, working in semidarkness. "Guess who I just saw?" Ruby said. "Helen. She dyed her hair. It's red in front."

"Why she want to do a crazy thing like that?" Bell said.

"She likes to have fun." Ruby looked out the window. "Ma, I'm going out for a while."

"You just went out. Where're you going now?"

"I don't know. The city."

"At this time? Too late to go out."

"I won't be long." Ruby left the laundry before she could change her mind. On the street, she pushed her hands into her pockets. She didn't know where she was going, but she headed for the bus stop. There was determination in the way she gripped the token in her hand and studied the bus map, although she knew the route to the subway by heart. Maybe she would visit her friends from school. They were always telling her to come over. They lived uptown. Or maybe she would head downtown and walk around and find a café where no one knew her. She would sit with a cup of tea in front of her or maybe even a drink until her date came along, someone new who would sit down next to her. They would talk about their day. Then, when it was almost time to go, she would ask him what he had eaten that day and he would tell her and then they would walk out together.

Chapter 11

*I*t was Friday night and the train was full of people headed into the city. Only the very old and the very depressed stayed home in Queens on the weekend. The rest of the bridge and tunnel crowd roused themselves after a week of working, put on their party clothes, got back on the train with thoughts of roast chicken or barbecued rib platters at BBQ and a couple of frozen daiquiris. The men on the train, young and old, watched three girls with fluffy hair cross and uncross their legs. One was wearing a skirt that rode up her legs and she kept tugging at it. She was young and still had hope that maybe one day, maybe even tonight, she would meet some big galoot on the dance floor who would love her just the way she was, big thighs and all.

For a moment, Ruby wished she had gussied up a bit more. Maybe she should have put on her other pair of jeans, the ones that weren't so saggy in the butt. But she was feeling cocky tonight, as if she could walk into a bar wearing an old house-dress and flip-flops and walk out with whomever she wanted.

The train pulled into stations downtown but Ruby didn't move. It was crowded and she was reluctant to stand up in front of all those people. She was afraid she might trip and catch her shoe between the train and the platform. At Lexington, a rush of people got off and another rush got on. At the last minute Ruby hopped off the train, walked up the stairs and waited for another train.

Two hours and fifteen minutes after she had left the house,

she found herself uptown near Nick's house. But she didn't want to see him tonight; if she saw him she might finally break down and cry. It felt dangerous to see him while she was living at home—she might be tempted to stay with him; days and weeks and then years would pass without her noticing, and one morning she'd wake up and look out the window and there, surrounding the house, would be the dreaded white picket fence. That was what Nick called her restlessness, like the weekend they went away to the country. They were in the canoe and she was rowing and wearing his jacket with the zipper. The water was very still. Once in a while they spotted turtles, and there, on the still lake, she felt unguarded for once in her life. That made her nervous and later, at Jeff's Corner, she picked a fight over a lamb chop. But Nick had known she wasn't fighting about dinner. "White picket fence?" he had asked. She nodded and said, "Stop harassing me."

So she couldn't live with him. She could never live with him. At night he got too hot and kicked off all the blankets and in the morning the pillowcases were stained with sweat. Over time, his pillows had gotten musty. At school, Ruby had used the old striped cases she had slept on most of her life, but after graduation she had bought herself a set of white cotton damask sheets from Macy's. She didn't mind him messing up his own, but she felt pure grief at the thought of giving up her clean white pillows. If only she didn't care about these things, then maybe she could live with him. So what if the pillows got a little stained, she told herself, but she wasn't convinced. As soon as she woke up, she would have the bleach out.

Tonight she wanted a stranger so she could start all over again. She left the train station and started in the direction opposite from Nick's house. She walked slowly, looking into each passing face, waiting for the shock of desire.

Finally she sat down at a sidewalk-café table but immediately felt conspicuous, like she was sitting in the middle of the sidewalk. If all she'd wanted was to sit on the sidewalk, she could have stayed at home and sat on a folding chair in front of the store. She sat at the sidewalk table and waited. No one came to bring her a menu. It wasn't that she was hungry, she just wanted to read the menu in case anything looked good for next time. The café was busy and Ruby knew that eventually the waiter would notice her and come and ask her what she wanted, but she couldn't sit still. She got up and started walking again, scowling at the couples hanging on each other. They took up the whole sidewalk and she found herself nudged closer and closer to the curb until she gave up and walked in the street. Ruby thought about Sara Ryan from her temp job that day and the way Sara had said about her husband, "He's such a goofball." She had said it with so much love that Ruby had to look away. Thinking about it again made Ruby feel strangely heartbroken. She scanned the people passing, suddenly hoping she'd run into Sara with her goofball husband. Ruby just wanted to see them together, maybe shake hands with the guy.

But Sara and her husband were probably having dinner in Westchester or some place like that. Ruby kept walking and finally spotted a table in the window of Magda's. As she walked in, she also spotted a cute guy in the back. She sat in the window and looked out at the people passing by. They all seemed intent on getting where they were going, as if they had to be at a specific corner at a specific time. Ruby drank her iced tea and wished she had remembered to bring a book or paper so she could write a letter. Halfway through her iced tea, she decided to stare back at the guy in the back, who was pretending to read a book. She wasn't sure she was interested in him. If she stared any longer, he would come over and ask her name. She looked away a second too late and he got up and came over to the cake display, which happened to be right next to her. He leaned close to the glass and studied the cakes and tarts and cookies. Then he stood up and looked at her. "You look really familiar. Don't I know you from somewhere? You ever had the mud pie?"

Ruby looked at him. Yet another white boy. Was there something stamped on her forehead that said "White boys especially welcome"? His teeth looked nice, though, and his shoes didn't turn her off. At least he wasn't blond. "I'm a coconut-custard kind of girl."

"I love coconut custard. Anyone sitting here?" He pointed at the chair next to hers. She pointed at the chair too but couldn't bring herself to say yes or no. He took her gesture for a yes and sat down. "Can I get you something?" he said.

"Nah, I'm fine."

"They have the best cappuccino. Not many people know how to make a really good cappuccino. You drink coffee?" He looked at her hand around her glass. She looked at his mouth, at the faint scar under his eye.

"I drink tea." They were looking at each other in a way so that they both knew they weren't talking about coffee. They talked some more about tea and then a little more about coffee and then they discovered they both liked carrot cake. He called the waitress over and ordered a slice with two forks. Ruby thought that was a bit forward, but when the cake came she couldn't help taking a few bites.

"So what do you do?" he asked her.

"This is it," she said. He laughed. "What about you?" she said.

"I'm a photographer. Street scenes, mainly." He didn't seem at all embarrassed by this.

"How many lovers have you had?" Ruby asked him suddenly.

"What? Why do you ask?" He looked startled.

"No reason. Just wondering."

"I don't know. Not so many. Maybe fifteen, twenty." He ate his cake and looked out the window. "What about you?" he said glumly.

"I don't know. Maybe fifteen. You haven't really seen me around before, have you?"

"No. Maybe. I don't know. Nice night out," he said finally. "Want to go for a walk? My name's Dave." His hand was large around hers.

"Maggie." Until then, Ruby had thought she might walk with him to the park and sit on a bench and lean her head on his shoulder and then they would kiss for a while and then go to his place. He was handsome and wouldn't be surprised that he had met a girl in a café who wanted to fuck without going on a date first. But as soon as the made-up name came to her, she knew she couldn't go through with it, even though he hadn't done anything to botch his chances. If she had said Ramona, or even Raquel, it might have been possible. But when the name Maggie came to her, loud and undeniable, she knew it was over.

"I don't think so. I have to go. Nice meeting you." Ruby shook his hand one more time. His hand felt so solid and he had nice nails. If only he had taken her other hand right then, he could have had her. He smiled at her like it was no big thing, but he was pissed. He could probably get another girl tonight, but probably not as easily as he almost got her.

"Another time then. Why don't you give me a call?" He waited until she nodded before looking through his bag for a pen. She took the number, folded it up and pushed it deep into her pocket.

"Well. See you around." Ruby waved good-bye and thought for a second about confessing her real name and taking his hand and walking out with him.

"Yeah. See you." He picked up his book again and kept his eyes on the page until Ruby left the café.

Out on the street again, she headed uptown. She wished she had thought to ask him what he was reading. A bus came and she got on it. What a close call that had been. It wasn't so easy to touch strangers anymore. Maybe she was getting old. When she had first gotten to school, she had gone around touching everyone who came near her. Once she got a taste, she realized what she had been missing for so long.

The bus stopped in front of Columbia. Ruby got off and walked around campus. When she saw a security guard, she looked straight ahead as if she were a summer student out for a stroll, yet she was afraid he would know she had no business being there. It was the same feeling she'd had when she first got to school, as if everyone was looking at her and whispering behind her back: "Go back to Queens. Go back to where you came from." She felt no one was fooled when she threw away her curling iron and abandoned her pink shirts and socks in the back of her closet, or even when she made the dean's list without seeming to study very much. Although she made friends, sometimes she looked at them and thought, Yes, you are my friend, but your parents have a house and sleep in the same bed and will send you to Europe in the summer and buy you a car for graduation, and yes, I am your friend, but I am your Chinese friend. She went to a few parties given by the Asian Student Union, but she felt everyone knew one another and that they were Chinese in a way she didn't know how to be.

Now she sat on the steps of the library. If only she still liked beer. The people around her were drinking and having a better time than she was. Sitting on the steps, she knew she would go to Nick tonight. She had met him four years ago on campus. She would never admit that she had felt lost at school; Nick seemed to know his way around. Besides, he had pursued her like no one else, and somehow she knew he would never leave her until she forced him to. And so, after months of telling him no, not yet, she fucked him. Not that they weren't having sex before. They had all kinds of sex before they stuck it in. After she got over her disappointment that she had waited so long for that rubbery awkward thrusting that was her first time, she grew to like fucking, but it was always something extra. What she liked best was to lie at the edge of the bed while he knelt on a pillow on the floor, his mouth between her legs. She liked to come that way.

If only she wouldn't fuck other people, they would be happy together, he said to her again and again. And sometimes she tried not to, but sooner or later she felt compelled. She would meet someone and they would be talking, but as it got late, she'd start to feel far away, and slowly she'd move closer and closer until there she was, sitting in some man's lap.

Or at least only fuck other women, Nick said; even that he could handle. She got mad when he said that, but it also made her feel sorry for him, that he didn't even know whom to be afraid of. Her affairs with men were harmless; she loved Nick as much as she could love any man, but she had a feeling that if she ever met a woman, she would leave him for good. But that didn't look like it would happen anytime soon; she was shy with women. She didn't have the confidence she had with men and she ended up talking with women and sitting too far away to touch. One time it was past midnight and the girl from Spanish class was sitting on Ruby's bed, touching the edge of her blanket. Ruby knew it was too late for talking and that since the girl was still there, that she was probably thinking about kissing too, but Ruby couldn't be sure, so she babbled on about some book she hardly remembered and tried not to stare too hard at the woman's mouth.

In front of Nick's building, she stopped and looked up at his window. The memory of the girl from Spanish class had made her mad at herself. Chickenshit, why didn't you kiss her? Or at least take your hands out of your pockets? she berated herself. She always got paralyzed when she liked someone too much. But now she stood looking up at Nick's window. His light was on. She felt so relieved she wanted to run up the stairs, throw herself against him and punch him as hard as she could. A woman in a short dress came out of the building and Ruby slipped in behind her.

Outside Nick's apartment, she put her ear to the door. She heard nothing, then footsteps and a door opening and closing. She knocked.

"Who is it?" He was trying to sound tough.

"It's me." When he didn't open the door right away, she added, "Ruby."

He opened the door and stared at her like he would eat her up right there in the hallway. "Sweetie," he said. He opened the door a little wider. She waited for him to say something else, but he just looked at her.

"You're not going to let me in?" she said.

"How come you didn't call?" he said.

"I don't know. I felt funny. You're not happy to see me."

"You abandoned me. I started looking for a new girl."

"Yeah, right," Ruby said. They laughed. He was devoted. "You better not or I'll kick your ass," she said. She walked to the kitchen. On the counter were a pair of dark blue bowls she hadn't seen before. They were almost too blue and dreamy for a man's kitchen. "Nice bowls. Got any drinks?" she said.

"You want tea?" He opened the cabinet. Neatly lined up were tins and boxes of all kinds of tea.

"You got whiskey?" She felt buoyed up, asking for such a butch drink.

"Whiskey?" He thought that was adorable. She stood real close to him. He put one arm around her and patted her on the back. "No. Not like that," she said and punched him, lightly.

"No hitting. Why do you always have to hit me?"

"Why do you have to be so cold?" She stood against the counter. They glared at each other. They got cranky when they hadn't fucked in a while.

"Oh, Ruby. Come here," he said finally. This time he put both arms around her and touched her back and moved his hips in close too. He put his face in her hair. "You smell like cigars," he said.

"You know my dad." She tried to move away. He pulled her back. "What, did you miss me?" she said.

"What do you think?" He walked to the living room. They sat on the sofa with their drinks. The sofa was a deep velvety red and made him seem like more of a grown-up than she would ever be, even though the couch was just a hand-me-down from his mother. They were quiet and Ruby looked around the apartment at the little changes he had made since she had been there last. Three weeks was a long time when you were used to seeing someone every day. Now that she was there, sitting on his couch and thinking lazily of getting up to see what was in the refrigerator, she felt silly for not coming over sooner.

He was looking at her and thinking that if only she weren't so fucking beautiful he could get some backbone and leave or claim her as his own, one or the other, because this was killing him.

"You look skinny. You eating?" she said.

"I eat. Sometimes I eat. Am I getting skinny? You have to eat with me," he said.

"You got new shoes." She was sad that he had gone out and bought a whole new item without her even knowing he needed new shoes.

"Don't say it like that. Do you like them?" He looked away, as if her answer wouldn't mean a thing to him.

"Not bad. Not bad at all," she said. Nick knew that was a rave coming from her. He sat up a little straighter and drank his whiskey. "Here, drink." He handed her glass to her. She drank and looked at him sitting in his house. On the table, he had arranged a bowl of plums and the room smelled sweet and summery. She looked at his hands holding the bottle as he poured out another drink. Those are the hands that touch me and make me come, she thought and looked away.

Before graduation, he had asked her to live with him. She told him she had to think about it but then never gave him an answer. Now, sitting on his couch, she thought: Yeah, you and me, babe, forever and ever.

"I'm drunk," she said. It was an invitation. He put his hands under her shirt and she looked back at him. She waited for the feeling of forgetfulness that she got when he touched her, but she kept remembering things like should she call her mother, but it was too late, everyone was sleeping.

She loved him best in bed and wondered if that was a bad sign. There was a sureness about him, so he seemed almost a different person from the gentle man who advised her on what shoes would suit her. She changed too in bed. The trapped feeling was still there, and now it felt just as dangerous but it also felt good. And that was the scary part, that in bed it felt good.

She put her arms over her head, with her wrists close together. He held her hands there with one hand and moved his other hand down her body. She pressed her legs together. "Now that I've got you here, I'll have to tie you up and keep you here," he said, very serious.

"No, no," she said, although at that moment that was all she wanted, to be forced to stay there always.

"Since you keep running away, I'm afraid I have no choice." He wrapped her wrists with the sash from his bathrobe and tied the loose ends to the bed. She closed her eyes and tried to move her arms. She shook her head back and forth.

"Then why are you so wet?" He pushed her legs open. "That's because my body is stupid and doesn't know any better," she almost answered. Then his mouth was on hers and she was reaching up to him.

This was what she needed. This was what she had had at school when she was happy. He was on top of her and she moved like she wanted to push him off. She tried to slide her hands away from the bed frame and for a moment his knots didn't seem tight enough and she was afraid that if she pulled hard enough, she would get away.

He was moving down her body, his mouth stopping here and there. But something wasn't right. Even while he was putting his mouth to that soft wet, she was starting to get that panicked feeling she would get at school when the books weren't thick enough to make her forget; she would go very still and would have to stop whatever she was doing, couldn't eat another bite or read another word. "I love you," she said, but she felt far away. Even though he was holding her down, she knew that when they were done he wouldn't be able to keep her there.

Then he was pulling on a condom and she watched his cock

disappear into it. He pushed into her and she stopped fighting. They started very slowly.

One minute she was making all kinds of noises and her hips were moving and the next minute she was coming and crying and wailing as she never did, wailing and crying for her mother and father behind the laundry, who had gone to bed hours before, lying in separate beds in separate rooms, knowing nothing about their daughter crying on a bed in Manhattan with her hands at her sides, a man they'd never met with his arms around her. She was crying now, not for her mother and father, who lived behind the store but for the girl who didn't anymore, the girl who had hid under the ironing table, watching the world outside.

Nick was touching her hair and she was wondering what would have happened if she had gone home with the guy from the café, not that she would rather be with him than with Nick, but she felt it almost didn't matter which bed she lying on. Nick touched her face. She curled away from him. "Ruby. Beloved. Are you hurt? Did I hurt you?" he said and looked down at his dick as if it were the source of all this trouble.

"No, honey. It's not you." And she almost laughed to think she could cry this way over him.

Ever since they first met, Nick wanted two things from her and he wanted them bad: he wanted to fuck her and he wanted to see the house she grew up in. She got annoyed with his obsession with fucking her, but she could understand it. Still, she remained unmoved by his begging and his threats. After eight months, she decided she wanted to fuck him too. She thought he'd be satisfied, but then he fixated on his other desire. He wanted to know where she came from, as if that would explain her. He wanted to know about the part she kept away from him, some small part he could never touch no matter how far he pushed his dick into her.

But she hadn't wanted to bring him home. He had such big eyes that were always staring at everything. Sometimes when he looked at her, she felt like there was something wrong with her.

If she took him home, he'd walk into the laundry and see the faded signs in the window and the old packages of laundry and her father sitting at the ironing table reading his newspaper with a magnifying glass. Then he'd walk into the living room and he'd see more laundry and he wouldn't miss the towels covering the headrests of chairs. In the kitchen, he'd stare at the dried-up fish hanging in the window and he'd look real hard at the roach powder sprinkled on the floor and the millions of bags and jars her mother had saved. In the yard, he'd see the scrappy vegetable patch, and then he'd think of his mother's beautiful cabbages and her sunflowers and the tomatoes that were the pride of her block.

The night she went to see him, she huddled close to the wall until she felt too cold, and then she turned to him and let him put his arms around her again. It was twelve-thirty when she finally stopped crying and said, "Okay. Maybe one day you can come home with me."

He sat up and looked at her. "You want me to?"

"I guess."

"You don't sound happy about it."

"No, I am. My father might be mean to you, though. He was mean to Lily's boyfriends—even Henry, a nice Chinese boy. Try not to get on his bad side. Don't talk about sex or even a shower. Don't say anything about drinking, even wine. Or parties."

"You worry too much. You'll see. Parents like me," he said. Ruby knew her parents didn't like anyone, especially some white boy who wanted to be an actor.

"It's not a regular house," she said. She thought of his mother's house and her kitchen with the rolling shelves, the pots on one shelf and the lids on another and her cream-of-carrot soup and the jar of pretzels that she nibbled on to keep her weight down. "There's no picket fence, no front lawn. You have to walk through the laundry to get to the house part. There's no couch, no coffee table. There's hardly anywhere to sit down. There's laundry all over the living room. The walls are green. The plates don't match. There's a washing machine in the kitchen. There's buckets of water all over the place."

"Ruby? Ruby. It's just me, sweetheart. You don't have to hide," he said.

When he said that, Ruby remembered watching her father getting the trash ready to put out on the street. He used the shopping bags that Bell brought home from the store. There were bags from Key Food and bags from Chinatown, which had Chinese writing on them. He was calm when he used a bag from the American supermarket, but when he used a bag from Chinatown, his face would get tight and his hands quick and angry as he turned the bag inside out so the Chinese lettering didn't show as much. "Why do you turn the Chinese bags inside out and not the American bags?" Ruby had asked him. "So people don't know this is Chinese garbage," he had said.

Nick was watching her and Ruby almost told him about her father and the trash, but then she said, "I guess it will be okay."

Chapter 12

At the dinner table, Ruby wanted to button Nick's shirt up a little higher. The curly hairs sticking out from his shirt seemed to scream: I'm fucking your daughter. Ruby could see that Bell had decided to be nice to the guy, he looked so nervous. "You want something cold to drink? Soda? Beer?" Bell asked him. The day before she had stocked up on soda and juice and had even bought a can of beer. The fellow sitting in her kitchen hadn't stopped smiling since he walked in. Bell realized with a start that she hadn't either.

It was the middle of June, and Ruby had been home for over a month. For the first few weeks, she had stayed put at night, but since she started working, she didn't come home until she knew Franklin had turned off the TV and gone into the bathroom with his newspaper, or else she stayed out all night while Bell counted cars driving past the laundry. Counting cars was an old habit of hers that had started when Lily started dating; by the time Bell counted a thousand cars, Lily would come home, Bell told herself. These days, even after Ruby called and said she was staying with her friend and not to worry, Bell kept her post by the window. One day Ruby had bought a sun hat for her and said it was for Florida. Bell had put it on her lap and the two of them had been almost giddy. Some nights when Ruby didn't come home, Bell held the hat in her lap and looked out the window and remembered the day she had brought Ruby home from the hospital, and it didn't seem so long ago to make Ruby old enough to stay out all night.

But now Ruby was sitting there in the kitchen with her friend. "Beer!" Ruby said. There had never been beer in the house.

"Lots of people drink beer in the summer," Bell said. Nick had perked up at the mention of beer but caught Ruby's warning glance and asked for orange juice. He handed Bell the apple-streudel cake he had carried on his lap all the way from Zabar's and was disappointed that she didn't open it right away and at least look at it. Twenty bucks he'd spent on that cake, but he had a feeling that Ruby's mother wasn't a raver. She had hardly looked at the huge bouquet of flowers he had brought for her and had stuck them unceremoniously in an empty juice jar. Now he watched her darting around the kitchen, rattling her pots with such authority, he couldn't believe this was the woman Ruby felt she needed to rescue. He forced himself to look away and took in the washing machine and the unmatched chairs and the water stains on the ceiling. This was where his sweetheart had grown up.

"Is that your room?" Nick pointed at the closed door.

"My room's in the basement now," Ruby said.

"I mean when you were little," he said.

"It's messy in there," Bell said.

"It's okay, Ma." Ruby let him peek into the room.

"God, it's tiny. All four of you slept in there?" He tried to check his disbelief. He didn't want her to feel like a freak or anything like that.

"Yup. Me, my mama, my sister and brother," Ruby boasted.

"Ruby. Go call your father eat," Bell said firmly.

Nick examined the striped pillows attached to each chair as if he were thinking about getting some for his own apartment. Then he moved to sit in Franklin's head-of-the-family chair. Ruby came back just in time to shoo him to another seat. Franklin had decided not to like Nick. When Nick first came in and said, "Hello, Mr. Lee, I'm glad to meet you finally," and offered his hand, Franklin had stared at it as if wondering how it had found its way into his laundry. *Finally?* What did the young fellow mean by "finally"? Then Nick handed him some fancy cigars and headed into the kitchen with a bakery box in his hands. Franklin had taken the cigars but wasn't going to soften up just because the guy brought over a cake and a few lousy smokes.

"You want a fork?" Bell said to Nick.

"Give him a fork," Franklin said.

"That's okay," Nick said.

"Ma. So much food." Ruby was relieved her mother had made Chinese food for Americans, neat and clean, not like the dishes she usually made, with claws and heads, skin and tails like it was still an animal.

Ruby had forgotten to tell Nick not to start eating until her father picked up his chopsticks. Nick reached across the table and helped himself to a plump morsel of chicken from the far side of the plate, the side right in front of her father. Ruby half waited for her father to rap Nick across the knuckles. No, no, Nick, Ruby said to him in her head, only pick in front of you, no matter what it is, even if it's the chicken head or chicken butt.

"This is great, Mrs. Lee. Even better than a restaurant," Nick said. Ruby took a small piece of chicken and touched it to her rice before putting it to her mouth. She looked over at Nick so he could see how to do it, but he was too busy eating. He had always been a bit of a slob, but it had never really bothered her before. His chopsticks went wide for a moment. Everyone was careful not to stare as he recovered his grip. Bell lifted the backbone from the fish in one easy movement, dunked pieces of meat into the sauce and then pushed them across the plate toward her husband, Ruby and Nick. Franklin picked up a piece of fish and laid it in his bowl, then ate it slowly.

Ruby watched Nick slap a piece of broccoli against the plate. No, no, Nick, no slapping. You can dab it a tiny bit, but no slapping. The only sound was eating and the sound of the television.

Bell got up to put more food on the table. "Forgot the soup," she said. "You ever eat this kind of soup, Nick? This is lotus root." She wanted to feed her dinner guest so he wouldn't look at her daughter so hungrily.

On the news, they had finished the first story, about a guy who shot two coworkers but who wasn't arrested until he stole a bag of peanuts, and were moving on to the next: "Eleven-year-old boy mauled and eaten by killer bear . . ."

"Did you hear about that one? Some crazy parent don't give a damn about their kid. Let them run wild like animals. What are those kids doing in the zoo at that time anyway? Yup. It's a damn shame what happen. So little he don't know any better."

"The bear didn't know better either. He thought the kid was dinner," Nick said and laughed. He stopped abruptly when no one joined him. Then he said, "But parents can't watch their kids every minute."

"If you had a kid, you wouldn't know if they're hanging around the zoo after it's closed? You think I let my kids run around like that?" Franklin's anger faded suddenly and he looked stricken, as if remembering how hard it had been to keep an eye on the kids before their mother came home from work; he'd tell them to play in front of the store where he could see them and later he'd look up and they'd be gone. "Wild animals," Franklin muttered again. No one said anything. They listened to each other chew and swallow. Franklin picked at his rice. "Your mother always make the rice too wet. It's mushy-like." He put down his bowl and laid his chopsticks across the top.

"It tastes good to me." Ruby lifted her bowl so she could scoop up a big mouthful. They listened to the rest of the story about how they had to kill the bear. Ruby got up and turned down the volume.

"You think that after all these years, she learn how to make rice." Franklin sucked his teeth.

"Dad," Ruby said.

Franklin brightened and turned to Nick. "So, Nick, you got any plans now that you finish school?"

"I'm working at a bookstore for now. But I'm thinking of going to acting school. I want to be an actor."

"Show-business life, eh? Excitement? Those show-business people all take drugs to keep them going." Franklin turned back to his food and shoveled the rest of the rice into his mouth. He filled the kettle for tea and turned the gas on high. The bakery box was sitting on the counter, red and white string tied in a sprightly bow. He looked with interest at the box but caught himself and moved to the backyard door. Suddenly, he reached for the cigar box on the floor, which held a pile of rocks and a slingshot he had made earlier in the week. He started to hurl rocks into the yard. "Those damn squirrels. They keep eating your mother's tomatoes," he yelled.

"Dad, what are you doing?" Ruby got up and tried to take the slingshot from her father.

"He's going to hit my plants, that what." Bell got up from the table. The squirrel slipped under the fence.

Franklin held up his slingshot and said, "I made it myself." Nick looked slightly sick. Then Franklin took out a twenty-dollar bill and handed it to Ruby. "You better go get a trap tomorrow. Take care of those things once and for all."

"No trap. Who's going to clean it?" Bell said to Franklin. But he was pushing the money at Ruby.

"I'm not going to buy a trap," Ruby said, but she knew she would. Franklin left the kitchen and everyone else sat down again.

"You can't catch a squirrel with a trap, it's against the law," Bell said. She picked up her bowl again. "Nothing wrong with this rice. Why he like his rice so hard anyway? Maybe because he have a hard life. What kind of rice do you like, Nick?"

Nick sat there as if he had never stopped to consider how he liked his rice. Finally he said, "My favorite is fried rice." Bell smiled but Ruby knew her mother was thinking about the time she told Ruby never to order fried rice in a restaurant because they use the white rice left over from people's plates to make it.

Bell got up and started to clear the table. Nick jumped up. "Can I help?"

"Sit, sit," Bell said roughly. Nick brought the dishes to the sink anyway and started washing them. Bell yanked plastic wrap from the box and wrapped up the leftovers, but she kept an eye on Nick and Ruby. Nick was washing and Ruby was drying and there was something about the way he held the plates out to her and the way she took them from him that made Bell feel slightly embarrassed. At dinner, the two of them had acted as if they barely knew each other, but suddenly they seemed like two people who had lived together for a long time. Bell went to the door and looked out at her garden. The weatherman had said rain, but she didn't trust him. If she didn't water at least once a day, everything would dry up.

"Remember the futon store?" Nick was saying to Ruby. "They closed down and now it's a Chinese restaurant. Kind of tacky-fancy. My mom will love it, just her speed." He made a face when he mentioned his mother.

"Your mother's coming for a visit? Where she live?" Bell turned to him with renewed interest.

"Boston. First she said she was coming for the weekend, but then she went ahead and got tickets for a week."

Ruby could see her mother was getting agitated and she shot Nick a stern look. "Hey, what kind of cake did you bring?" she said. She picked up the box, weighing it in her hands. "It's heavy."

Bell paid Ruby no mind. "You don't want your mother to visit?" she said to Nick.

He sounded tired now. "She's afraid of the city. She hates to walk. When I'm at work, she won't leave the house. I don't even have a TV for her. She hates to read. She opens the fridge and complains that I eat weird things."

"Buy something she like to eat. You know what she like to eat, don't you?" Bell had never met the boy's mother, but she felt a sharp pain in her stomach just thinking about her. "Maybe she just not used to the city. I was scared of the city when I first come here," she said.

"Mrs. Lee. Not everyone gets along with their mother as well as you and Ruby," he said.

"That's right," Ruby said, although she felt like a fraud. Of course they got along well, Ruby told herself, but what came to mind was her mother picking through the laundry basket so she could rinse out Ruby's panty hose in the bathroom sink. Ruby wished she wouldn't do that.

Nick looked at Ruby. She wouldn't look at him and he wondered if she was still upset that he had made a slob of himself at the dinner table. It wasn't like her to hold a grudge for such a little thing. The bouquet he had brought took up almost the entire counter. He had chosen lilies and stocks and birds-of-paradise, not realizing they would be too showy for Ruby's mother's kitchen. Ruby studied the flowers while her mother said, "Yup. I'm lucky to have a daughter like her," and then got up and went into the bedroom. She came out with the sun hat on her head.

"See the hat she got for me?" Bell said with pride. Nick praised the hat.

"It's nothing. It's not a very nice hat. I looked, I couldn't find the kind I wanted," Ruby said. In the bright light of the kitchen, the hat looked flimsy.

"It's a good hat," Bell said.

Ruby took the hat from her mother and had to restrain herself from rolling it up and throwing it on the floor. It was a dumb hat, not at all what she had been looking for. "Why don't we throw this one away and I'll get you a better one?" Ruby said.

Bell snatched up the hat and put it back on her head. "Don't you throw away my hat. This is my best hat."

Nick touched the brim of the hat. "Ruby. The hat's fine."

Ruby was close to tears. "Okay, okay. It's a good hat," she said, not believing it for a minute. Bell took the hat off, held it in her lap and patted it. She went into the bedroom and hung it on the nail where Van's mirror used to hang.

After they finished cleaning up, Ruby and Nick got out the folding chairs and sat in the front of the store. "How'd I do?" Nick said. He pulled at a loose string on his shirt.

"Stop that. You'll make a hole." Ruby took his hand away from his shirt, then looked into the store before she held his hand. "It's okay. I should've prepped you better. You can't pick from the far side of the plate."

"Now you hate me." He was finally at her house and she seemed farther away than ever.

"Don't be silly." Ruby knew she didn't sound very loving.

"Let's go downstairs, to the basement," he said. He had that dead-serious tone that meant he wanted to go to bed.

"With them right here?" Ruby said.

"Right, right." He looked so dejected that Ruby almost liked him again.

"Did you see the kitchen? I'm going to paint it."

"I'll help you." He felt she was giving him another chance.

Bell came out with pieces of cake wrapped up in napkins. "Here, try some. It's good," she said. Nick got up and tried to make her sit but she wouldn't. "I have some work to do," she said. The way Nick and Ruby were looking at each other made her feel sorry for them, as if Ruby had just discovered that she wasn't as much in love as she had thought and was trying to hide it, while Nick looked determined to win her back.

Bell went back inside and sat at her sewing machine before she realized she didn't have a thing to sew. She sat in the dark and watched the young people out in front.

Nick and Ruby sat outside the store and ate their cake. She told him about growing up, with her and Helen the only Chinese girls for miles around. Helen was the popular one; her hair feathered just so, she wore lots of eyeliner and knew how to flirt. She was always trying to dress Ruby up, do her face, teach her to dance. Ruby hated parties; at first she went because she loved her friend, but later on she went in the hopes of finding someone who would drape his legs over hers in the back of the bus on their way to the movies. Helen had told her about the leg trick in a tone of indignation that she didn't feel. "And then we were sitting on the bus and he throws his leg, like this, over mine. I was like, excuse me!" Helen had thrown her leg over Ruby's to show her. The solid warmth of her friend's leg on hers had startled her, but Ruby was sorry when she took it away.

Nick watched her as she talked. She looked younger and not as sure of herself. For the first time he saw her easily as a wallflower and he wanted to scoop her up from her lounge chair and take her away. Now she was telling him about going to the laundromat after school and ironing handkerchiefs and hand towels that her father would unfold and iron over again. He told her about his piano lessons and about driving his father's car to concerts in the park, where he smuggled in a thermosful of wine to drink with the girl he was dating, whose hair smelled of strawberries. He knew talking about piano lessons when she was talking about laundromats would rile her up; he wanted his feisty girl back.

"Spoiled little fuck," she said, a little too seriously.

"Little matchstick girl," he said. Teasing had always been their way of being affectionate, but today something was wrong. Suddenly he thought of the flowers that were sitting on the counter in the kitchen. "Your mother likes carnations. That's what you said, carnations."

"She liked them," Ruby lied. She didn't like to lie. The street lamps lit up just then and she leaned slightly away from him. He got up to leave and tried to kiss her good-bye. "Not here," she said and reached for his hand. They shook hands solemnly and it started as a joke, but suddenly their handshake felt oddly appropriate. She walked him to the bus stop and kissed him hard to shake off the strange feeling she had. People passed them and looked away, some shaking their heads, a few smiling to themselves. Nick moved his hands slowly to her breasts and she went to push his hands away, but then she closed her eyes and moved closer. She knew she should stop, that one of her father's customers or maybe Helen's mother might go by and see her and before she knew it, her parents would know she had been acting trashy on the corner. Finally the bus came and she stepped away from him. He walked with difficulty onto the bus and sat by the window. She waved at him, her mouth a little open.

Then he was gone and she walked home, smoothing down her shirt and wiping her mouth with the back of her hand. She sat outside the laundry until the fireflies came out and then the kids with jars to catch the slow, dreamy bugs. Store owners pulled down their gates and locked up for the night, then they came out and leaned against cars and parking meters and talked about last night's fight. Then the women came out, so eager for one another's company that they left the dessert dishes in the sink and didn't bother to take off their aprons.

Ruby sat there after the kids had gone inside with their jars of fireflies to light up their rooms. From inside the store, Bell was watching her. There was something about the way Ruby was looking past the cars that made Bell hesitant to go out and sit with her. A cup of tea, Bell thought and went to the kitchen to put the water on.

Across the street, people were starting to arrive at the night-club that Franklin was always railing against. They were dressed like movie stars and Ruby knew that even if her father hadn't forbidden her ever to set foot in there, she still could never go. Bell came out with two cups and a tin of popcorn. "Here's some tea. Want some popcorn? It has cheese. I have another kind, I think it's caramel flavor." Lately, Bell had taken to buying big tins of fancy popcorn. Every night she ate a handful as she watched TV, and when the tin was empty she washed it out and filled it with sugar or crackers or zippers.

They ate popcorn and drank tea and finally Ruby said, "So what do you think?"

"About Nick?"

"Yeah, Nick."

"You tell me. You know him longer than me," Bell said. Ruby

felt sad suddenly. She caught a glimpse of the time when she and Nick wouldn't be together and she and her mother would be sitting outside in front of the store on a summer night and Ruby would say to her, "Remember that guy Nick? Remember the first time he came over for dinner and he brought you those flowers that gave you a headache?" But he did love her to pieces and sometimes when she was with him, she believed she wouldn't leave him one day.

"He's all right," Ruby said.

"We better take the chairs in now," Bell said. She got up and folded the chair she had been sitting on. Ruby jumped up and folded her chair too and dragged both chairs inside.

The floodlights from the dance hall lit the night sky over the laundry and the bus stop, which was empty now, and as far away as the house where Van lived with his wife and three children, where he sat in the backyard and looked up at the sky and remembered the first Santana concert he had been to. As he watched the bright light in the sky, he dreamed of the rock-and-roll barbecue he had always wanted to have. Jeannette would never allow it, but she was leaving to visit her family in Milwaukee. His friends would bring their guitars and drums over and they would drink and jam like they used to before they all got married. His guitar would feel strong and sweet in his hands and all his friends would be there and they would rock and roll right there in the grassy yard. Then he remembered that his mother had called him a few weeks ago. The swing he had hung from the tree that afternoon for his daughter Sylvie swayed back and forth in the wind. He lifted his face to catch the breeze, his eyes half closed, as he dialed his mother's number in his head and invited her and Dad and Ruby and Lily over for the barbecue. For once they would all be together.

Chapter 13

*F*ranklin stomped into the kitchen. The flowers on the counter had been in his way all week. He reached for the tea and before he knew it, he had knocked over the flowers. He tried to catch the jar but only succeeded in bumping his leg against the cabinet. He cursed in Chinese. After he had exhausted his Chinese curses, he said, "Goddamn," over and over. No one came out of the bedroom, so he said it louder. He could kill himself, for all anyone cared. Even Ruby didn't care about him anymore, she always took her mother's side. Cursing the whole time, he cleaned up the mess, then rooted around under the sink for the homemade liniment. He sat heavily in a chair and groaned as he rubbed the oil on his leg and finally he left the kitchen, limping mightily.

It was Saturday and Ruby and Bell had both worked all week. They sat on the bed and waited until Franklin went back out to the laundry. Then Bell said, "Goddamn," in exact imitation of her husband, drawing out the *God* and following with a quick little *damn.* She sucked her teeth too.

Ruby cracked up. Sometimes she forgot that her mother was funny. "Do it again," Ruby said.

Bell had to stop laughing first. "Goddamn. God*damn* it." Cursing sure felt good. She could see why her husband liked it so much, and for a moment she felt a little affection for him. She remembered that she was out of fruit; in the summer, Franklin liked a few slices of melon after dinner.

"What's the matter with him? Why's he so grumpy?" Ruby said.

"We better go get some fruit." Bell got a few dollars from her sock drawer and was back to her businesslike self.

Franklin rolled up his pant leg when he heard the two women walking toward the laundry. He opened the bottle of liniment and rubbed on some more. Bell started to walk out, then stopped and said to Ruby, "Ask your father he need something from the store."

"Dad, you want something from the store?"

"Get some half-and-half."

Up the block, the neighbors who lived in Louie and Sheila's old house were planting even more flowers in the tiny garden, floppy petunias with purple-and-white stripes. They had saved all their lives to buy a house, and by God, they were going to decorate it.

"Dad's in a good mood," Ruby joked.

"You know your father. Act just like a baby when he don't get his own way."

"His own way? What's he want?" Ruby looked down at the cracks in the sidewalk, at her feet stepping over them. *Step on a crack, break your mama's back.*

"Oh, you know." Then she was quiet.

"What?"

"Never mind. Look, those are nice ones over there." Bell pointed out some roses that Ruby didn't think were anything special.

At Grand Union, the fruit was cheap but it was hard and small. They went to the greengrocer on the corner and Bell paid a little more for three cantaloupes and two honeydews that smelled soft and clean. She nestled them carefully in the bottom of the cart. "That's a lot of melons." Ruby worried that the fruit would go bad before they could eat it. She didn't realize her mother had chosen the melons carefully so that by the time they finished one melon, another would be perfectly ripe.

"Everyone has to eat." Bell patted the melons like children's heads.

As they crossed the street where the light was always broken, Bell reached for Ruby's hand. Her mother's hand was cool and slim, the same size as hers. They held hands, fingers interlaced, and her mother's hand in hers felt small and reminded her too much of the women she had fallen in love with and been rejected by. When they got across the street, Ruby let go of her mother's hand and stuck out her elbow instead. They were almost there when Ruby stopped. "The half-and-half."

"Oh." Bell stood on the sidewalk, then turned back toward the store. "Your father. Everything has to be his own way."

Ruby understood then that her mother wasn't just upset that Franklin sat at home while everyone ran around doing his errands. "What do you mean? What way? What's he want?"

Bell looked slightly past Ruby's shoulder. "You know. What all men want."

"What?"

"You trying to tell me you don't know what men want by now?" Bell pushed the cart in front of her like she would roll it into the street.

There was only one thing Ruby could think of, but she was sure her mother couldn't mean that, so she shook her head. "Is he upset because you don't cook crabs for him? He keeps asking for them. If it was up to him, he'd eat crabs every day. I don't blame you. Who wants to cook crabs?"

"No, no. Not crabs. Sex." She spat the word from her mouth like a watermelon seed.

"Sex? No. You two don't do that anymore. Do you?"

Bell was quiet for a moment, then said, "I guess I can tell you now. Don't tell your sister. I don't know what's wrong with him. He's an old man. My friends, their husbands don't bother them anymore. But your father . . . he act like he can't live without it." There. She had finally told somebody and she was glad.

Ruby looked down at the melons jostling against each other.

They would get bruised if her mother wasn't more careful with the cart. Ruby tried to picture her parents having sex, but she felt hopelessly puzzled and hurt somehow, as she had when her friend Blanca had explained the facts to her in second grade. At night Blanca used to open her bedroom door so she could hear the noises from her parents' bedroom. Then in the morning, she'd stare at the hickies all over her mother's neck. "Open your door. Then you'll hear it," Blanca told her. Ruby was convinced that the red and gold furniture in Blanca's house drove her parents to do such crazy things to each other. She wanted to tell Blanca that she didn't have to open her door because she knew where her mother was all night long. Her mother was sleeping in the bed next to hers and she never had hickies.

On the way back to the store, Ruby looked at her mother's soft pale neck and wondered how they approached each other at night when they never touched during the day, not even accidentally. She tried not to think about it, but now that her mother had started, Ruby had to know.

"So where do you do it?" Ruby said casually.

"In his room," Bell said matter-of-factly. Ruby had pictured her father coming to her mother, sidling up to her thin bed in the middle of all her clutter.

"Does he call you to come to him?"

"No. When I'm ready I go to his room." Ruby tried to picture her mother wanting it, sneaking off to her father's room to get it.

"Do you do it a lot?"

"Maybe every couple of weeks."

"Every couple of weeks. That's a lot," Ruby said. Bell just shrugged. "Do you kiss first? What about touching, like a back rub or something? You know, to get in the mood." Ruby tried to keep her voice steady.

"Sometimes. When I'm not too tired." Bell didn't look at Ruby.

"Do you like it?" Ruby didn't look at her either.

"Sometimes. When I'm not too tired. These days I'm tired all the time. I don't go to his room for a long time. That's why he make noise, bang around the kitchen, knock things down."

"Do you come?" Ruby looked down at her hands, which were minding their own business, switching a ring from one finger to another.

"What's that?"

"You know. At the end, when the guy . . . when the stuff comes out and it feels real nice. Women do that too. But without so much stuff. Usually." Ruby spoke slowly and deliberately, as if she were giving Bell a recipe.

"Oh, that. I heard about that. No, not me. I don't need that." Bell held herself a little straighter, differentiating herself from the women who did.

"You don't have to go to his room if you don't want to," Ruby said.

"He smoke too much. His whole body smell smoky. Who want to go near him?" Bell suddenly felt like crying.

"Ma." Ruby took her mother's hand and patted it. They walked in silence. At the deli, Bell went into the store and Ruby waited outside. As Bell was walking down the aisle, the man at the cash register said, "Need some help, gorgeous?" He had joked with her before, but today Bell felt ashamed, as if the guy saw the same thing in her that made her husband want sex all the time, even though she was old now and hardly ever put a dress on anymore. "No, thanks," she said.

Outside, Ruby pushed the cart back and forth like she was rocking a baby. She watched Bell in the store and wondered whether her mother kissed her father's cigar mouth and whether he liked her body, round and soft from three children. Did he touch her so she knew she was beautiful, or did he think about the women he saw on TV as he pulled down her pajama pants and got on top? And did her mother feel anything? Did she stroke his back and arms, strong from lifting buckets of starch? Did she wrap her legs around him, or did they just hang in the air, unloved and unloving?

Bell came out, holding the bag away from her, as if the cold would hurt her body. She frowned and said, "That store. They raise the price again."

"I never heard you. All those years and I never heard you."

Bell tried to smile. "You know, I been thinking. It's not so bad. You don't have to worry about me."

Ruby gave the cart a dejected little kick. Bell reached for Ruby's arm and they walked home slowly, like an old married couple. It was late afternoon by the time they got back. As they walked into the laundry, Franklin stood up and shoved a piece of paper at them. "What's this?" he demanded.

Bell took the paper from him as if it were a snake. There wasn't much writing on the blue paper. "What's it say?" she said to Ruby.

Ruby scanned the letter. "It's from Louie and Sheila. They say they're waiting for us. The weather is great. They're going to take us to their friend's private beach. We don't need to bring anything, just ourselves." The letter said to bring "just your beautiful selves," but Ruby couldn't bring herself to say that in front of her father.

"Who's going to Florida?" He snatched the letter back. No one answered him. "That's what I thought. I didn't think anyone was going anywhere."

"Me and Mom might go," Ruby said. Bell tried to get Ruby to be quiet by looking hard at her. She didn't think it was a good idea to tell Franklin their plans.

"The house looks like a pigsty and all you two can think about is going away." He looked as if he would tear up the letter.

"That letter wasn't for you," Ruby said.

"Any mail that comes to my house I can read," he said. The veins in his neck looked like they were going to pop any minute.

"That's my letter," Bell said. Franklin and Ruby both turned to look at her. She held out her hand, and as if in a trance, Franklin gave her the letter. "I have to put the cream away now," Bell said and marched back to the kitchen.

That evening after dinner, Bell cut into a honeydew. Her knife didn't slide as easily through the fruit as it should have. She sawed it in half, then spooned out the seeds. She cut thick slices and then cut the slices into squares. Ruby put a few toothpicks on the table. Lily had come down from her apartment and sat at the table with Sunday's newspaper in front of her. She turned right to the coupon pages. "Ma, you need this? It's detergent."

"Leave it there. I'll use it," Bell said. Lily cut the coupon out and laid it on her mother's pile. There were a lot of good ones this week. When the supermarkets had double coupons, sometimes she really racked up.

Bell bit into the melon that had seemed so ripe in the store. "Too hard. Should wait a few more days. I don't know if your father going to eat it. Ask him if he want some canned peach," Bell said. She put a few pieces of fruit into a bowl and stuck some toothpicks into them. Ruby took the bowl out to the living room.

Franklin tasted a square of melon. "Not too good," he said, but when Ruby reached for the bowl, he said, "I'll eat a few."

Ruby went back to the kitchen. Bell was cutting up the melon and putting it into plastic bowls. "This one just like the one your father bought for me in China. See, in China you don't get fruit every day. Just on the holidays. Even apple and orange, we don't get too much. But your father, he buy a honeydew melon. Cost about thirty dollars because they don't grow it there. You can buy ten, eleven chickens for that money. But he want to buy a melon. When we open it up, it's hard inside. Not even sweet. My mother laugh at him."

Bell had that peaceful look on her face that she got when she was touching food. She looked young, like she did in the photograph of her at age sixteen. Ruby had had different rooms at school, but in each one she kept the silver-framed photograph by her bed. Next to the photograph were flowers and candles and fruit. Ruby's friends would ask in hushed voices who the woman in the picture was.

"That's my mother."

"Oh. She's pretty. When did she pass on?"

"What are you saying? She lives in Queens with my father." Ruby would wonder what gave them that crazy idea. Now the picture was on the little night table by Ruby's bed in the basement.

Ruby watched her mother's hands touching the melon and, next to her, Lily sorting her coupons. Ruby ate a few pieces of melon. It was crunchy but it had some flavor.

Lily had a pile of coupons now and she started to sort them in her Leatherette wallet organizer she had gotten by sending in labels from ten cans of tomato sauce. The wallet had seven different sections; Lily held a coupon for Poppin' Fresh biscuits and wondered if it should go in the bread section or the frozen section. She looked up at Ruby and said, "Don't look at me like that. Last time I saved ten dollars."

"I was just wondering if you had one for cookies. I'm sick of those oatmeal ones." Ruby pointed at the blue tin on top of the refrigerator, where her father kept his stock of cookies.

Lily looked at her to see if she was serious. Satisfied that she was, Lily said, "You want cookies? I got lots of cookies." She emptied the snack section and handed Ruby a few coupons. They looked at each other, it seemed, for the first time since Ruby had moved home. "What do you really think about marriage?" popped into Lily's head, but she didn't say it because Franklin came into the kitchen then.

He looked out into the backyard, then said to Lily, "Don't forget that trap tomorrow, the kind with the spring door. I want to catch those squirrels." He seemed to have forgotten that he had already told Ruby to buy the trap. Ruby didn't remind him.

"We don't need a trap. It's against the law. Someone will see you and then you'll be in trouble," Bell said.

"I want to eat some tomatoes this year," he said and shoved the money at Lily. Lily put the money in her pocket and looked down at the floor. Ruby felt bad for her.

After Franklin left, Lily took out the money and threw it on the table. "I'm not buying a trap," she said. Ruby and Bell nodded but they both knew, as did Lily, that tomorrow Lily would go to the hardware store and that she'd stand in the crowded aisle and ask to see the traps. After asking lots of questions, she would pick one trap over another, and as she was paying she might think of the time she had almost walked out in high school and it would strike her as funny that she used to go riding around on the back of her boyfriend's motorcycle with her hair flying behind her and that one night she had talked about getting her own bike so they could ride across the country together.

Chapter 14

The day after Lily bought her father's squirrel trap, she stood in front of her closet. Her heart began to race when she reached for the dress she wore for parent/teacher conferences. The slate-blue linen with buttons up the front made her feel like a lawyer. For months, she had shopped for a wedding dress, not a white gown with yards of lace, but something simple that she might wear again. But nothing had seemed right until that morning, when suddenly her linen dress seemed like the perfect dress to get married in.

She was tired of sleeping alone in the one-bedroom apartment above the laundry that she had lived in since college. She was tired of watching Hector get dressed after their quiet lovemaking. The ceiling and walls were thin; when Lily was close to coming, she'd push her face into the pillow.

No one had ever said that Hector wasn't allowed to stay the night, but the one time he had, years ago when they had first met, Franklin rang Lily's bell in the morning and raged at her for not buying his *Sports Eye*. He looked forward all week to sitting at the ironing table, checking off in red his two-dollar bets, but they all knew he wasn't yelling about his sports newspaper but about the fact that Hector hadn't trudged down the stairs the night before, stopping by the laundry to say good night as he usually did.

The day Lily put on her slate-blue dress, she called Hector and said, "Let's go. Let's do it."

"Today?"

"The license is going to expire any day now. And I've got my linen dress on, the one you like."

"What about the reception, the dinner?"

"No party, no family. Just me and you."

In the end, Hector put on his suit and got into his Honda and drove down Flatbush to the Brooklyn Queens Expressway. Under his suit, he had on a brand-new pair of shorts. Before he rang Lily's bell, he stopped at the shoemaker's next door to the laundry and sat in his stockinged feet while the shoemaker shined his shoes to a high gloss. "I'm getting married today," Hector said.

"Married? In that case, you need some new taps. Won't take but a minute," the shoemaker said. Hector wiggled his feet on the floor. He didn't want to keep Lily waiting. But he wanted to look spiffy. When his shoes were done, he laced them up quickly and practically ran to Lily's door.

At City Hall, they put rings on each other's fingers, said yes to the magistrate, then kissed each other, a brief public kiss. As they walked out, Hector put his arm around her shoulders. Lily put her arm around his waist. His jacket was pleasantly rough. She waited. This is my husband, she thought. We will live together above the laundry. He will bring over his bachelor furniture and we will find a place for it. He will not leave me at night. The word "husband" seemed strange to her. She waited and waited but she felt no different from the way she had felt before.

Hector talked about taking everyone out to dinner. "Did I ever take you to Seven Seas? They have the best steaks. Your father will love it. Will your mom eat a steak?" Hector's parents had met Lily's parents a few times before. He was talking about the baked potatoes at the steakhouse when he noticed the curious look on Lily's face.

"How're you holding up?" he said.

"Good, good," she said. This is marriage, she thought, her hand on the soft part of his waist hanging over his pants.

Absently, she played with that little piece of fat until, embarrassed, Hector caught her hand and held it there, her thumb tucked under his belt, her hand resting on his shirt.

As they were walking into the laundry, Lily dropped her arm from around his waist. She told her father she had just gotten married.

"No one says anything around here," Franklin fumed.

"We didn't want to make a big deal out of it," Lily said.

"Well, I guess we should shake hands," Franklin said to Hector. They shook hands and Franklin clapped him on the arm. "I guess we're like family now," Franklin said.

Bell heard the commotion and came out to the laundry. "How come you two don't tell anyone?"

"We didn't want a fuss," Hector said.

Then Franklin put on his shoes, Bell put on her pleated blue shirt and even Ruby changed out of her beat-up jeans into her newer jeans, and they all went out to Seven Seas Restaurant.

"What do you think about the steaks? Aren't they great? I told you they were great," Hector said.

"Too big. But tender," Bell said.

Franklin was quiet at dinner. When the check came, Hector and Franklin both reached for it. "I'm the boss around here. So I get to pay," Franklin said. Hector looked disgruntled but said thank you.

At home, Lily and Hector called out good night and went upstairs. Bell went out to the yard and watered her vegetables. Ruby was walking toward the basement door, when her father said, "I guess it's too late to do anything now. Just between you and me, I think it's a big mistake. A big mistake. Just friends, okay, but getting married? Yup, you can't mix two different kinds of people. Maybe it start out fine, but one day he want potato and she want rice. People like to eat their own food."

"Look. They could cook both. One extra pot, no big deal." Ruby knew her father was telling her to find a nice Chinese boy to settle down with and she wanted to tell him not to hold his breath.

"And what if they have kids? They won't be anything, just mixed up."

Ruby didn't think they should get married either, but it wasn't because of mixed-up babies. Lily seemed smaller and quieter around Hector. Maybe it was his cologne. Lily had been embarrassed to ask him not to wear any when he came over, but Bell couldn't bear to be in the same room with him because of it. She started coughing as soon as he walked into the house.

"I have to go downstairs now," Ruby said.

"How's your friend? Mick?" Franklin said.

"He's fine." Ruby didn't bother to correct him. She left him fussing with the *TV Guide* and went down to the basement.

Days later, Lily came down to borrow a can of tuna fish for lunch. Ruby went to the cabinet to get it for her. Then she told Lily what her father had said about Hector. As soon as she said it, she was sorry. She had thought they could laugh about how their father found fault with everything and everybody, but instead Lily just got quiet. "What does he know?" Ruby said.

Lily didn't answer for a long time. Then she said, "He used to take me to the movies. Before you were born. Ma would try to drag me to Sunday school but I wouldn't go. One time I was crying because Ma left and then Dad woke up and he took me to the movies. He let me get anything I wanted."

"What did you get?" Ruby said.

"Oh, candy. Popcorn."

"What kind of candy? Whoppers? Twizzlers?"

"Yeah," Lily said softly.

Ruby couldn't tell if Lily had really gotten that kind or a different kind altogether. She pictured Lily and their father sitting in the darkened theater, passing candy back and forth, Lily's shoes not quite reaching the floor.

"Remember we used to say we were never getting married?" Lily said. When she and Ruby were kids they swore they'd have lots of lovers with names like Miguel and François who would take them away to warm places and teach them new and wonderful customs. The closest Ruby ever came to this was when Nick took her to the Jersey Shore. She thought that was pretty exotic.

"Hector's a good guy," Lily said.

"He knows a good steak," Ruby said.

"He's bringing his stuff over today. No way it'll fit in that little apartment."

"Get rid of that couch. It's a monster."

"He wants to buy a house someday."

"With a lawn and everything?"

"He's always wanted a house," Lily said. She paused and then said, "You never lived upstairs."

"Don't you ever get depressed living up there?"

"You think I live up there because I want to?"

"I thought you wanted to save money."

"I've hated that carpet from day one. The noise, the bugs. The walls; you can hear everything. You know I never liked it up there."

"It's not so bad."

"Easy for you to say."

"I thought you liked it up there."

"You're the baby. You should've stayed." Lily looked up and when she saw how miserable Ruby looked, she laughed.

"You're laughing at me?" Ruby said.

"You're a mess. You owe me. You have to live upstairs and put in your time."

"How long?"

"I'm *kidding*. Anyway, come up later if you want, watch some TV. Ask Ma too. We just got a twenty-one inch. We've got lots of snacks."

After Lily went back upstairs, Ruby went out to the laundry and took her father's newspaper and his red pen. In the backyard, she sat on a lounge chair and marked apartments that sounded good.

Chapter 15

Summer was more than half over. Lily had gotten married and Hector had moved his furniture upstairs. What didn't fit in the apartment had ended up in the basement. Hector believed in family and invited Ruby and Bell to come up and watch movies. Lily would pass around bowls of pretzels and chips and cookies. Hector invited Franklin too, but Franklin said he liked to watch his own TV.

When everyone was gone, Franklin checked the squirrel trap. It was set among the tomato plants and so far the squirrels had taken the peanuts without getting caught. Franklin had started tying the peanuts to the trap. He still hadn't caught one squirrel yet. He and Hector talked about getting a different trap.

Ruby had been working for a month, but she barely had enough saved for two tickets to Florida, never mind the hotel that looked out onto the water and the restaurants she wanted to take her mother to so she could sit down at a table and have someone bring her her food. Her mother preferred her own cooking to anyone else's, but maybe she had never been to a restaurant that she liked.

Ruby didn't know why she didn't have more saved. She wasn't spending it on clothes, that was for sure. Her outfits were getting rattier and she mended them at work with Scotch tape and staples. Half the time her skirts were falling down and her nylons were gathered around her ankles. One morning she threw them all out and walked into work flaunting her bare legs in the hopes that they would send her home. Her legs were noted but overlooked; it was hard to get a good temp these days.

When her outfits couldn't be repaired anymore, she found clothes in the basement and wore them to work. Her father gave her a beige cardigan that a customer had left behind years ago. Beige wasn't becoming on her, but she wore it anyway with her long black skirt that was too narrow at the bottom. Such outfits made her sullen and spiteful; she was as efficient as ever, but she didn't try to smile anymore.

She almost didn't go in to work the day she found Van's old employment files. She had just gotten her period and as soon as she sat down to the breakfast her mother had made for her, she leaked. "Lord, Lord, Lord. Lord, please." Of course, for once in her life, she wasn't wearing black. As she was rinsing her skirt in the bathroom sink and while she was drying it with the hair dryer, she was on the verge of calling in sick. She even picked up the phone and put it down again. It was just a dumb job, but somehow she had her father's sense of honor when it came to work. If she said she would do the job, she would do it, god-damn it.

No matter how hard she scrubbed, she couldn't get out the stain. Then she remembered the dress her mother had given her at the beginning of the summer and even while she was fighting the idea, she knew that when she walked out of the house, she would be wearing the black dress with the white dots and the little round collar.

Stuben Engineering Company had scheduled her for the week. She had no idea what they engineered. It could have been steamships or bridges or car seats. She had worked there last week too and on Friday they had offered her a permanent job. That had scared her out of her wits, but she had answered quickly that she was starting cooking school in the fall, but thanks anyway. She didn't know where the cooking-school idea came from, but after she said it, it didn't seem crazy at all.

She was in the filing room, sorting old files. If the record was clean, she threw it out. If it had bad spots, she put it back in the file. That's what the file man had said, bad spots, as if he were talking about fruit. Ruby didn't think that was very fair, so when the file man wasn't looking, she threw out the bad files too.

Soon she could glance at a file and tell if it was good or bad. The file man went to lunch and she called Nick. "I'm a traitor. They've got me in the file room. They keep all the naughty files forever so they can give a lousy reference to the poor slob trying to get a new job."

"Look. You're a poor slob too. A job's a job."

"God, you should see the dress I've got on. I got my period today. What do you think about cooking school?" she said.

"I've always wanted to be a cook."

"I meant for me."

"Oh. Like French or something?"

"I don't know. Maybe French."

"You love food. You should do it. That temp job's killing you. Are we painting next week?"

"She has to pick a color. She's thinking yellow. Someone's coming. Got to go. Call you later."

"Love you."

"Me too."

The file man came back from lunch. He smelled minty. Ruby was sorting quickly, almost without looking, as her father did when he checked collars for spot cleaning. The next folder was her brother's. Van Lee, it said in big letters. From the weight of it, she knew it belonged in the file drawer. She waited a long time before the file man left the room, then she put the file in her bag.

She read that Mr. Lee was continually late. That wasn't news to her. His clock would stop, the second hand ticking the same minute over and over again and he would wake up late. Then he had to have his coffee and pull out the hairs that had turned white in his sleep. Some mornings, the bathroom mirror had been thick with hair.

Mr. Lee was caught plastering the office with his artwork, drawings of creatures who peeped over brick walls and pointed long arms at things like tuna and black ants. When asked what he was doing, he replied, "Enhancing the office environment."

Mr. Lee rewired the building's elevator musical system so that rock music played at a painfully high volume all morning while maintenance men worked quickly to repair the damage.

Mr. Lee came to work in jeans, T-shirt and sneakers. When warned that he was not exempt from the dress code, Mr. Lee came in wearing a purple polka-dotted tie, orange bell-bottoms and a lavender shirt. Ruby remembered that outfit. He had looked sharp in his colors.

Mr. Lee did not report to work for three days without calling in sick or notifying his supervisor. When asked where he had been, he replied, "Frisco."

Van had worked for Stuben for all of five months, yet there were pages and pages in his file. Ruby thought about what strangers had written about him, strangers who knew him as the oddball Chinese guy who worked in the mail room. This was what she knew: Van had adored both his sisters, had fought with his father, and had so disappointed his mother that she refused to speak to him. He had three children, a wife and a house. He worked in the basement of a bank and was trusted with keys to the safe-deposit boxes.

Ever since she had moved to the basement, she would look at the things Van had left behind and she'd feel like calling him and asking him out for a drink. At first he would be surprised to hear from her, but then it would be like old times, except that she was old enough to drink now. When he lived at home, he would take her to Dunkin' Donuts. They sat in his car in the parking lot and checked out the girls. "What about her? Do you like her?" Van would ask. "Yeah, what a babe," or "Nah, not my type," Ruby would answer. Van got a kick out of her answers and he would ruffle her hair. Sometimes he went out and talked to a girl. Ruby drank her iced tea with sugar that never quite dissolved. She opened and closed the window and waited. High five if he came back with a phone number. When she grew up, she would buy a car and cruise babes and get phone numbers too, she told him.

After she had moved to the basement, she wanted to call him. Now that she had found his file, she felt she could. They would meet in the city at one of Van's favorite bars where he knew the owner, who would come over and Van would introduce her. "This is my baby sister." The owner, a young guy in a beret, would sit with them for a minute and maybe he'd give them drinks on the house and then he'd leave them alone. Van would tell her a little about the band that was playing that night. Ruby would tell him about how she had ended up working at Stuben too and they would laugh about how a dumb job could haunt you forever. It would feel a little like a date and maybe afterward they would go for dinner.

She had his file. But her mother had called him and he hadn't called her back. Ruby couldn't believe he had blown off his own mother. She remembered the Siamese fighting fish he had given her for her fifth birthday. One was bright blue and the other red as a fresh cut. One day Van lifted the partition between them. "Hey, Ruby. Baby sister. Want to see something?" At first her fish swam up to where the glass had been and wouldn't go past that point. Then they lunged, tearing each other to bits. Van slipped the panel back and Ruby took her hand, already curled into a fist, and hit his leg hard. He could be so mean. The blue fish sank to the bottom of the tank. It died that night. The red fish wasn't really hurt but it died the next day. To make it up to her, Van took her to the Bronx Zoo to watch the bats drink blood. That was a good time and it hadn't mattered to her that Van was broke and that she spent all the money that customers had given her for being cute. Ruby didn't really blame him for leaving and not coming back, although she had cried and clung to his leg when he left.

It was only three-thirty but Ruby felt done with working.

Her dress felt like cardboard. The file man told her to hold all calls. He was watching her from his glassy office. "Shut up," she said, under her breath. The phone rang and Ruby took a message from a guy who wanted to joke with her.

"Who was that?" The file man poked his head out of his office.

"George. George Gallagher. He said to call him."

"George Gallagher? Why didn't you tell me?"

"You said to hold your calls."

"Yeah, but not for Georgie."

"My mind-reading abilities have deteriorated immensely in the last few years."

"Hey, watch yourself." He pointed a finger at her.

"If you would prefer that I not work here, that can be arranged." She hated every hair on his toupee.

"Calm down, just calm down. Who said anything about you not working here? Christ." He went back to his office.

Ruby sat at her desk. The phone was ringing and then she was gathering up her bag and her sweater. On second thought, she left the sweater draped over the chair. At the reception desk, she said, "Just going to the ladies' room." Then she walked down the hallway and out the glass doors. She took the elevator down and strolled out of the building. No one followed her and she walked away and was pleased not to answer any phones or type any letters. Very pleased.

She was so pleased she walked all the way downtown to her favorite bookstore, where she ran into Manny. He looked good. She told him so. At school, they'd had crushes on each other and once they'd even given in and slept together. He never told his girlfriend Claudia, but every time Ruby saw her on campus she felt guilty. Ruby had told Nick and he had threatened to leave her. Now Manny and Claudia had broken up after four years. Manny still looked sad about it. In the bookstore, they talked like good friends, and when he touched her arm to ask if she wanted to, she didn't move away.

Two nights later, Nick was looking at her, but he wasn't listening to her telling about how she had left the office in the middle of the day. Her shoulders were covered up by her hair and he looked at her mouth and her nose and her eyes, trying to decide if she was really worth so much suffering. There was that radiance about her that meant she had been fucked recently, and fucked well. It had been some time since he had fucked her. She also had that look like she was going to tell him about it soon. Her eyes were pretty but her nose was a little on the flat side. He would be better off without her. But that mouth. He was weak and hated himself. If only he could harden his heart against her.

She was just about to tell him about running into Manny at the bookstore when she stopped. Maybe she didn't have to tell him. Other people fooled around and never said a word about it and they stayed together. "Stop looking at me like that," she said.

"Like what?" He tried to make his face look friendly.

"Like you're judging me. Like I'm a fucking used car." She was getting mad now. That always helped.

"You know what? You have to decide." He wasn't angry and he wasn't pleading with her. There was a resolve in him that Ruby hadn't seen before and she felt a little respect for him. It gave her a jolt to realize she hadn't respected him before. Each time she cheated, she had waited and hoped and feared that this time he would put his foot down. Now that he had, she went quickly to indignation. No man was going to tell her what she could and could not do. Underneath her indignation she felt terribly afraid when he said, "Ruby, what do you want?" He said her name and asked her the question that nearly broke her in two; she didn't know if she was more afraid of wanting him or of not wanting him. But he had asked her plainly, as if she could just say what she wanted and then get it, like a candy bar.

He had been waiting for her answer and then he stopped waiting and slowly started to pull away from her although he hadn't taken his hand from hers. She looked at him and thought he was handsome even though he didn't think so. He would stand in front of the mirror and study his face. "I've got beady eyes, no chin and a big nose. What do you see in me?" She was looking at Nick and thinking about Manny and how she had so easily followed him home and how she had stood still and watched his hands as he undid her skirt. They had kept the lights on and had watched each other. Afterward, she had tried smoking for the first time. Now, as she sat on Nick's bed, it suddenly occurred to her that she had no idea how to love.

Nick talked in that calm way he had about love, his love for her and how no one would ever love her more than he did and all she had to do was say yes and he would be hers always. Then he was talking about her love; he knew she loved him, she just had to stop fighting it. She listened to him; he seemed so sure. "But I don't know how," she said. Her heart felt like a little crumb heart that would never open.

He was giving her a week to decide. She looked around for her shoes and put them on and left him standing by the window. By the time she got to the train station, walking slowly and looking into store windows along the way, he would have drunk half a bottle of very good red wine that he had been saving for the dinner he had planned on making for her. Brisket. It wasn't a romantic food, but he had planned on lighting candles anyway. By the time she had made her way home, after having decided absolutely yes, then absolutely no, then yes again, he would have drunk the whole bottle.

Chapter 16

*A*ll week, Ruby walked around the house and the streets of Springfield and thought *if only*. While she was on the phone with her agency, explaining that she had left work abruptly on Friday because she hadn't been feeling well and that she didn't know when she'd be going back, she was thinking *if only*. As she sat in Dunkin' Donuts and ate a French cruller, as she looked at the Want Ads, as she walked on the streets and looked at couples and at people walking alone, as she cooked the food her mother had put aside in the refrigerator for dinner, as she sat at the table and watched her mother and her father and sometimes Lily and Hector, she thought *if only*.

If only she and Nick didn't live in New York, if only they lived someplace far away from everyone she knew, then she could say, "Yes, you and me, babe." If only she were fifty years old and tired of affairs. If only he weren't so white and didn't sweat up her pillowcases. If only he were a woman. Or if he were more of a man. Or if he could just learn to cook a good pot of rice.

But he made a mean omelette. He was a good kisser. Trying so hard to decide only made her more confused; what was more important, omelettes or pillowcases? When she thought about saying yes, all the walls in the house seemed to press too close to her and she had to go out walking. On Saturday morning she left the house and passed without seeing the shoemaker's and the barber's and the deli and the houses with the tiny lawns that she had coveted as a child. She walked to Woolworth's and walked up and down the aisles and bought a bag of by-the-pound candies.

When she got home she went down to the basement to call Nick. Maybe if she heard his voice, she would know. She picked up the phone and put it down. The file she had stolen from work was hidden in the bottom drawer of her dresser, under her fancy white sheets. She took out the file and leafed through it, wondering what Van was doing. Before she could talk herself out of it, she had picked up the phone and called him.

"Van? It's me, Ruby."

"Hey, baby sister. I was just thinking about you. I'm having this barbecue, a rock-and-roll barbecue. I want you to come, and Mom and Dad and Lily. If you guys can make it." Then he said quietly, "How's Mom and Dad?"

"I guess they're okay. The same. Listen, I was working this temp job and guess what? I found your file."

"You're old enough to work? Take it from me, stay away from work. It's no good for you. What'd those bastards have to say about me?"

"Silly things. Like how you wore funny clothes. And put pictures on the wall and played loud music. Same things you did at home that drove Dad nuts."

She paused.

"Van?"

"Yeah?"

"I think Ma was kind of upset you never called her back."

"I was going to call, but then I got back late from work and the next day Jeannette's sister came for a visit and then—oh, lots of things. Was she upset?"

"You know her, she doesn't say much. But you can tell."

"I think about you guys all the time. But with the kids and work and all . . . I've got this new boss and Sylvie goes to acrobatics on the weekends and Dylan's in high school already." He sighed. "I don't know. Listen, what are you doing right now? You want to come over and jam? We need a drummer."

"I've never touched a drum in my life."

"You can keep a beat, can't you? That's okay. Just come to the barbecue. We'll get the grill going, throw on some burgers, some chicken. I'll make my special sauce. Tell Mom and Dad. And Lily, tell Lily. Labor Day, okay? Around four."

After Ruby hung up the phone, she sat with Van's file in her lap. Then she went upstairs. The kitchen smelled of chicken soup and bleach. Bell was making lunch and Franklin was washing a load of laundry. Bell was standing at the sink and Franklin nearly pushed her out of the way, then poured stain remover on the shirt he had in his hands. The smell of the stain remover made Bell grip the counter.

"Van's having a barbecue. He wants us to come," Ruby said.

A big smile broke over Franklin's face and he said, "A barbecue. How about that? Maybe he's finally growing up."

Bell looked as if she had been hit in the stomach. "Barbecue? That kind of food will make you sick. No good for your ulcer."

"One barbecue's not going to kill me. How do you like that? Van doing something for the family. When's the last time he came for a visit?" Franklin marveled.

"Remember he say he's coming for Easter. What happened? The food got cold. Did he show up? He don't even call." Bell's eyes were bright with fury.

"The past is the past," Franklin said firmly.

Bell shook her head at him. Then her shoulders sagged and she said, "Maybe I'll cook some noodles and bring it to the barbecue."

Ruby had stood silent while her parents talked. It was strange to see them talking to each other. Now her mother opened the cabinets and looked desperately inside them, as if she would start cooking for the barbecue right away. Her father smiled to himself, set the washing machine to "permanent press" and walked out to the laundry.

"You better go tell your sister," Bell said.

Ruby called Lily then and told her about the barbecue. "He's so strange. He doesn't talk to us for years and then he invites us to a barbecue. What should we bring?" Lily said.

After Ruby hung up the phone, she went back to thinking about Nick. She felt cornered again and walked all the way to the travel agent on Smith. She sat in the hard plastic chair. Every time she crossed her legs, she hit her knees against the desk. The brochures were shiny and blue. Watching the travel agent write down prices of hotels and flights made Ruby feel dreamy and she thought it would be nice to bring a pie to the barbecue.

She walked home with travel brochures in her pocket. When she got home, her father asked her to make his afternoon snack. Her mother was in the backyard, picking tomatoes. There was still a month before the days would turn cool and her mother would be coming home from work in the dark. Before the first frost, her mother would pick all the green tomatoes and line them up on the windowsill. When they turned red she would make tomato and pepper steak.

It was on one of those cool days that Ruby had made her first loaf of bread. That was the year she and Helen Hong had picked John Travolta to lavish every ounce of their eleven-year-old lust on. His disco hips drove them crazy and they saved their fifty-cent allowances until they had enough to buy the *Saturday Night Fever* sound track. Customers would hear the Bee Gees crooning behind the laundry, and if they looked into the living room they would see two girls doing the hustle. Maybe they were a little awkward, but they were too excited to care. They couldn't wait until they were old enough to go out at night; by then they would know how to dip and twirl away from the stores that were their homes, dipping and twirling into the arms of men wearing tight flared pants. How they hustled as they waited for breasts—big American ones they wanted—to fill out their spaghetti-strap dresses—red, of course.

Helen would go home to her house above the restaurant, the house with the two little rooms. Her brother slept in the kitchen on the striped cot and everyone else crowded together in the other room. After Helen left, Ruby, still sweaty, would look through the Betty Crocker *Bread Book*. The golden loaves had a warm orange glow about them, which Ruby tried to duplicate, following the recipe with painstaking care, even bringing the desk lamp from the living room into the kitchen. "So dark in here. You can't see nothing," Bell said and tried to turn on the overhead fluorescent.

The first loaves she baked were hard and dense. Or they were burned on the outside and raw in the middle. Ruby learned that yeast died in hot water and refused to grow in cold water. Either way, her bread didn't rise. After many heavy loaves and pounds of wasted flour, she learned to flick a few drops of water on her wrist. She could tell when the water was just right—not too warm, not too cool. After that, her bread rose to perfection, bread so fragrant and chewy that her father would cut another slice and tell her he was going to close the laundry and open up a bakery. Her mother would take the extra loaf to the factory and cut it up into chunky pieces and give everyone a slice. Bell would say, "My daughter made this. No, the little one. Yes, very smart." By the time she was sixteen, Ruby still hadn't been kissed, but her bread was soulful, better than any bakery. You didn't need butter, it was so good.

It had been years since Ruby had baked. Her mother bought dinner rolls these days. Ruby cut a roll in half and unwrapped a slice of cheese and put the whole thing in the toaster oven. When the cheese drooped at the corners, it was done. She took a little bite. The roll was stale and toasting only helped so much. In the store, her father was on the phone with his bookie. He motioned for her to leave the roll on the table, then huddled in the corner and placed his bets.

Ruby hurried out of the store, leaving her father to bet in peace. She walked up the block and stood outside the new bodega. For years, Diamond Aluminum Siding had run a brisk business, the miniature houses in the window lit up all night long. Their customers were the same ones who brought their laundry to Franklin. But slowly, anyone who could buy a house didn't want one in Springfield. They moved to Long Island, usually to Nassau. The people who stayed behind didn't have money to fix up the houses that weren't their own, but that they rented year after year, and so Diamond Aluminum closed and Rodriguez's bodega opened up.

The sign above Rodriguez's was new and shiny, but the inside was already taking on a haggard look, much like the men who sat on crates outside the store. La Chinita, they called Ruby, and she searched her memory for a snappy comeback she could say in Spanish but ended up walking stiffly past them, with her eyes straight ahead, as if she were busy thinking about yeast and flour and raisins.

At home, she cleared the table and went to work. Cinnamon swirl with raisins had always been a favorite. She made a well in the flour, poured in the yeast and added the water. *Knead just until smooth and elastic.* That had always been her favorite part. The dough was sticky, so she added a light sprinkling of flour, not too much or the bread would be tough. She pushed and pulled the dough, pounded it with the heel of her hand, dug her knuckles into it. Finally, the two halves of dough clung to each other when she pulled them apart. If she went on kneading, that would make it tough too. So many things could ruin a good loaf; it was amazing that it ever worked at all.

Let rest until doubled in size. It was resting now on top of the stove in the big white bowl. The dough rose up, slow and steady. It rose above the rim of the bowl. A finger pressed into it made a neat belly button. *Punch down and let rise again.* This was hard to do, to punch it down after it had worked so hard to rise.

While the bread was baking, Franklin whistled around the house. Bell got out the mop and washed the kitchen floor. It had not been washed in some time. Afterward, the gold swirled into the green linoleum and seemed to shine. Franklin had a cheerful news story for once. "There was this truck delivering shoes in New Jersey. All of a sudden, it turned over on the highway. No one was hurt. But shoes everywhere! People stopped their cars and picked up whatever they wanted. And they were expensive shoes too. Not cheap ones." He told the story and when he got to the part about the shoes being expensive, everyone laughed. The timer went off with a sharp little *ping.* It was time to check the bread.

The two women sobered up as if the bell had suddenly reminded them that the summer wouldn't last forever and that Ruby would move out someday. The bread was cooling on top of the washing machine. It was deep brown and shiny from the egg she had brushed on top. Bell put away the leftovers from dinner. There were lots of leftovers. Everyone had been saving room for the bread.

Before the knife cut all the way through, Ruby knew it was no good. She started talking fast. "Oh well, I guess it didn't work. Maybe I'll run up to the bakery and get a pie. How about apple? Is apple good? Maybe a crumb cake. A crumb cake, that's a good idea." She stepped in front of the bread so no one could look at it. The inside was sticky and raw. Slice after slice she cut. Surely the whole thing couldn't be ruined. Franklin and Bell were watching her cut up the loaf. When they saw the look on her face, they both looked down at the floor.

"It doesn't matter. Maybe you're just a little rusty." Franklin looked everywhere but at the bread.

Ruby went over each step in her head. She had done everything right. Sifted the flour, measured carefully, preheated the oven. And somehow, it still hadn't worked. Bell came over and picked through the slices. The part near the crust was not so raw and she ate a piece.

"No, don't eat it." Ruby started to gather up the bits of broken bread.

"Here, taste it. This part is good." Bell held out a piece to Ruby. Ruby shrank away and then started washing the pans. "Here, you try it." Bell held out a piece to Franklin.

"No, don't give it to him." Ruby scrubbed harder at the pans. They needed soaking, that's what they needed.

"It's not so bad," Franklin said. He chewed slowly, as if afraid he might find bones in it.

"Maybe it was old. The yeast." Bell nodded vigorously. "A little old."

Franklin latched on to that. "Yeah. The yeast. It must have been old. Where'd you get it? That little store. They always sell old things."

"Stop eating it. Just throw it away. I'll go to the bakery. What time do they close?" Ruby said. Maybe the yeast was a little old. Maybe that was it, she was thinking.

Bell was still picking through the bread, cutting the raw parts away. "No big deal," she said after a long time. Ruby wondered where she had gotten that from.

"No big deal," Franklin said.

Chapter 17

*A*fter Ruby had finally finished washing the pans, she crept down to the basement. If her mother told her one more time that the bread wasn't so bad, Ruby would scream. The basement was smaller and darker than ever. She looked for a long time at the photo of her mother in the gold dress, standing straight as a soldier. It was the last thing she saw before falling asleep. She dreamed she was eating dog. It was roasted and chewy. Later, she dreamed she was having sex with her mother. Her mother was close to coming, but then her father woke up and was clearing his throat in the bathroom. Her mother pushed her off and said she had to go to work.

Ruby woke up, remembering the time when the kids at school had asked her if she ate dog for dinner. "Chinese restaurants cook dog meat all the time," they said. Ruby thought they were crazy. After all, she would always save scraps from her dinner to feed Beauty, the shoemaker's beagle. She knew Chinese people ate pigeons, turtles and frogs, but dogs, no way. She had gone home and asked her father about it. He said, "Yup, dogs are a real delicacy. But you don't eat your own dog. You need your dog so you know if someone trying to come into your house. And you don't eat your neighbor's dog because that's not too neighborly. But if you find a dog from another village, that dog you can eat."

After her father said that, Ruby went to the library and found a book on food rituals. She read about a tribe of people who grew yams and piled them up in the yard. When you visited your neighbor, you brought along a basket of yams that you had piled up, and when you left, they gave you some of their yams that they had piled up. You weren't supposed to eat your own yams. Or your own dog. Or your own sister or mother. Your own yams, your own sister, your own mother you may not eat. Other people's sisters, other people's mothers, you may eat.

Ever since Ruby could remember, her mother had grown vegetables in the backyard. Her mother's friends grew vegetables too. They would come over and give her a bag of tomatoes, beans and squash, and she would give them a bag of hers. No matter what the weather had been like that year, they would all apologize for their vegetables. "Not enough rain this year. The beans are kind of tough. And the tomatoes, not so sweet."

Your own tomatoes, your own mother, you must not eat.

Ruby woke up from her dream. The photo of her mother was looking at her. Ruby reached over and wiped the dust from the frame, then turned it slightly toward the wall. The newspaper was open on the floor. She picked it up and wondered if the apartments advertised were as good as they sounded. She doubted it. But there was a one-bedroom that she could almost afford. It was walking distance from Nick. If she would just live with him, it would save her the trouble of finding an apartment. But then she'd have to live with him.

In the back of the newspaper were ads for phone sex. It promised hot times. Maybe if she had one last fling, she might be able to commit. She thought about calling Manny. He had called her a few days ago but she hadn't called him back. She was a little embarrassed by how easily she had gone with him that night at the bookstore. She had kissed his neck as if she were starving. Later, he said her name and touched her face. She had always wanted Nick to touch her face. She knew if she asked him to, he would be happy to do it. But if she had to ask, it wouldn't be the same.

Maybe one last fling would help her make up her mind. One last fling and then she would commit. But she didn't feel like calling Manny. He would be nice to her. He might touch her face again and then she'd be undone. A stranger would be better. But she didn't want to go out and find one.

She turned back to her newspaper and wondered if phone sex would be allowed under the new arrangement. It wasn't actually touching another person. She didn't feel much in the mood, but the hot line was free for women, so she called up and listened to the ads from men who were hoping to talk to the women they had seen in the newspaper ads. "I'm wearing a black lace teddy," she said, although she was wearing a white T-shirt and pajama pants that her mother had made. All the men she talked to happened to be handsome and well endowed. She touched herself idly. A couple of hours passed and then a new guy got on the line (a millionaire, he said). He wanted to know if any ladies out there were feeling lonely tonight. She hung up the phone.

With so many jerks out there, Ruby couldn't figure out what she thought she'd be missing out on if she said yes to Nick. And she knew she didn't want to lose him. She had left too many of her things at his house—clothes, panties, books. If only her things weren't mixed in with his, she might be able to leave. Her stomach felt like a fist when she thought about taking all her clothes from his closet and from his dresser drawers. It was that feeling in her stomach that finally made her get on the train to Manhattan on Sunday morning.

Then she was walking on Broadway, looking into every face that passed. Her eyes were full of tenderness and regret that she would never know their names or what was inside the packages they carried. A few people looked back at her and maybe they wondered what made her look so sad on that beautiful Sunday morning. At the bakery, she looked with longing at the little strawberry tarts and the apple turnovers and fancy cakes like Easter bonnets. She lingered there as if saying good-bye to all that was dear to her. How she envied the people who walked right into the store and pointed confidently at something in the window and came out with a cardboard box that they held carelessly by the string.

All week, she had thought of reasons why she shouldn't show up at Nick's door on Sunday morning, yet there she was. On her way to Manhattan, she still didn't know what she would say to him. By the time she got to the uptown number-one train, she found herself thinking about his bedroom. It smelled of eucalyptus leaves and there was a thick blue rug by the bed. There were no chairs, so she would have to sit on the bed. If they went into the bedroom she would be lost, but if they stayed in the living room she might have a fighting chance.

For days she had tried to keep busy, had looked in the paper for a job (which she didn't find), called her friends (who told her gaily that they felt quite abandoned by her), had pushed the shopping cart in the supermarket for her mother (who noticed that Ruby looked troubled and didn't ask her about it, though she did buy a nice cut of beef to make some pepper steak for her). No matter how she tried to keep busy, she still missed him.

As she reached his block, she took one last look at the trees and the street signs and the cathedral and the cherries and watermelon and plums of the green market, at the dogs and the Manhattan people and the stores that were closed for the day. She stood outside his building, then sat down on the curb. He lived in a building where people walked past each other without saying hello. She looked up at his window and for the first time in her life wished she were a smoker. She would take her time smoking one last cigarette, and then she'd go inside.

But she had never learned to smoke. She got up from the curb and let herself into his building. In the elevator, she slumped against the wall. Her legs were heavy as she walked down the hall to his apartment. She let herself in. As the door to the bedroom opened, he lay there, clutching a blanket around his waist. "Jesus. You trying to give me a heart attack?" he said. She had a feeling he had been lying there all week.

"Here I am." She gave a little shrug, as if she didn't care one way or the other.

"What's that mean?" he said.

"Yes."

"Yes what?"

"You and me, babe, forever."

"You and me," he said slowly. Then he came to life. "You and me?" he said.

"You and me." She was in despair.

He got out of bed and put his arms around her. "I love you," he said into her hair. Then he stepped back. "You're not happy."

"No, I am happy," she said and gave him a ghastly smile. "I tried to buy breakfast but I couldn't go in."

"We can go out. Get some eggs, pancakes if you want." They went over to the bed and soon they were fucking. It was hard to say who started it. As he was coming, her face was pressed against his arm and she thought that he didn't smell as nice as she remembered. Afterward she felt a little better and thought maybe things wouldn't be so bad after all.

At breakfast, they both ordered omelettes, and at the last minute Nick ordered a waffle too. She knew he wouldn't finish all that food and started to get nervous. She hated waste. But then she thought, This is a celebration. She would help him eat the waffle.

"What do you want to do today?" he said, looking wonderingly at her.

"I don't know."

"How about the Cloisters? We had fun there last time."

"Maybe." The way he was looking at her was starting to make her edgy.

"Want to see a movie?"

"Not really. Maybe we could go for a walk," she said, just to say something.

Then the waiter brought them their food. The omelettes looked fluffy yet cooked. That was a good sign, she thought. She hated a runny omelette. As she buttered her toast, she felt a little hope rise up in her. Finally she had made a decision; now she could get on with the rest of her life.

After breakfast they walked in the park. Nick seemed especially tall that day; maybe it was his new shoes. She thought people were staring. An old Chinese couple walked past them. She felt a little embarrassed. They went back to his place in the afternoon and fell into bed again. Even though she had a great big orgasm, she felt like she was pretending.

It was dark by the time she said, "I have to go."

"How come?"

"I have to go back to work tomorrow. I'm broke."

"I have money."

"I need my own money."

"Baby, don't be so uptight."

"I have to go. I'll come over tomorrow, after work."

"You want lamb chops tomorrow?"

"Let's see tomorrow, okay?"

At the train station he bought a token so he could wait on the platform with her. When the train came she sat by the window so she could wave to him. As the train pulled away from the station, her face closed up again like a pocketbook snapping shut and then she looked like everyone else on the train.

By the time she got home, whatever hope she'd had at breakfast was gone. The restless feeling was worse than ever. This time she had brought it on herself. Her own treacherous legs had taken her to his house and out of her own back-stabbing mouth she had declared she would forsake all others. And now she didn't even want him anymore.

The day after Ruby went to see Nick, Franklin caught a squirrel. He was eating chicken soup and a grilled-cheese sandwich when he heard a loud snap. For the past week now, he had tied the peanuts to the bottom of the cage, but the squirrels were still getting away. Franklin ran out to the yard when he heard the metal door slam closed. The squirrel raced around the cage, then started gnawing on the door.

"You think you're so smart. Not smarter than me," Franklin said, shaking his finger at the squirrel. The squirrel chattered back and threw itself against the cage.

"That'll hold you," Franklin said and went back to his lunch.

Later that night, Bell was in the kitchen cooking dinner. Van had just called to make sure everyone was coming to the barbecue. Although she had been gruff with him on the phone, after she hung up she turned on the radio and hummed a little. Hector and Lily said they were coming down for dinner. Ruby said she'd be home too. Bell was trying to decide if she had cooked enough food. At the last minute, she decided to make beef and peas too. That only took a few minutes.

Franklin came in to get a cup of tea. He held his hand to his ear. "Did you hear that? I think that's the trap." He looked at Bell. She was busy with her beef and peas.

"I think we caught something," Franklin said. "You better go out there and take a look."

"I'm cooking."

"But the trap."

"What about you?"

"I get dizzy when I go out there." Franklin watched her uncertainly. He didn't know why she wouldn't go out and check the trap. At dinner he mentioned the trap again, but Bell still didn't do anything. Hector said he would check the trap after dinner, but after dinner he drove to the store for ice cream.

After the ice cream, Ruby went to Nick's house. They walked to Augie's, a bar they used to go to. She was wearing her black tank dress that showed everything. Nick thought she looked great. A guy at the bar thought so too and looked at her for too long. Nick used to get mad at that sort of thing, but now he just smirked and put his hand on her leg.

"Don't do that," Ruby said.

"Do what?" Nick took his hand from her leg and picked up his drink.

"Touch me like that."

"Like what?"

"Like this." She grabbed his leg.

"Was I?

"Uh-huh."

"Oh. Sorry."

They settled back into their seats. Ruby ordered french fries. "My mom picked a color. For her kitchen. Sunrise. Either that or lemon mist."

"What time should I come?"

"You don't mind?"

"Course not."

She felt shy suddenly. He put his arm around her. She moved closer to him. He touched her hair. "Touch my face," she almost said. Instead, she leaned forward slightly to put ketchup on the fries. She stayed over that night.

All that week, Franklin didn't stop talking about the squirrel trap. Bell was trying to ignore him. At night, when she got off the bus, she would look into the store to see if he had a customer. If he did, she tried to sneak past him before he could say anything to her. It's just a little squirrel, she told herself, but she couldn't bring herself to go out to the yard.

Franklin started waking up earlier and stood by the backyard door while Bell packed her lunch. "I think we caught something," he said almost every morning.

One night Bell said to Ruby, "Your father trying to make me crazy. Every day he bother me about that trap. He pretend he don't know if he catch something or not. But he know."

"Why doesn't he check it himself?" Ruby was getting mad at her father.

"He say he get dizzy when he go outside. He always go out in the yard." Bell had *told* him not to get a trap.

"Ma? You ever think about leaving him?" Ruby picked at her nails as she waited for her mother to answer.

Bell looked unsure. "I don't know," she said. She thought about it, then said, "I never think about that."

Slowly, Ruby looked up from her nails to her mother's face. Her mother meant what she had said. All that time, Ruby thought her mother was just waiting for the right time to leave. For so long, Ruby had wanted to take her away. *And her mother didn't think about that.*

Ruby sat up straight in her chair. She felt light suddenly. Slowly, she shook her head and said, "Goddammit. How do you like that?" Ruby slapped her leg. Then she grabbed her mother by the arm. Her mother's arm was strong and solid.

Chapter 18

Two thousand four hundred dollars. That was what Ruby had saved by the end of the summer. For seven hours a day at her temp job, she settled her face into an expression of glum politeness. Each week she took her check from the tissue box on the counter where her father left her mail; she went to the bank and deposited it. She didn't spend much except for lunch and a few accessories at Strawberry's so no one would notice that she only had three outfits. Sometimes, as she waited at the copy machine for the warm pages to fall into her hands, she remembered that her mother didn't think about leaving and she felt surprised all over again.

In the end, Bell broke down and went out to the yard. She found the dead squirrel in one corner of the trap. It had started to smell. She had planned to nudge it into a plastic bag and then hose down the trap, but after seeing it, her dinner threatened to rise up in her. In the laundry, Franklin opened a new bag of roasted peanuts. He ate one. If he let himself, he would eat the whole bag. They were bad for his ulcer. Besides, they were for the squirrels. He took some laundry string and wrapped it around a peanut.

Bell opened the metal door. Even with her rubber gloves on, she didn't want to touch the squirrel. She had always hated how they dug up her yard and ruined her tomatoes, but as she squatted down to look at the tiny face, the matted fur, she felt sorry for it. Her husband was waiting in the laundry to set the trap again. Something snapped in her. She picked up the trap and threw the whole thing into her trash bag.

Franklin came into the kitchen, whistling. The peanuts he had rigged up were in his pockets. Bell was in the bathroom, washing her hands with hot water. Franklin looked out into the backyard. The trap wasn't among the plants or near the trash or by the fence that separated their yard from the shoemaker's yard. He walked over to the bathroom and banged on the door. "You finished washing the trap?" he yelled.

Bell dried her hands carefully before coming out. Franklin tried to look into the bathroom.

"You're not going to find it. It's gone," Bell said.

"I paid good money for that trap," he said without vigor.

"We don't need a trap." Then, gently, she said, "Getting cold anyway. Soon there's no more tomatoes."

The day after Bell threw away the trap, Franklin ignored her when she called him to breakfast. She had made oatmeal and a boiled egg on toast. "You don't want to eat?" she said.

"Not hungry," he answered. At ten o'clock, he came into the kitchen and got himself a bowl of cornflakes. For three days, all he ate was cornflakes.

"Dad's not eating," Ruby said to her mother.

"He's no baby. If he wants to eat, he can eat," Bell said, but that night at dinner she said in a loud voice, "Tell your father his ulcer going to get worse if he don't eat." Franklin stamped his feet before coming into the kitchen. Ruby kept looking at his stomach to see if he was getting skinnier. He ate a few spoonfuls of rice and a couple of string beans and went back to the living room.

After he left, Ruby said to her mother, "He's still upset you threw away his trap?"

"It's about time I threw that thing away." Bell was triumphant.

Ruby waited to feel triumphant too. All her life, she had waited for her mother to stand up to her father. But now Ruby couldn't understand why she felt so sad and small. "He told me he didn't want them to get your tomatoes," Ruby said.

"He want to eat tomatoes is one thing. He don't want to clean the trap is another thing," Bell said. She looked around the kitchen. "It's cool enough, we can paint soon. Maybe after we paint, then we can go to Florida," she said. She went into her bedroom and came out with a pair of shorts she had made. They were just like her pajama pants but shorter. "What do you think of my short-shorts?"

"You never wear shorts," Ruby said.

"Maybe it's hot in Florida. You want a pair? I can make you one."

Usually, talking about Florida cheered Ruby up, but that day she was too busy thinking about the squirrel. "How did it look? In the trap," Ruby said.

"Don't talk about that. Of course it didn't look too good."

"What'd you do with the trap?" Ruby thought her mother might have hidden it somewhere in the basement. She felt uneasy about going downstairs if it was there.

"I threw it away."

"You didn't put it downstairs?"

"Who want to keep a thing like that?"

Ruby believed her mother but she couldn't shake the feeling of not wanting to go to the basement. "I think I'm going to Nick's tomorrow. After work."

Bell folded her shorts back up. She felt deflated suddenly. "Call if you stay over there."

The next day Ruby was almost glad to go to work. In the morning she typed a few letters, then took out her cooking-school brochures. The course descriptions stirred her more than anything else had in a long time. She lingered over the softly lit photos of food: eggs in a wire basket, tender young asparagus, a whisk and an empty bowl. And cooks got to wear that snazzy white jacket and those wide black-and-white-checked pants. The hat looked sort of silly, but it was still better than the polka-dotted dress that she was wearing. In the afternoon she talked with the temp next to her. He was a musician. She showed him her cooking brochures. He gave her a demo tape and his phone number and told her to come to his next gig. In the old days, she would have gone and afterward would have gone home with him. It had only been one week since she had given up her affairs. She didn't know how long she'd last.

After work she bought a sunflower and went to Nick's. On his bed was a neatly folded stack of laundry, nestled in brown paper. "What's that?" She felt broken.

He had meant to put the laundry away before she came over but hadn't gotten around to it. "So? I had my laundry done. I've been running around. I didn't have time." He got up and started putting the laundry away. It was cleaner and brighter than when he did it himself. Lots of people dropped off their laundry. He felt Ruby watching him.

"You paid people to do your laundry?" Ruby said. He felt caught. He knew Ruby was touchy about laundry; she believed firmly that you should wash your own dirt and that it was wrong, somehow, to pay someone else to do it. Once he had argued that her father would have gone out of business if everyone felt the way she did. She told him he was missing the point and then she wouldn't kiss him for the rest of the night. Now he wished he had remembered to put the damn laundry away before she came over.

"Where'd you bring it?" She hoped it wasn't the Chinese guy up the block. She hoped to God that she wasn't in love with someone who brought his clothes to the Chinese laundry. "Did you bring it to Wing Wah's?" she asked.

"I don't know. The guy on the next block."

"Oh." That was all they said about the laundry. In the shower she was thinking of how she would tell him, but he was waiting for her when she came out. The towel he had left out for her smelled different. The laundry had been put away and the brown paper folded up and pushed into the trash can.

"You're mad all the time. Is it the you-and-me-babe thing?" he said.

"I thought I could do it."

"You were wrong?"

"It's not working. You know me, I get restless."

He was quiet, then said, "My mom said you would never change."

"Your mom hates me."

"She doesn't hate you." He sighed. A big drawn-out sigh that was only a little exaggerated. "Let's see how it goes." They put their arms around each other but it wasn't the same. The longing in her was desperate and she wanted to say, "Let's live together." Or "Let's break up now." Instead, in a light tone, she said, "What do you want for dinner?"

A week went by and Nick waited for Ruby to go back to her cheating ways. When they went out, he watched her closely to see if she had eyes for anyone else. When she didn't come over, he called her early in the morning. She sounded happy to hear from him. At the end of the week he started to feel that he wasn't such a fool, after all.

After being released from their agreement, Ruby didn't think about affairs as much as she had before. Van's barbecue was coming up on the weekend and she was busy thinking about that. She thought about making a pie but was afraid after the cinnamon-raisin bread. Pies were easier than bread, but crusts could be tricky.

On the day of the barbecue she walked up to Hillsdale Bakery. She was thinking Dutch apple, but when she got to the store, there was a lovely open-face peach pie in the window and she knew that was the one. As she walked home she thought of cooking school and of learning to make a pie with a flaky crust. If Van's barbecue became an annual family event, maybe next time she'd bake her own pie.

At home, Lily and Hector sat at the kitchen table, a bakery box in front of them. They had bought a pie too. Bell had cooked a big pot of noodles and three racks of spareribs. Her ribs were always a big hit. Ruby came into the kitchen and put the pie on the table.

"You got dessert too?" Lily said.

"A pie. Peach," Ruby said.

"I almost got peach. But then I saw the apple. Everyone likes apple," Lily said.

"Two pies is okay," Hector said.

Bell served up small bowls of noodles. "You better eat something before we go. You know your brother, always late. We won't eat until midnight."

From his room, Franklin yelled, "Don't eat too much. You people better hurry up. It's late. It's not nice to keep people waiting." He reached under the bed for his shoes, the same pair he'd had since Ruby was born. He got out his shoe brush and buffed the tan suede until it was soft and clean. He put on a pink shirt. It wasn't a color he would have chosen himself, but lately he had taken to wearing clothes left behind by his customers.

In the kitchen Bell was packing up the food she had made for the barbecue. She also had packages of cookies and candy for the kids. In a separate bag, she had packed the last dress she had made for Sylvie. The other ones were too small by now, but the blue one with the lacy hem should fit just right. At the last minute, Bell ran into her room and changed from her faded flowered shirt into her pleated blue one with ruffles.

Finally, everyone piled into Hector's car. As they reached Van's block, they could hear music blasting. Lily and Ruby exchanged looks. Bell looked down and fussed with her bags. The music got louder as they got closer to Van's house. Parked in front were five motorcycles. "I always wanted a Harley," Hector said.

They gathered up their packages and walked to the front of the house. Franklin rang the bell. "I guess they're all in the back," he said. They walked up the driveway and then they were in the yard. Van was there playing his guitar. Five other guys made up the rest of his band. Van's eyes were closed and his head bobbed up and down as if he were saying yes, yes. At the end of the song he opened his eyes and saw his family standing close to the house, clutching bags and boxes. He lit up and moved toward them. "Lily. Ruby. Mom. Dad." He hugged and kissed them, then shook hands with Hector. He introduced them all to his friends. "Joe's a teacher like you," Van said to Lily, pointing at his bass player. Joe and the rest of the band waved.

"What do you want to drink?" Van led them to the kitchen. "Beer? Soda? Juice?" He handed out cans of soda. Franklin and Bell made a face when he popped the tab on a Budweiser.

"Where's Jeannette? Where's the kids?" Bell asked.

"She's gone. Went to visit her family. Took the kids. Come on out to the yard," Van said. The door closed behind him and he went back to playing the guitar.

Franklin got up and went out to the yard. He sat in a lounge chair and tapped his foot faintly. He got up and inspected the swing that Van had put up for Sylvie. He sat back down, watched his son and waited. Then he went up to him and said a few words in his ear.

Ruby had never met the guys in the band and the other people sitting in a half-circle drinking beer and listening to the music. She drank a cream soda although she wanted a beer. The music was loud. She didn't like rock, but she thought the band sounded good. Franklin came over and sat next to her on the bench. "I told him. I told him it's fine he want to play with his friends, but he invite me here and I'm hungry." He looked pained as he watched Van playing his guitar.

"What did he say?" Ruby asked.

"He said in five minutes."

Franklin still looked confused. Ruby wanted to stay with him but had just realized that her mother wasn't in the yard. Ruby went back into the kitchen. Bell was sitting there, the food she'd brought piled up on the table. Besides the noodles and the ribs, she had made a big salad. Chinese people usually don't like to eat raw things, but it was a special occasion, so she had bought some lettuce and cucumber and added tomatoes from her garden and bought a big bottle of French dressing. Bell got up and started to look through the cabinets.

"Tea, where's the tea?" Bell said. Lily and Hector sat at the table and watched her searching the cabinets. Bell sat down. "I can't find the tea," she said.

"You want tea, Ma?" Ruby said.

"You want some?" Bell said. There was a pleading in her voice, so Ruby said yes, although tea was the last thing in the world that she wanted at that moment. Ruby got up and looked through the cabinets. There was cereal and rice and cookies and plates. Finally, she found a tin of lychee tea.

"Oh, lychee tea," Bell said. She tried to hold her hands steady as she filled the kettle with water and put the gas on. "I wonder where Jeannette keeps her teapot." Bell looked in the cabinets she had just looked in. She found a plastic jar and practically seized it. "I guess I'll use this." The tea leaves fell slowly to the bottom of the jar.

Before the tea was fully brewed, Bell poured it into cups and handed them out to Lily and Ruby and Hector. Then she spotted a bag of carrots on the table. "Oh, look. Baby carrots. You want one?" No one did. Bell put a carrot in her mouth. It made a loud noise in the kitchen. She ate quickly and then looked around for something else to eat. In the yard, the music stopped. Bell looked up. Then the next song started. Bell reached for another carrot.

Franklin came into the kitchen. "It's time to go," he said.

"We just got here," Lily said.

"Maybe we should wait. Maybe he'll cook soon," Ruby said.

"He act like he don't even know we're here," Bell said.

Then Van came in. "Well, I have to go now," Franklin said.

"What? You just got here," Van said.

"You let your guests go hungry," Franklin said. His voice got louder. "You don't even put the coals on yet."

"I'll do it now," Van said. He took the freshly washed grill from the dish rack and marched out to the yard. He threw the coals on and poured lighter fluid over them. Then he picked up his guitar.

Bell started packing up the food she had brought over. "Finish your tea. We better go. We'll take this back and eat it at home." She hesitated and then picked up the packages of cookies she had brought for the kids.

"Can't we leave that here?" Ruby said.

"Those charcoal take at least forty-five minutes." Franklin left the house and went to stand by the car. Bell picked up both boxes of pies and followed him.

"The pies too?" Ruby said.

"Can't we leave the pies?" Lily said.

"Those people don't want to eat pie. They're too busy drinking," Bell said, pointing toward the yard.

Ruby went out to the yard. She stood by the gate and watched Van jump into the air and land lightly on his Converses. Van and his bass player looked into each other's eyes as they played. When there was a pause, Ruby went over to him. "Hey, Van. You guys sound great. But I think we have to go. Mom and Dad are a little freaked out," Ruby said. Lily and Hector had come out too and were standing next to her.

"You're leaving? This isn't working out. Did I fuck up? I fucked up." He took his guitar from around his neck and laid it lovingly on the grass.

"You know Dad. He never liked rock and roll," said Lily.

"I thought maybe he would like it this time. Why don't you take them home and come back?" Van looked at Ruby, Lily and then Hector with eyes so bright and hopeful that they all looked away from him.

"Well . . ." Ruby said.

"Come on, Ruby. Do it," Van said vehemently.

Ruby looked down.

"Lily? Hector? Come on," Van said.

"I better go start the car." Hector left.

"Maybe another time," Lily said.

"Come and say good-bye to them," Ruby said.

Franklin and Hector were sitting in the car. Van walked up to them. "Dad. I'm sorry. I messed up." His voice was thick. Ruby and Lily milled about on the sidewalk, nearly bumping into each other. Ruby looked at Lily's face and saw that she was trying not to cry too.

Franklin pointed at him. "I always knew you had no sense. Jumping up and down, playing that guitar like you're still a kid. Go back and play with your friends."

"I'll tell them to stop. What if I tell them to stop playing?" Van said.

"You don't even know what's important, your friends or your family," Franklin said.

Van looked down at the ground and when he looked up again at his father, he was crying. "Family. It's family," he said.

"Go and play with your friends. They're waiting for you."

"No, the family is important," Van said.

"Let's go," Franklin said to Hector. Hector started the car. Van wiped his eyes with the back of his hand. Ruby covered her mouth to stifle her own crying and Lily stood by a tree and blew her nose. Bell stood by the car, panicked by the sight of all three of her children crying on the sidewalk.

"Come on. Let's go. Another time," Bell said. She tried to herd Lily and Ruby into the car.

Ruby ran to the car and knelt there. She put her arms on the car door and put her head in the window. "Dad, don't go. Not like this. Can't you see he tried?"

"I haven't seen my friends in two years. I just thought we could all get together," Van said.

"You never had any sense," Franklin said. "Come on. Let's go," he said to Hector.

Ruby hit the car. "No, don't go," she said.

Ruby went to Van. "You know Dad. Nothing ever makes him happy."

"I'm sorry," Van said.

Bell went over to them. "Why don't you come over some other time?" she said to Van.

Van nodded. He looked at his father, where he waited in the car. "I really fucked up," he said. He breathed in deeply. "I guess I should go back to my friends now," he said. His friends had come out of the yard and were standing in front of the house.

"We'll try again another time," Ruby said. She hugged her brother. Lily hugged him too.

"Come on. We have to go now," Bell called from the car. Lily got in the car, and then Ruby got in after her. Van stood by the side of his house and waved at them. Then he walked over to his friends.

At home, Ruby couldn't stop crying. "You don't feel well?" Franklin asked her.

"I'm sad," she said.

"Playing the guitar is one thing, but why he have to jump up and down like he's trying to be a rock star?" Franklin said.

"Dad. He's just feeling it. He's into it."

"He can't even play."

"That's not true. You didn't listen. He *can* play."

"You think I did wrong?"

"I can see why you got upset, but did you have to break his heart?"

"Break his heart? Whose heart is broken? You tell me, honey."

Ruby looked down at the worn-out places on her father's shoes and wished he wouldn't call her honey.

Chapter 19

*F*ranklin was quiet at dinner. It was the night after the barbecue. He had a few news stories he could tell, but they seemed too long and complicated. Bell had cooked a sea bass. She opened the fish up like a book; she removed the backbone. Clinging to it were tiny shreds of meat. She ate those carefully.

Last night she had slept better than she had since the day she had called Van for his birthday. Since then, every night, just as she was starting to doze off, she would think that the phone was ringing and she would snap awake. The house would be quiet. But last night, she had gotten a good night's rest. She saw that her husband looked as if he had spent the night tossing in his bed. Bell pushed a few pieces of clean white fish toward him.

Franklin put down his bowl and rubbed his chest.

"What's wrong with your chest? Is it your heart?" Ruby said.

"I have a tightness," he said.

"Want me to call Dr. Chang?" she said.

"I'm okay now." He patted his chest a few more times, then shook his head. "The old ticker," he said. Bell looked at her husband and knew how he felt. Before the barbecue, as she was chopping scallions and turning the ribs, her chest had tightened too. "It's over now," Bell wanted to say to him.

Ruby was telling him to go to the doctor. He said, "Yup, the old ticker won't hold out much longer."

Bell thought he was taking it a bit far. He had always known how to make people feel sorry for him. He knew Ruby was upset that he had lit into Van, so now he had to pretend he was having a heart attack so she wouldn't be mad at him anymore.

"I didn't finish those shirts today." Franklin didn't look at his wife.

Ruby knew her father was playing her, but she still felt for him. "Tomorrow's Saturday. Customers are coming. Those shirts won't be ready," he said.

"Oh, Dad. Come on. Let's go finish them now," Ruby said. She picked up her tea and walked out with her father to the store. Bell watched them go. They hadn't finished their dinner. The food would grow cold. Bell sat there for a long time before she got the plastic containers to put the food away. As she was putting the lid on the last one, she thought again about the barbecue. Her whole body felt soft. She jumped up and made room in the refrigerator for the leftovers. But there was so much food. More than they could ever eat. Bowls stacked on top of other bowls, ribs crammed in sideways next to the milk, and noodles, yards and yards of noodles. Her eyes filled as she looked at all the food she made for the barbecue and brought home again. She reached for a bowl of noodles and grabbed a handful. The noodles were cold in her mouth. She swallowed quickly so she wouldn't choke as she started to cry. She watched her hands reaching out for the bowl.

In the store, Franklin's mood had lifted. He turned on the iron and waited for it to warm up. Ruby turned on the other iron. "You have to use a hot iron. Otherwise you never get the wrinkles out," Franklin said. He had told her that a hundred times before, but each time he acted like it was new advice.

Ironing at night reminded Franklin of working late in his father's laundry when he first came to New York. His father had been living in New York, and once in a while, when he felt like it, he sent a few dollars home to his wife in China. He had never met his son, having left China for the United States before the boy was born. Eighteen years later, Franklin arrived at Ellis Island and met his father.

Franklin sat in one room and his father sat in another. The immigration people had a lot of questions for the young man. *Where were you born? Where is your house located? How long has your father been in America? Who occupied the house on the sixth lot of your row in your village? How many rooms do you have in your house and what directions do they face? Who sleeps in each room? What is your mother's maiden name? Did she have bound feet? How many water buffalo were there in the village? How many male, how many female?*

My house is the second house in the fourth row. The ancestral hall is in the third row facing east and there are this many water buffalo in the village; this many males, this many females. My mother did not have bound feet.

Franklin's father was easily irritated at their questions. He became belligerent and shouted at the officers. "How the hell am I supposed to remember all that? Everything changed after I left. If you don't believe he's my son, send him back." The officers were ready to do just that, but one examiner wanted to see something. He put them side by side. They had the same eyes, the same sharp nose, the same point to their chins, the lips as pretty as a woman's.

"It has to be his son. Let him in," the man said.

That was years ago but Franklin still remembered the man's hand on his face, turning it this way and that. Franklin touched his finger to the iron and started on a pair of blue-and-white boxers. "My father don't like to work much. Nah, he don't like work. I used to work at night. I was so tired I don't want to cook, so I eat a few banana, a few orange. When I first met your mother, I thought I was getting a good cook, but she don't even know how to cook a pot of rice," he boasted. He liked to take credit for teaching Bell to cook.

"Couldn't you find someone here?" Ruby was suddenly angry that he had gone to so much trouble to get a wife so far away and bring her to this place.

"Who is there for me? Back then, there's only three Chinese ladies in all of Chinatown. All married and here just temporary. Their husbands doing some kind of business." He folded the boxers and reached for a shiny black shirt, the kind that men wore open at the chest with a thin gold chain around their necks, maybe a tiny cross nestled in the dark curly hair.

"But what about the woman in the picture?" Once Ruby had found a picture of a white lady in a fancy hat. On the back it said: "To Franklin. With love, Yvonne."

"What woman?" He tossed a red shirt to Ruby. Red gave him a headache.

"Yvonne."

"You saw that picture? Who said you could look in my drawer?" He pretended to be angry. "Yvonne. She was a good friend of mine. She worry about me that I eat too much fruit. Sometime she come to visit and bring me something nice to eat. A very nice lady."

"Why didn't you marry her?" Ruby's voice was low with hatred toward the woman in the picture; she hated the sharp tiny face beneath the hat, hated the tenderness in her father's voice when he said her name.

"What're you talking about? She's a white lady." He was quiet. Ruby saw that he was ironing the same sleeve over and over, the rest of the shirt still wrinkled. She didn't know if she should say anything.

"I don't know what happened," he said, ironing and ironing.

Ruby ironed too.

A small room in Chinatown when there weren't any ladies padding along the streets in wide black shoes, scarfs wrapped around their heads, arms full of shopping bags. Back when Chinatown was filled with loverless men, my father's room had blue walls and a bathtub in the kitchen. Two cots with thin mattresses, one for his father, one for him. My father is sitting on his bed, looking up at the whole bunch of bananas hanging in his room, plucking a fruit when he is hungry. And a crate of oranges. He alternates between bananas and oranges so he won't get bored.

One day he picks the last banana from the hanging stalk. He sits on his milk crate, peeling his last banana and thinking about a woman, the beautiful young woman in the photograph. My mother. He'll have to buy another crate of oranges soon. In the top drawer of a small wooden desk where he studies his English lessons is the photograph. He drags his crate over to the window to catch what little light makes it to the bottom of the air shaft. He holds the photograph in his hands, careful not to get fruit on it, and looks at the woman, who is young and pretty and wearing a nice dress. She is not smiling, but then again, people in China don't smile for photographs.

Soon she will be with him, cooking dinners—rice and soup, fish and vegetables and chicken the way his mother made. Maybe then his stomach won't hurt so much. Maybe she will even rub the tiredness from his shoulders when he finishes work. Her arms will be real and warm, not stiff cardboard as in the picture, and she will put her arms around him and kiss him and touch him like the women in the movies that he goes to see on Canal Street on Sundays. He closes his eyes and thinks of the woman in the photo and swallows the last bite of his last banana.

It was his father's idea. The old man said, "Why don't you go back to China and get a wife?" Franklin hadn't thought much about marrying before. He was thirty years old. At first he hadn't especially wanted a wife. What he wanted was to please the man he called Father. If he got a pretty wife, his father might look at him with new eyes and say, "Son, you did good." So at first it was for his father, but after he got the picture, he started to want her.

After months of waiting, he is finally there. The woman in the photograph stands in front of him. She is wearing the same dress but is not nearly as still. Even when she's sitting, she seems to be moving. This woman is soft and pliable beneath her stiff dress. He wants to give her something, something that will make her look at him. The melon, he'll give her the melon. He has it right there in his bag. He holds the honeydew melon, so round and heavy he almost drops it. He holds it out with two hands for what seems a long time.

She takes it from him and he thinks she wants to laugh. Her mother, who is standing behind her, comes forward and takes the melon from her daughter. She places it on the table for all the neighbors to see what a lovely gift her future son-in-law has brought. She smiles and rubs the melon as if it were her daughter's belly with all her grandchildren inside. It's the same melon she has seen in the store, the one in the glass case for twenty dollars. She has never tasted melon before but has heard that it is wonderful. She smiles but then thinks of how many chickens that would have bought.

The young people do not sit next to each other in the room filled with family and friends. "What is it like in America? Do you have a very big house? Do you eat meat every day?" He answers that he has been in the army, that he will open a business to make enough to live on and that he misses Chinese people to talk to and eat rice with.

The young woman watches him whenever she thinks no one is looking. She peeks at him through an amber stream of tea that she pours into his cup. Cup after cup, he drinks. His movements are quick and angular like his face. His nose is long and sharp. She tries to imagine them kissing; it seems his pointed nose would cut her soft round one like a knife slicing tofu.

Her relatives tell her how lucky she is to marry an American citizen, that she is lucky he is so kind to marry her for her good looks alone; her family has lost nearly all they owned when they fled to Hong Kong, afraid they would be on the wrong side when the revolutionaries came. She would bring nothing to the marriage except the clothes she wore and a guarantee that he would be her first and only. That, and a few pieces of jewelry that her mother has saved for her. Her mother unwraps the soft cotton and shows her the gold locket, the tear-shaped pendant, the two bent gold rings. "Put them away in case you need them someday." She presses the silk jewelry pouch into her daughter's hand.

Franklin's hair as he bent over his ironing looked especially white, as if he had bleached it with the Clorox he rubbed into shirt collars. Ruby looked up at the wedding picture, propped up between the cigar box of buttons and a pile of white hand-kerchiefs. In the photo, his hair is very black. It's hard to believe his hair was ever that black. He wears a dark gray suit. Bell is wearing a long white dress that trails on the floor. They stand side by side in their rented clothes. He has his arm around her waist. His hand is so stiff it looks rented too.

Next to the photo are smaller ones. They are honeymooning in Hong Kong. They pose in front of fountains and statues, try-ing on smiles. They are just learning that they should look happy in pictures. There is one of them in front of their hotel. Bell had told Ruby that the hotel was fancy, that their room was big enough for a whole family to live in. You never had to shop, someone brought food if you called on the telephone. Someone came to clean the room and brought new towels every day. Who was that dirty?

Franklin saw his daughter looking at the wedding picture. "Your father was a handsome man, don't you think?" He had stopped ironing that one sleeve and his hand was slow and steady as it guided the iron across collar, shirttail, pocket. She looked at the photograph, trying to see it as a picture of a man and not her father. He wore a custom-made herringbone suit and had dashing good looks.

Ruby was struggling with a flannel shirt that fought her on every wrinkle, unlike the shirt her father was ironing, which unfolded easily under his hand. "Dad. I've been looking at cook-ing schools. They teach you to make all kinds of things." The part that she had just ironed got creased as soon as she moved on to the next part.

"A cook?" He was scornful. "What happened to journalism? Cooking, huh? Well, let's hope you can stick with it this time. Not start something and leave it like you always do. Like your brother," he said. Ruby knew she should be used to his grousing, but for once in her life she wanted him to say, "Gee, that's nice."

"So, what do they teach you over there in cooking school?" he said skeptically.

"Oh, you know. Knife skills. Sauces. Baking." Ruby moved the iron quickly over the shirt. She thought of the time her father was talking to the leprechaun (a loyal customer who wore a derby). "Yup, she sure is a smart one. She got ninety-eight in math, a hard subject." That was right after he had yelled at her for missing out on the two points. She had stood in the darkened living room, peering out at him.

Now she reached for another shirt, an oxford. She ironed quickly, not caring if it got creased again.

"Hey, you're not doing it right." Franklin came over and took the iron from her.

"I never could, could I, Dad?" she said quietly.

"Look. First of all, your iron is too cool. You need a hot iron. Go slow, like this." He put his hand on top of hers, guiding it slowly across the collar, down the arm. "There. After you do the sleeves, then you do the back. Otherwise the whole thing gets wrinkled again."

He stepped back to his own table. "Now, after you finish the back, you can do the front. See? Go slow here between the buttons." The iron moved across the shirt.

"Dad?"

"See how easy it is with a hot iron?" he said. Her hand still felt the pressure of his and she glided smoothly over the next shirt.

"See, that's better. Slow and easy. Everyone's in a hurry these days." He straightened the pile of pressed shirts, wrapped a band of white paper around each like a belt. Then he wrapped the pile in brown paper, tied it with string and snipped the ends.

Ruby put down her iron and looked up at the neat stacks of laundry. The packages on the top shelf had been there for years, like family. The paper was crumbling and the pastel tickets had faded, but you could still read quite clearly: "Not responsible for items left over thirty days."

When she was little, she would climb to the top and read the dates stamped on the tickets. Some were more than ten years old, some twenty. Her father had marked the contents on the ticket: five shirts, one tablecloth, two sheets, four pillowcases, three towels. She wondered what had become of the owners.

Sitting at the ironing table doing her homework, she would try to get her father to open up the packages. He wouldn't. "Maybe they come back for it someday and then what will I do?" he said, even though it was printed on the ticket: "Not responsible."

Now he saw her looking up at the shelves. "Remember I always wanted you to open up those old packages?" she said.

"Sure, I remember. I was thinking the other day I should open up some of those old things. I guess no one going to come and get them now." He pushed the metal trash can over to the shelves, bruising his leg. He rubbed at the spot through his pants, then climbed onto the trash can. She stood below with her hands out. "Here's one been here seven years. Look at this one, eleven years. This one only six. Maybe I'll leave this one," he called down to her. Gathering up the chosen packages, he climbed down and put them on the ironing table.

Ruby drank the last of her tea, which was quite cold. She stood next to him, remembering how badly she had wanted this when she was a kid, but as soon as he started to open the first one, she wanted to stop him. The knots untied easily, guided by his hands, brown and weathered as the paper wrapping. He pulled apart the paper to reveal a glimpse of white and pastels. He pulled out a white cotton shirt, a man's. "Here. You wear shirts like this, don't you?" She took the shirt from him. It was so creased and yellowed she couldn't imagine it ever being fresh and white. "And here's some sheets and pillowcases. I think they'll fit on your bed downstairs." She took them but didn't look into his eyes.

As he opened the next package, she couldn't take her eyes off his hands, his brown hands unwrapping the brown paper, crackling and breaking with age. The next package must have belonged to a woman who liked fancy things but didn't have much money. A yellow blouse lay in the wrapping. Ruby touched it. It was warm and soft like skin. The lace doilies made her think of white grandmothers. There was a nightgown too, beige and lacy with a low neckline. She held it up to the light and wanted to cry. It had been so long since anyone had worn it. "Maybe your mother can use these," he said, loosely rewrapping the package. Ruby took them, knowing they would end up in her mother's bottom drawer next to all the nightgowns and scarfs and handkerchiefs that she got for Mother's Day, which took her kids so long to pick out at Rene's Boutique, the saleslady saying that blue was always in style, everyone looked good in it, you just couldn't go wrong if you picked blue.

Chapter 20

The ginkgo leaves were starting to turn yellow outside the store. Bell went out in her slippers and knocked a stick against the branches to shake the big round seeds to the sidewalk. Then she gathered them up and made soup. Lily went back to work. There were four kids in her class who didn't speak English. Every time she took the kids out to the playground, she pointed at the bathroom. "Bathroom," she'd say. By the end of the week, every kid knew the word and she had fewer accidents to clean up. She kept meaning to call Van but was tired when she came home in the evenings.

It was September and Ruby was busy looking at apartments. She didn't have the money but she liked looking anyway. She had saved enough for Florida, and in a couple of months she'd have apartment money too. That seemed a long time to wait.

Nights were cooler now and Bell had left a light blanket on Ruby's bed in the basement. One day she and Ruby were in the yard picking the last of the tomatoes. Bell had taken to leaving peanuts out for the squirrels so they would leave her tomatoes alone. It seemed to be working.

Bell picked a half-ripe tomato from the vine. Ruby followed behind her, placing the tomatoes in the apron she was using as a basket. The sun was watery. Bell turned the collar up on her shirt. That morning she had put on panty hose under her pants to keep warm. "I bet it's still hot in Florida," she said. All summer she and Ruby had talked about Florida, but Bell would never say for sure that she would go. "We'll see," she always said.

But today there was something different in her tone that made Ruby take notice. "It's getting chilly here," Ruby said.

"I feel sleepy when it's cool. My bones get soft. Soon I'll be too old to go anywhere." Bell didn't really seem to believe that she was getting too old. In fact, ever since she had gotten rid of the squirrel trap, she did her exercises in the yard and looked so lively that her friends at the factory asked her if she was taking any new tonics.

"So, what about Florida?" Ruby asked her.

"I think so," Bell said.

"Really?"

"You want to?"

"*I* do. Do you?"

"Yeah."

"I have money saved up."

"I have money too."

"I want to give you something. Just one time."

Bell hesitated. Ruby said, "I'll get the tickets, okay?"

With great effort, Bell said, "Okay. You can get the tickets." Then she brightened and said, "I'll have money for the hotel."

"If I need it, I'll ask you."

Bell looked determined. Ruby knew her mother would end up paying for something. Just letting Ruby get the tickets was a big deal.

Bell looked around at her tomato plants. "That's it until next year. Might as well take these down." She touched the leaves with her gloved hand. "Maybe we'll wait awhile. I like to look outside and see something green."

In the kitchen, Bell lined up the tomatoes on the windowsill. Then she went to the cabinet and took out color charts. "What do you think of yellow?" Bell said. She was sick of cooking in a green kitchen. She pointed at lemon mist.

"Lemon's nice."

"It's not so dark like green."

They decided to paint before they went away so the house wouldn't look quite so shabby when they came back. Ruby called Nick and told him when to come over. Bell and Ruby went up to the hardware store with the cart and bought the paint. They left it in the living room under some laundry that had been hanging there for a long time. Bell thought Franklin would be mad at them for spending money, but when he saw the paint, he said, "This place sure could use a paint job."

While the paint was still sitting in the living room, one day after work Bell stopped at Gertz and bought a suitcase for their trip. It was brown and sturdy and had lots of compartments. It had wheels too. Bell folded up the shorts she had made and placed them in her suitcase. She also packed the two skirts she'd found at Gertz's end-of-summer sale.

"You need a suitcase? I can get you one. What about a bathing suit? Gertz has bathing suits on sale," Bell said to Ruby.

"You think we should tell Dad soon?"

"He'll just get mad."

Ruby went to work and tried to shop on her lunch break. An hour wasn't enough to run to the store and pick out a bathing suit, take off all her clothes and try it on, only to find that it looked terrible on her. Perhaps it was the glaring lights of the dressing room that made her look so awful. She tried to recall what she had read in *Glamour* about choosing a bathing suit, but nothing came to her.

All summer, Ruby had worked on convincing her mother to go on this trip, but now that she had said yes, Ruby didn't know why she didn't feel happy about it. When she first moved back home, she had felt coerced. Moving home was the last thing she had wanted to do, but she had no money and nowhere else to go. But no one was forcing her to go on vacation and stay in the oceanfront room and drink piña coladas by the pool. But somehow she still felt coerced. She was angry in the dressing room as she adjusted bathing-suit straps, as she tried on sandals, as she tried to choose one beach bag over another.

If she tried on one more bikini she would scream, she swore she would. She decided she'd have better luck finding a bathing suit in Florida. She stopped looking and instead started looking at apartments after work. The first thing she did when she walked into an apartment was to go to the window and look out. There were people in their apartments across the street. They would be her neighbors and she watched them anxiously; they had homes; they knew how to live.

When she came home at night, she sat at the kitchen table and told her mother about the apartments she had seen. "The ceilings were too low, I felt like I was going to bump my head. The kitchen window had a gate over it like a jail. There was light, but the floors were linoleum. The rooms were kind of big, but the landlord lived downstairs; he seemed nosy." Bell tried to check the relief she felt each time Ruby came home and said the apartment wasn't quite right for her.

Ruby noticed that whenever she talked about apartments, her mother would rub her arm. She only rubbed her arm when she was nervous. Ruby became more and more fussy about where she wanted to live. Every apartment had something wrong with it.

The day before they were going to paint, Ruby went out to the laundry. Franklin had his hands in the starch water. His hands had toughened over the years and he hardly felt the hot water now. The puffiness around his eyes was a little more pronounced. His back was as straight as ever. "Dad, you want some tea?"

He looked up reluctantly. "Not too much sugar." He handed her his cup. As she waited for the water to boil, she remembered how she had first learned to bring him his tea. Her mother would place the cup of tea in an empty pot so if Ruby spilled, the tea would fall into the pot and not on the floor. Her father had been proud when she had learned to walk without spilling. "Didn't even spill a drop," he'd say. Skipping back to the

kitchen, swinging the pot like a baton, she could forget that he
was the same father who could be so stern that they would wait
for him to leave the room before they started breathing and
talking and moving again.

Now, as she put his cup down on the iron rest and watched
him starch, she could forget again. He plunged a shirt into the
starchy water and held it there as if he would drown it. But then
he pulled it quickly from the water and rubbed sorrowfully at it
as if he had changed his mind and now wanted to revive it.

"Dad?"

"Yeah?"

"The lemons are big this year." She pointed at the lemons,
big as oranges, wrapped in nylon mesh, which seemed a little
out of place in the laundry, a bit too racy, like a fishnet stocking.

"The guy next door always come in asking for one, but I tell
him it's not ready yet. If you want one, take one. And there's lots
of oranges this year. Sour, but you can make jam." He drank some
tea.

The oranges only grew as big as Ping-Pong balls. Ruby
picked one and peeled the thin skin, opened it up gently and ate
a section.

"Sour." She made a face but then got used to it. She ate it
slowly, section by section, her teeth aching. "Hey, Dad?"

"Yeah?"

"Me and Ma are going to Florida."

"Florida?"

"In a couple of weeks. You want to come?" Ruby didn't know
where that had come from; it just popped out of her mouth.

"You know I get plane-sick."

"Why are you so mean to her?" Ruby said quietly. The sound
of starch water being wrung from shirts stopped suddenly.

"Is that what she tell you?" Franklin said just as quietly.

"God. She doesn't have to tell me. I've got eyes." She was
almost yelling. The next part she said quietly. "You might lose
her, you know. Maybe she'll come and stay with me when I

move out." Ruby knew her mother had said she didn't think about leaving, but Ruby still liked to think about it. She sidled along the counter, stopped behind the big lemon tree. The trunk was as thick as her wrist, not like when they first got it, no thicker than her pinky then.

Franklin shook the starch from his hands and dried them on his apron. "Your mother belongs here. In this house. Your mother's not going anywhere."

"What do you care if she goes? You never say one nice thing to her. She's tired of it."

Franklin sat down and covered his eyes with his hands. "I'm tired too. Sometimes my eyes are so tired I can't keep them open," he said, not taking his hands from his face.

"Maybe you should eat something? You want to eat something? A sandwich?" She wanted very much to go to him.

Instead, she went to the kitchen and came back with a toasted cheese sandwich. He had gotten up and gone back to work. "I can't eat all that. You take half," he said, tearing the roll and handing a piece to her. They ate without talking. Then he went back to his starching and Ruby stayed in the store until he finished the last shirt.

On Sunday, Nick came over in his old khakis with the holes in them and an old white T-shirt. Ruby met him at the bus stop. She hadn't seen him in a week and when he stepped off the bus she threw herself at him and gave him a big kiss. When she stepped back she saw that he had on his painting outfit and she felt shy suddenly.

"You'll miss the flea market today," she said.

"That's okay. I can miss a week."

"How's your back?"

"My back's fine. You don't want me here?"

"You hardly know my mama."

"So. She's your mom."

Ruby stopped arguing. But she still felt funny about Nick coming to paint the kitchen. Bell had cooked in the morning and then draped the stove with a sheet. Nick walked into the laundry. Franklin was prepared to snub him, but Nick was ready for him today. "Hey, Mr. Lee. How're you? Got you a few cigars." Franklin opened up the box cautiously, then sniffed a cigar. He smiled despite himself.

"That's a pretty good cigar," Franklin said. "Go on in and get a cup of tea."

"You hear about the horse that slipped on that ice pocket? You think that was a setup?" Nick said.

"I bet on that horse!" Franklin looked appreciatively at him. Ruby pulled Nick by the arm.

Bell made up a plate for him. "Hiya, Nick. You sure you don't have something to do today?" She fed him rice and steak and broccoli. Everyone else had eaten lunch already.

"This is it," he said.

The kitchen hadn't been painted in over twenty years. Bell didn't know why she had ever chosen green in the first place; she had thought it would look fresh like new grass, but she had been wrong. The walls were a sickly green, like the cuttings that she gathered on her walks in the neighborhood and put into jars on the windowsill.

Nick started on the ceiling near the living room. Ruby painted near the backyard. It seemed she hadn't been painting long before her arms were aching and she longed to stop. Ruby tried to get her mother to sit down, but she wouldn't.

Bell's arms were aching too, but she didn't dwell on it. Ruby saw the slight trembling in her mother's arms and it made her heart hurt. Bell was sitting on the short bench, painting the baseboard. Once in a while she got up and shook out her legs. She swung her arms in front of her like a boxer warming up.

"Hey, Ma. Why don't you take a rest. Let me and Nick finish."

"You think I'm an old lady or something?" Bell painted and painted. Ruby watched her, overwhelmed that her mother was working so hard. "I'm only fifty-nine. A spring chicken." Bell wished her daughter would stop looking at her like that.

They painted all afternoon. Lily and Hector came downstairs. "Hey, how's it going?" Lily stepped over a pan of paint.

"It's going," Ruby said. She introduced Nick and Hector. Hector extended his hand but looked worried about getting paint on his new black jeans and his black turtleneck.

"Looks good. You guys should've said you were painting today. I would've helped out," Hector said.

"Too many people get in the way," Bell said with a wave of her hand.

"You sure?" Lily said quickly. The smell of paint made her dizzy.

"How's it going upstairs?" Nick knew from Ruby that Hector didn't like the apartment he had moved into a month ago.

"I'm asleep, right? And then all of a sudden I hear these two guys. They're right outside the window. One guys says, 'Fuck you.' And then the other guy says, 'No, fuck you.' All night long, it's 'Fuck you,' 'No, fuck you,' 'Fuck you,' 'No, fuck you.'" Hector was almost yelling. Lily nudged him with her foot. "Sorry. It's a little noisy upstairs," Hector said.

Lily practically pushed Hector out the door. "He's a funny guy, your brother-in-law," Nick said. Bell had started on the cabinets.

"Are you hungry? I'm hungry," Ruby said. She wasn't really hungry, but she couldn't bear to watch her mother roll more paint.

"I'll make you something." Even though her kitchen was one big mess, Bell managed to whip up big plates of food. "You two better eat outside. More air."

In the yard, Ruby and Nick sat on the steps and held their plates on their knees. His face was covered with specks of paint. Ruby licked her finger and rubbed at his face. That afternoon was the longest time they had spent together without touching. Ruby hadn't realized how accustomed she had grown to touching his arm or his shoulder or coming up from behind him and pressing against him. When he had handed her a bucket of paint, she had gone to kiss him but then caught herself.

The first coat had dried by the time they finished rolling. "You think we should wait?" Nick said.

"Nah, it's dry enough," Ruby said. They started on the second coat. It grew dark outside and Bell turned on the overhead lights. She worked on the corners and the detail work. Then it was dinnertime and the kitchen was almost done. Ruby set the rollers and brushes to soak.

Franklin came into the kitchen. He had smoked one of his fancy cigars in the afternoon and was quite impressed. Perhaps he had misjudged this Nick fellow after all. The kitchen was bright and almost cheerful. "Looking good, looking good. Hey, how about you go up to the Chinese restaurant and get some take-out? I don't know how your mother can cook in here," Franklin said. Bell and Ruby both stared at him as if he had just suggested going to China for dinner. Years ago, he and Ruby would get on the bus and go to Kentucky Fried Chicken and bring home a bucket, but that was years ago and that was fried chicken. They had never gotten take-out food from the Chinese restaurant before, but suddenly Ruby had a big craving for the sweet spareribs and egg rolls and wonton soup and all the gringo food her mother would never cook.

"I could eat Chinese food," Ruby said.

"I can cook," Bell said.

"Maybe it'll be fun to take out," Ruby said.

"You want to?" Bell said.

"Don't cook, Mrs. Lee. You painted all day."

Bell hesitated. "Okay, if you people want to."

Ruby and Nick washed their hands and walked up to Moon Palace. They ordered soup and ribs and lo mein and butterfly shrimp, roasted chicken and a bottle of soda. Bell had the table set when they came back. She insisted on pouring the food into dishes.

"Too spicy," she said, but seemed to enjoy the wonton she had put into her mouth. She slipped a nice fat shrimp into Franklin's bowl. He acted as if he didn't see it, but when he finally got to it, he ate it slowly and thoughtfully.

"So it's all finished?" Franklin looked around at the walls.

"We have a little more. Just the trim; maybe go over the cabinets one more time," Ruby said.

"It's getting kind of late. Not safe to travel. Maybe your friend should stay over and go back tomorrow. He can sleep downstairs. You can sleep in your mother's room," Franklin said.

"I *am* kind of tired," Nick said. He looked at Ruby. She shrugged, then nodded. She didn't really want him to leave.

Bell said, "You must be tired. Better you sleep here tonight."

"I have some pajamas you can wear." Franklin passed the soda to Nick.

"You want some soda, Mom?" Ruby asked.

"Just a little. That's enough," Bell said. She hadn't drunk soda since her children's birthday parties. Now she drank it with a spoon, doubtfully, as if she were afraid the bubbles would hurt her.

Franklin picked up two pieces of the tender white breast and laid them in Ruby's bowl. "One for your mother," he said.

"This chicken's not bad," Ruby said.

"It's a little salty," Bell said.

After dinner, Franklin found a pair of new pajamas in his dresser and gave them to Nick. "Still in the package," he said. Nick put them on. They fit in the waist but his legs stuck out. "That's okay. Like short-shorts," Franklin said. Bell picked out a clean set of sheets. "I have some toothbrushes. Which kind you like?" Bell held a new toothbrush in each hand. Nick picked one and then he and Ruby went down to the basement.

Chapter 21

Ruby and Nick sat on the edge of her bed. The TV was on. She picked paint out of his hair. "I'm sleepy," she said and flopped down on the bed. He flopped down beside her and tried to look into her eyes. She got up and changed the channel. "Want to see pictures of me when I had Farrah Fawcett hair?"

"Come here, baby."

She sat down again. "You don't want to see pictures?"

"Give me a kiss first," he said. She listened for her parents. Her father's TV was on loud. She didn't think it was a good idea to kiss a boy in her mother's basement. But they had just painted the kitchen and her parents were upstairs and she hadn't touched him all day. She kissed him. His mouth was warm. She wanted more. He rolled on top of her. She started to open her legs. Just one more minute, she said to herself. Ten minutes later, he had his hand down her pants. Just one more minute, she told herself. She moved around under his hand. Then, with great effort, she pushed him off.

"You trying to drive me nuts?" she said.

"We'll be quiet."

"They hear everything." She got up and changed the channel on the TV. They watched a show on tap dancing that they weren't so interested in. His hand was moving very lightly across her breast the whole time.

"I don't want to sleep upstairs," she said.

"So don't. Stay here."

"You heard my dad. *'Nick sleeps downstairs. Ruby sleeps upstairs in her mother's room.'* "

"So come back. After everyone's asleep."

She didn't answer. His hand was still moving across her breast. It was hard to keep her hips from rising off the bed. She said quickly, "I saw this apartment the other day. A walk-up. Fourth floor. It was kind of sweet."

"Come back later, after everyone's asleep."

"I can't find a bathing suit. I looked and looked. Maybe in Florida. Okay, okay, I'll come down later. But just cuddles, okay?"

"Okay," he said a little too quickly. They watched a show on animal intelligence.

At eleven o'clock, Franklin turned off his TV. He coughed deliberately, then paused and coughed again. In the basement, Ruby got up abruptly. "What's the matter?" Nick said.

"That's my dad. He's telling me to come upstairs."

"He's just coughing."

Franklin got up and stamped his feet a few times as if they had fallen asleep. He coughed again.

"He gets on my nerves," Ruby said. "See you later." She kissed him and trudged up the stairs.

"Time for everyone to get some sleep," Franklin said.

Bell was in bed already, but when Ruby came in she sat up and turned the light on. "Your friend need anything?"

"He's okay."

"Kitchen looks nice and clean. Like new." Bell felt shy suddenly. She watched Ruby getting into bed. Ruby's eyes looked too bright for bedtime.

"Your arms tired? After all that painting? Let me see your muscles."

This was one of their old games that they hadn't played in a long time. Ruby rolled up her sleeve and flexed. Her mother squeezed her arm and said, "Big and strong. What about the other one?" Ruby flexed her other arm and her mother admired it. They laughed. All of a sudden Ruby sobered up, remembering that she had a date with Nick in a few hours.

"What's the matter, you tired?" Bell asked her.

"A little. Not really."

"Well, better get some rest." Bell reached for her book. She had gotten it from the library last week. It was a yoga book. She had taken out yoga books before; she couldn't read the words but would study the pictures carefully. This was the first one she had found in Chinese. She thought she had been doing it right before, but now that she could read the words she realized she had been doing it all wrong. "You ever do yoga?" Bell said. She put her glasses on. "You have to breathe."

Ruby watched her mother get into a half-lotus position. She wanted to run down to the basement and tell Nick that she couldn't come down to see him later.

"Try it," Bell said. Ruby went into a full lotus but it felt like a lie.

"How come you moved out of Dad's room?" Ruby said suddenly.

"His room? You used to cry at night."

"How was it, sleeping by yourself again after sleeping with him all that time?"

"Of course you sleep better if you sleep by yourself. He used to kick me."

Finally, Franklin went to bed. Bell put down her book and turned off the light. Ruby listened to her mother's breathing. She could hear her father in the room next door. He always fell asleep quickly. Her mother, though, often stayed awake for a long time.

Ruby was getting sleepy. When she closed her eyes, she saw herself painting the kitchen over and over again. Tomorrow, after they were done, she would go back with Nick. She wanted a big plate of pasta from Antonio's that she couldn't quite finish, but they would pack it up for her and she would eat it for breakfast the next day. Nick would get shrimp scampi, as he always did. Maybe after dinner, they'd get a bottle of wine and drink it on the lawn by Reid Hall the way they used to.

She had to make sure everyone was sleeping before she went downstairs. No one would know. It wouldn't cause any harm, she thought. After all, they had worked all day, dripping sweat in the kitchen as they rolled out the walls, as they stood on the counter to cut the ceiling, their faces splattered with tiny specks of paint. They had not touched except to hand over a brush. And then in the basement, she hadn't wanted to stop. But she had.

I deserve this, she thought as she waited for her mother to fall asleep. Ruby closed her eyes. She told herself she could have a tiny nap, and before she knew it, she was asleep. The soft stirring between her legs woke her. Her mother was breathing evenly a few feet from her. Ruby pushed the covers off and stepped quietly into her slippers. Her mother had left the night-light on in the kitchen. It was past three in the morning.

In the bathroom, she brushed her teeth. Then she put tooth-paste on Nick's toothbrush and filled a cup with water. In the kitchen she grabbed a pot.

The basement was pitch-black. She turned on the light at the top of the stairs and made her way down. Nick was sleeping all sprawled out on top of the covers. His hair was one big mess. She went to lie down next to him, then stopped and pulled the spare blanket over him. As she was turning to go, he roused himself and caught her arm. "Where were you?"

"I fell asleep. I should go back up."

"Five-minute cuddle," he said.

Reluctantly, she sat down on the bed. He felt so warm. She moved a little closer. He put his face against her neck and breathed. "You smell good," he said.

"Baby, look." She tried to keep her head from tilting back and offering her neck to him. But he knew how to touch her and soon she wanted to kiss. "Okay, okay. Here. Brush your teeth." She handed him the toothbrush and cup of water.

He laughed. Then he brushed his teeth. She handed him the pot so he could rinse. Now that he had brushed his teeth, her resistance was gone. A noise came out of her as she went to kiss him.

Her parents were upstairs in their separate rooms. That made her move slowly at first, hesitantly. Each creak of the bed seemed amplified in the dark basement that smelled like old rain. She moved as she had never moved in that house. The sheets were smooth under her and she reached her hands up as if to pray. All that touching and moving and breathing was almost painful, like being woken from a deep sleep.

Upstairs, Bell lay in her bed. Even before she opened her eyes, she knew Ruby wasn't in the room sleeping. She listened for her in the bathroom but heard nothing. The robe she reached for and tied around her waist was more to busy her hands than to warm herself. She had a good idea of where her daughter was and what she was doing, but still, she had to know for sure. As she walked out to the living room, she told herself that it wasn't too late, that she could go back to bed and lie there until just before sunup, when Ruby would come sneaking back to bed. But Bell was driven out of her warm bed and as she opened the basement door and stood at the top of the stairs, she had to listen hard before she could make out the whispering and the rustling and the noises and sighs her daughter was making. Bell tied her robe a bit tighter and listened for a brief moment, but long enough to take in the knocking of the bed, the creaking and that her daughter sounded as if she was enjoying herself. Then Bell closed the basement door again. She didn't exactly slam it, but she shut it so that the door moving back into its frame was heard from the back of the basement.

Ruby heard the door closing. She shut up and stopped moving. Her hand on Nick's shoulder told him to stop. When he saw the look on her face, he lost it. Her heart was beating so fast she thought she would pass out. Then she figured that her mother would never come downstairs or open the door again, so she went ahead and finished up.

The next day, they didn't look at one another at breakfast, but her mother still cooked and served it up and smiled and said how nice the kitchen looked. Ruby wondered if she had imagined the closing of the basement door. She had only stayed a few minutes longer for fear that she'd fall asleep. As she walked up the stairs, she could smell sex all over her. She stopped in the bathroom to wash her face and scrub under her arms and between her legs.

After breakfast, Nick and Ruby finished the kitchen. Bell left to work on her new curtains, pale yellow with orange flowers. After she left, Nick stopped painting and went over to Ruby. She was painting listlessly.

"Are you sure? Are you sure she heard?" he said.

"Positive. Maybe not. Maybe she didn't. Nick, she heard," Ruby said.

"Maybe I should go out and apologize or something."

"Don't make it worse."

Outside in the laundry, Bell worked on her curtains. Now that the kitchen was painted, she couldn't hang the same dirty brown ones again. As she sewed, she wondered how she was going to talk to Ruby. She had gotten used to having Ruby around again, although all along she had known it would end someday.

Nick left in the afternoon. Franklin shook his hand and told him to come back soon. Bell smiled at him but looked just past his face. After he left, Bell and Ruby walked back to the kitchen. Ruby was thinking about going out for a walk when Bell said she wanted to talk to her. For a few moments during the day, Ruby had been able to convince herself that her mother hadn't heard, but now all hope was gone.

"You're a big girl now. No good to live with your ma anymore," Bell said.

Ruby wanted to throw herself at her mother and deny that she was grown, that she was acting grown but she was just play-acting. Bell went on, "Somebody told me there's lots of hurricanes in Florida now. Not a good time to go. Tell you what. You take that money you saved up and you get your own apartment."

"No. We have to go to Florida." Ruby couldn't understand why her mother was speaking to her so kindly, as if she wasn't mad at all.

"We'll go to Florida. But later. Not right now," Bell said.

"I'm sorry, Ma. I don't know what's the matter with me." Ruby put her face in her hands.

Bell put her arm around her daughter and patted her on the back. She rocked her back and forth.

Chapter 22

A few weeks before her mother's sixtieth birthday, Ruby moved out. She signed the lease the same day she went to see the studio apartment at the Mary Elizabeth Inn, a women's hotel near Claremont Avenue. The best part was the parlor with old velvet chairs and couches and a grand piano. Men weren't allowed in the rooms, but they could visit in the parlor up until eleven o'clock at night. Nick got mad at her for moving into a building where he couldn't stay over. Ruby argued that she was always at his place anyway. She didn't tell him she liked the idea of living in an all-women's building.

The day Ruby moved out, Bell got up early and made sticky rice. It was ready when Ruby woke up.

"Good day for moving. Not too hot, not too cold," Bell said. But whenever she looked at Ruby's boxes piled up in the living room, there was a stone in her throat. She had to fight to swallow it.

Ruby sat at the table. "You're not eating?" she said.

"Me? I ate."

"You don't want to sit with me?"

"I have to make oatmeal for your father."

Ruby waited, but after the oatmeal her mother went out to the yard and pulled a few scallions from the ground. She sliced them up into thin green and white circles and then she fried up a few slices of ham, huddling close to the stove as if she were cold.

"Ma, what are you cooking now?" Ruby was desperate for her mother to sit still for one minute. Bell looked up from the stove, startled by her daughter's tone.

"I'm making you some fried rice," Bell said. In the pan, the ham lay curled up like tiny pink cradles.

"There's food in Manhattan."

"Maybe it's dark when you get there. No good to go looking for food in the dark." Bell tasted the rice and then seasoned it again. When it was done, she packed it up in containers and wrapped them in clean dishrags. She packed the rice next to the soy sauce chicken wings and the grass noodles with shiitake mushrooms. Tonight her daughter would sleep in her own apartment. She was only moving to Manhattan, Bell told herself, it wasn't as if she was moving to the other side of the world. Even so, she couldn't stop cooking. Suddenly, she said, "In China, that's why families fight all the time. Too close together. Everyone living in one house."

Ruby finished eating and Bell cleared away her bowl and chopsticks and cup. The sink was full, so she put them on the counter. Ruby patted the chair next to her. "Ma, your tea's getting cold."

Bell sat down uncertainly. She took a few sips. Then she jumped up again. "I better make you some soup," she said. It might be dusty at her daughter's new apartment. Bell got out her jars of dried things and took out some lotus root and red dates.

"I'll come back all the time. It won't be like when I was at school," Ruby said.

Bell got some chicken bones from the freezer and added them to the big pot of water. "This soup is good for your throat. Nice and cool." While the soup was cooking, Bell thought of other dishes she could make. Her bobby pins had come loose and her hair stuck up in places. She didn't seem to notice.

"Ma, your hair," Ruby said. Bell swatted the top of her head. Ruby wanted to go over to her and smooth her hair back into place. "Maybe you need a haircut," Ruby said. Bell had stopped going to the beauty parlor years ago, when her one tube of lipstick ran out. Then she had started cutting her hair herself. It was easy except for the back.

Bell patted her hair again. Then she moved her chair closer to Ruby's. "Maybe *you* need a haircut," Bell said. Opening and closing her fingers like scissors, Bell reached for her daughter's hair and pretended to cut.

Ruby flushed; she felt pleased and shy. Bell said, "My hair's dirty."

"Go wash it," Ruby said.

Bell was uncertain again. Her head felt terribly itchy and in need of a wash all of a sudden. Then she thought, What the hell, it's just a haircut.

In the bathroom, Bell thought of her own mother. It was true that her mother had tried to give her away when she was born, but afterward she had relented. Bell's older sister had cried so hard that her mother finally said they would keep her. Growing up, Bell had listened many times to the story of how her sister had saved her. At first she had felt a gratefulness tinged with shame, but later on all she felt was shame. Even now, alone in the bathroom, she felt it. She felt it when Ruby looked at her with a certain softness in her eyes that Bell found almost painful. With a steady hand, Bell filled cup after cup with water, pouring it over her head until the water ran clear.

Ruby went to her mother's room to get a comb, brush and scissors. Now that she was leaving, the clutter in her mother's room looked worse than ever. The empty popcorn tins that her mother was saving so she could put pistachios and candy and tea in them to give away as Christmas presents lay scattered around the room. The Florida brochures stuck up out of her mother's sun hat. Piled on the folding chair that served as a night table was a clean pile of clothes. Ruby almost pounced on it, grabbed an undershirt and folded it. Then she reached for a pair of pajama pants. She matched the socks. Soon she had a neat little stack. The room was still a mess, and the movers would be there in a couple of hours.

She grabbed the brush from the dresser and left the room. Her mother had come out with her hair wrapped in a towel. Ruby stood behind her. The comb slid right through her hair. Drops of water collected at the ends and hung suspended for a moment before splashing to her neck. Ruby held a small section of hair between her fingers; she closed the scissors around it. Her mother's hair was tougher than it looked. Ruby felt she was hacking at it. She took smaller sections and tried to cut them evenly, but she was afraid she wasn't doing a very good job.

Bell wasn't afraid. It didn't really matter to her what her hair looked like. Her daughter's hands moving slowly across her head made her feel pleasantly sleepy. The ladies at the beauty parlor used to push her head one way and then the other, yanking at her hair as if they were trying to pull it out. Ruby bent close to see if both sides were even and Bell could feel her breath on her skin.

Tufts of hair lay scattered on the kitchen floor. Ruby cut and cut. She cut very little at a time but she felt confident now. She put her hand against her mother's neck so the cold scissors wouldn't shock her.

More than an hour had passed since Bell sat down with the towel wrapped around her shoulders. Ruby put the scissors on the table. She combed her mother's hair with her fingers. That wasn't really part of the haircut, she just wanted to. Bell's hair dryer was heavy and old but it still worked. It looked a little like a cake mixer. The noise from the dryer was loud and they didn't try to talk above it. Ruby's stomach felt peculiar when she looked at the balding spot on her mother's head, which had been browned by the sun.

With the comb, she lifted her mother's hair and tried to curl it under. The comb felt clumsy in her hands and soon she abandoned it and used her fingers. She put one hand over the top of her mother's head so the dryer wouldn't burn her.

Bell was looking down at the bag of food she had packed for Ruby. She couldn't stop thinking of more dishes to cook. The noise from the hair dryer shut out the sound of her husband's footsteps.

Ruby kept drying but she and her mother waited for Franklin to make some remark about how filthy it was to cut hair in the kitchen, the hair would get in the food, and why couldn't they do that out in the yard? He looked at them for a second and then he went to the refrigerator and got the Entenmann's, cut a piece of pound cake and wrapped it in a paper towel. Munching on his cake, he pointed and said, "Hey, that's not bad." He nodded and then he went out to the store.

Ruby and Bell looked at each other. "He must be getting old," Bell said, not unkindly. In the store, Franklin got the broom and started sweeping under the ironing tables. There wasn't much dust today. He looked toward the kitchen, squared his shoulders and went in. Without saying anything, he started sweeping the hair into a pile. He whistled a little. "It's like a beauty parlor in here. Maybe I need a haircut too," he said.

"Your hair grows fast." Bell watched her husband sweeping up her hair and she felt confused for a moment and then angry. She had always known he could be nice if he wanted to. But now Ruby was holding a mirror in front of her and one in back. Bell turned her head this way and that. She couldn't see the back but the front looked real fine.

And then for a moment, before all the hair was swept up and the scissors had been put away, the three of them were joking and Franklin laughed first and then Ruby joined in and finally Bell did too. They were hesitant but it was better than nothing. When they stopped, Ruby looked down at the floor, which was swept clean now, and her heart was a small tight thing. She had always prided herself on her memory; she remembered every little thing that happened, but now she was desperate to remember another time, any other time when the three of them had stood in the kitchen or the living room or the store or any other place and had tried to be warm and kind to one another. But she couldn't remember one time. After one more hearty laugh, she walked quickly to the bathroom and stayed there until her father returned to the store and her mother went back to cooking.

And then, after what seemed a long time since the haircut, the movers were gone and Ruby was finally alone in her apartment at the Mary Elizabeth Inn.

Almost furtively, she drew close to one wall as if she would kiss it. Her cheek was practically touching the freshly painted surface when she pulled away and stooped down to touch the dark wood floor. It was warm and smooth. Until that moment, she had never realized how much she hated the green linoleum of her mother's kitchen, green with gold swirled into it like a crazy marble cake. She had swept and mopped that floor so many times without realizing just how much she hated it. She went to the door and locked it, then leaned heavily against it, as if someone were chasing her.

As she leaned against the door, she waited for the big cry that had threatened her the whole time she had waved good-bye to her mother and her father standing outside the store, both in their slippers. Her mother had stared at the license plate, memorizing it in case the movers were kidnappers. The truck started to move away and her parents waved at her and she waved back. It was hard to see them through the cloudy window of the truck.

Only after the truck turned the corner did Bell and Franklin drop their hands to their sides. Bell went right to the kitchen and opened the refrigerator. She didn't take anything out. Instead, she got the watering can and went out to her husband's store and watered each plant just until water dripped from the bottom of the pot. Franklin watched his wife. Her back was hunched over. "Stand up straight," he wanted to yell at her. Bell finished watering and headed back to the kitchen. For once, she wanted to consult with her husband about what they should eat tonight.

In the truck Ruby had wanted to cry and then again when she signed in at the front desk and while she waited for the movers to bring up her bed and the last of her boxes. But now that she was finally alone, all she wanted to do was to touch every inch of her new apartment.

Then she remembered the food her mother had packed for her. The shopping bag was squashed between two boxes. It was tied with bakery string. Ruby took a long time undoing the knots. The food was still warm. She lined up the containers in the refrigerator. The last container had soy sauce wings. Ruby wasn't hungry but she took out a wing. She pulled a chair over to the window and sat down. Her mouth felt too dry to eat, but she kept taking bite after bite.

It was evening and people were walking home from the train station. They carried small bags of groceries, not a big bag of everything they needed, but just the things they needed to get through the night, maybe a few tomatoes and a cucumber to throw together with the slightly wilted lettuce at home. Other people stopped at the Taquería on the corner. They came out with their dinner in paper bags.

Lights were starting to come on in the apartments across the street. Ruby chewed on another chicken wing. She always hoped to see people having sex, but so far the closest she had come was the time she had seen a woman taking off her shirt. One minute the woman had a tight black T-shirt on and the next minute she had both arms stretched above her head and then she was naked. Ruby had stood frozen on the street below until the woman moved away from the window and then Ruby had walked on.

But today, no one was taking their clothes off. A man who looked as if he worked for the electric company walked into a room and turned on the television, plopping down in front of it without taking off his jacket. In another apartment, a woman opened a can of chili. Other apartments were still dark.

Ruby had been looking into one of the darkened apartments for some time when she realized that it was just as easy for her neighbors to look into her apartment. She stepped away from the window and then peered out again. Everyone was going about their business. But that didn't mean they wouldn't spy on her later. She felt calmer when she got her list out and wrote: "Buy curtains."

The apartment was a cracker box, self-contained, no extra rooms or hallways to worry about. She waited for a feeling of relief or joy or even remorse, but she felt nothing except a mild worry about her laundry. She had meant to do it the day before she moved out but hadn't gotten around to it.

If she wasn't going to cry, she might as well eat another wing. She did and then she washed her hands and moved her furniture around until it was dark. It was late at night before everything was in its rightful place, but finally the bed found a place by the window, the desk and bookcase formed a tiny study in one corner, and she put the palm tree between the kitchen table and the bed to separate the kitchen from the bedroom. The last thing she did was to find her fancy white sheets and put them on her bed. By then, it was too late to do laundry.

It was also too late to buy curtains. She looked out the window again and panicked at the thought of people spying on her while she slept. But no one was watching. She told herself that no one wanted to spy on a Chinese girl from Queens anyway.

The phone company said they would turn on her service by Friday. She went down to the phone in the lobby to call her mother.

"You got there okay? How is it?" Bell said with forced cheerfulness.

"It's great, nice and clean, just painted. I mean it's kind of small, but it's okay."

"You eat yet?"

"I ate that chicken. How're you doing, Mom?"

"Fine, fine. Well, you better go get some rest now. You must be tired."

"I'm not tired. Did you eat?"

"Kind of. Your father eat in the living room today. I guess he like to watch his program. Well, getting late. Better get something hot to drink." And then Bell hung up.

Ruby stood in the hallway, holding the phone. Her father had eaten in the living room. Ruby hadn't thought that they would go back to their old ways so quickly. She hung up the phone and dragged her feet along the carpeted hallway.

The room was a mess, boxes half unpacked, others taped shut and piled in the center of the room. Suddenly, she was tired. Her bed looked so white and clean that she felt too dirty and sweaty to sleep in it. But the shower curtain was packed away somewhere, so she got under the sheets and tried to stay in one spot so she wouldn't dirty the whole bed.

In the morning, she inspected her sheets. They were still clean. She made the bed and told herself not to be so neurotic. It was Tuesday and she had forty-five minutes to get to work. Almost all her clothes were in the hamper. She fished out a top that she thought was less wrinkled and dirty than the rest. The window seemed especially big and bright. She crouched behind the palm tree to put on her clothes, but it was hard to get her skirt on, so finally she stood up and dressed with her back to the window. Let them look at her backside, she thought.

Then she went to her temp job at Marshall & Potter. She had worked there so much that summer that they called her the permanent temp. The hem of her skirt was unraveling. She was running late, so she packed her sewing kit and later, at work, sat at her desk and mended her skirt. Surely tonight she would do laundry.

It was a slow day at work. The high point of her day was running into Sara Ryan at the copy machine. Ruby had met her earlier in the summer. Before she could stop herself, Ruby asked Sara about her husband just to watch Sara's face light up. Ruby kept asking her questions to keep her there as long as she could. Sara didn't seem to mind; she thought Ruby seemed a good kid, although maybe a little confused. Ruby went back to her desk, feeling dreamy. Looking at her cooking-school brochures made her feel even dreamier. She thought of the day her agency would call her and she would tell them she was working at Le Cirque and didn't need their dumb temp job anymore, but to come by and she'd give them free dessert.

After work she stopped at the ninety-nine-cent store. She needed things for her apartment. Super Savers had everything a girl starting out in the world could want. With a few dollars in her pocket she could buy anything in the store. But the problem was she couldn't decide which things belonged in her new house. Together, all the things in the store were bright and cheap and lovely, but separately they were just bright and cheap.

"It's for garbage," a guy who worked there yelled at her after she had examined every trash can in the store. The ones with pop-up lids cost more but they seemed worth it. After opening and closing every trash can, she bought a twenty-gallon white one with a foot pedal and a pop-up lid. Her hands would stay clean and her trash would be tucked away where no one could see it.

There were checkered curtains and flowered curtains and even a striped pair, but she couldn't settle on one. She felt angry suddenly at the big window in her apartment. After all, she wasn't doing anything wrong. So what if people looked in and saw her. She marched over to the cashier and slapped money on the counter for her trash can and left the store.

On the way home, she stopped at a café. She was in one of her moods when anyone who touched her could have her. Ever since she had fucked Nick in her mother's basement two weeks ago, she hadn't felt the same about him. He was contaminated now. She had seen him a few times since, but things weren't the same.

The café was crowded, but she didn't see anyone she liked. She didn't feel very choosy, but she still couldn't pick anyone. She would just drink her tea. Her refrigerator was filled with food her mother had made. Unfortunately, she was sitting right next to the display case. Before she could stop herself, she had ordered a grilled veggie sandwich with smoked mozzarella and a side of rosemary potato salad. The bill was fifteen dollars, but she paid it with a flourish; she felt a little reckless spending money when she had food at home.

For the next few days she went to work, then stopped at the ninety-nine-cent store, then the café. By the time she got home, it was too late to do laundry. The last wash was at seven-thirty and there was no folding after nine. So, for one more day, she wore a crummy pair of underwear, one that was too tight and cut into her thighs or one with no elastic left. When she had worn the last lousy pair, she went to Truma's and bought three new silk panties. She told herself she needed panties anyway.

After she had been in her house for five nights, she tore herself away from her fancy sheets and went to see Nick. He didn't seem contaminated anymore as they walked up the street to the Lemongrass Grill. Ruby told him about her apartment and said she would have to smuggle him in one night. Later, Nick talked jokingly about marriage, but she knew he was serious. She loved him but was too young, she said. He laughed and said he didn't want to get married either. At the table next to them, a young Chinese couple ordered a whole fried fish.

Ruby and Nick ordered pad thai and string beans with basil. It was good but Ruby kept staring at the fish at the next table. It lay curled on the plate as if it had been caught and cooked in the middle of swimming along, minding its own business. There were pickled carrots and daikon on the side and ginger and red chili sauce on top. The girl who had ordered the fish had short hair and glasses. Her eyes lit up when the waiter placed the dish on the table. Then she picked up her chopsticks and no longer seemed to hear her boyfriend, who was intent on telling her about a paper he was working on. The boyfriend picked at his curried chicken. The girl ate the fish by herself, with great enjoyment.

"They have fish," Ruby said.

"We could've gotten that."

"My mom never taught me." She looked again at the food on the other table.

"What's so hard about it?"

"Look. See how she breaks off the tail and gets the meat out without choking on a bone? See how she pulls off the fin and slides her chopstick in?"

"You don't have to get all worked up. You need sex or something?"

"No. Maybe."

Ruby watched the girl finish the last bite of her dinner, put down her chopsticks and start talking with her boyfriend again. Ruby ate her string beans. She complained that they were too hot and drank lots of water. The couple at the next table paid their bill and the waiter took away the dish with the head and tail and bones on it, but Ruby kept thinking about that fish.

Later, they went to Nick's place. Ever since the night she and Nick had sex in the basement, Ruby would freeze up every time they were in bed together. She still wanted to have sex, but now they did it on the sofa or on the rug in front of the sofa or even in the kitchen. Nick didn't mind, although sometimes he missed fucking her in his big comfy bed.

A week later, Ruby called home to ask her mother what she wanted for her birthday. Her mother would turn sixty in a week, but whenever anyone asked, Ruby would say, "My mom? Oh, I think she just turned fifty." She had said that for some years now and wasn't purposely lying, it was just that sixty seemed lean and dry as leather, but fifty was round and plump like her mother's upper arms, like her stomach behind her apron.

The day her phone service was finally turned on, she called home. Her father answered the phone. "Is that you? Your mother's not here. Out, out, out, all the time, out. I don't know where she go. She don't tell me. When I ask her, she say shopping, but she come home empty-handed, maybe a couple of oranges. Gone all day for a couple of oranges?"

"How're you doing, Dad?"

"Me? Fine, fine. I have a soreness in my arm, can't even lift it. I put some Tiger Balm on it. I ask your mother to rub it for me, but she don't rub hard enough. You have to rub it hard, you know."

As her father talked, Ruby looked out the window and wondered where her mother was. Her mother was hardly home anymore and Ruby needed to ask her things. Like how to make soup to build up her blood and how long you can keep bean curd and how to make her sea bass in black bean sauce. Not that Ruby had the ingredients, but just listening to how she made it would be enough.

"So, how's everything with you? Everything okay?" Franklin said.

She hardly knew how to answer. He had never asked her how she was before. "I'm okay. Just setting up."

"Did you eat anything? Who do you eat with?"

"Who do I eat with?"

"You eat with somebody?"

"Sometimes I eat with friends. Sometimes I eat by myself."

"Oh. By yourself. I see." He seemed saddened by her answer.

"But sometimes I eat with people. Remember Nick? We had Thai food the other day."

"Nick? Right. Nick."

"Anyway, I want to know how Ma makes her sea bass."

"When she come home, I tell her you call."

Chapter 23

After she hung up the phone, her boxy apartment felt too quiet. From down the hall, she heard a neighbor opening her door. Ruby jumped up and grabbed the half-filled garbage bag from the kitchenette and walked casually down the hall as if she just happened to be on her way to the trash chute. She had never lived in a building with a trash chute before. In fact, she had just found out about taking the trash out by opening a slot in a wall as if you were mailing a letter but instead you tossed in a bag of garbage and walked away without worrying about turning bags inside out or about dogs getting into your trash and littering the front of your store so you'd get a ticket. What would they think of next?

Her neighbor made a sound of impatience as she locked her door. Ruby waited for her to look up, but the woman turned and walked briskly toward the elevator. The sign by the trash chute warned against incinerating paint cans, oil-soaked rags and camphor balls. Ruby stopped to consider the contents of her garbage bag before sending it down the chute. Then she went back into her apartment. She had only wanted to say hello.

A walk, she would go for a walk. Her clothes lay scattered around the room and piled up in the closet. She still hadn't done laundry. She pulled on a pair of jeans and a T-shirt that was an awkward length. Her clothes didn't actually show dirt and they didn't exactly smell, but there was a grubbiness about them, as if they'd picked up the smells from everywhere she'd been—smoke, sex, old food.

As she was lacing up her boots and wondering when she'd start feeling at home in her apartment, the phone rang. She jumped for it. It was Miranda. Ruby hadn't seen her all summer. Miranda was having a last-minute party, would Ruby like to come? "You saved my life," Ruby told her. If Miranda hadn't called, there was a good chance Ruby would've ended up in some crowded bar.

Ruby stood in the deli, trying to decide between beer and flowers. At school, Miranda had coached Ruby on how to use a tampon. She had also advised her to get rid of her pastel clothes and her beige pumps. Ruby had been glad for her friend's help. Drinking was important but so was ambience, she thought, as she decided to get both the beer and the flowers. She hoped it would be a dark party with dancing and not a bright party with talking and bad music, like the last one she had gone to.

When she got there, Miranda berated her for disappearing all summer, then kissed her on both cheeks. Ruby handed her the gladiolus, which were just starting to open, and the six-pack. Miranda gave her another kiss and ordered her to get her butt over to the kitchen and get herself a drink. She sure looked like she could use one, her friend said affectionately.

Ruby headed for the kitchen. In the living room, a few people were trying to dance. Ruby stood in the doorway and watched. She felt grateful suddenly that later she wouldn't have to stand on the corner trying to find a cab that would go to Queens.

Hazel was standing in the kitchen. She was drinking a beer and just starting to feel that being single wasn't so bad after all. Girls were a distraction she didn't need at the moment. Then Ruby came into the kitchen and Hazel changed her mind. Hazel had a weakness for beautiful women in frumpy clothes. They both stood absolutely still and their eyes went wide, as if they were in shock. They looked away at the same time.

Hazel wasn't pretty like the girls Ruby usually lusted after.

She was tough. Ruby had never wanted to kiss a smoker before. Hazel drank her beer as if she were in a big hurry. Then she lit another cigarette before she had finished her first one. Ruby realized that Hazel was even more nervous than she was. That made her relax just enough to walk over to her without tripping.

They said hello and then they just looked at each other. "You need another drink?" Ruby asked her finally. Hazel squeezed close to the counter so Ruby could open the refrigerator. Ruby took out two bottles. She had to concentrate to get them open. "So, what do you do?" Ruby asked her and then kicked herself for asking such a dull question.

"You ever look at toy boxes? Like on the side, it might say 'Collect All Ten Action Figures.' That's me. That's what I do."

"You love your job, I can tell," Ruby said.

"God. I keep saying I'll get my portfolio together one of these days. You know how many people are looking for illustration work in this city?"

"A lot?"

"About six." They laughed. Ruby couldn't tell if Hazel was just being friendly. She wasn't. "What about you?" Hazel said.

"I'm a temp." Ruby wanted to tell her about cooking school but was afraid she'd blurt out that she was dying to cook for her, that she was seized with a sudden desire to shop at open markets for her, to buy only the most beautiful string beans and patty-pan squash and red bliss potatoes and herbs from Amish farmers. She also wanted to run out and buy some phyllo dough and wrap up something fancy in it and bake the whole thing until it was golden brown. "I might go to cooking school," Ruby said. "Maybe you'll come for dinner some night. I'll cook." She told herself not to be so forward. At least she didn't say she wanted to kiss Hazel, which was what she was really thinking. Hazel's lips looked round and soft, not like the thin line Ruby was used to kissing.

Ruby watched her hand reach out and touch Hazel's sleeve. Right after that, Hazel reached out and touched the front of

Ruby's hair where it was white. "Where'd you get that from? Your high-powered temp job? Or heartbreak?" Hazel asked.

Ruby stood very still and when Hazel took her hand away, Ruby wanted to say, "Do that again. Touch me again." She watched Hazel smoke. "Heartbreak. I went away to school. Left my mom," Ruby said suddenly.

"Oh, honey," said Hazel. Their joking tone was gone now. People came into the kitchen for beer.

Hazel and Ruby talked and looked at each other. It seemed an agreement that they would leave together at the end of the evening, although no one said anything about it. But Ruby couldn't believe it and then she started wondering whether there was an agreement after all and suddenly she felt foolish. She told Hazel she had to say hello to someone and then she fled.

Outside, she walked a few blocks and then she stopped. It was too late to go back. Hazel would think Ruby was stupid, running out and then running back, as if she couldn't make up her mind. When Hazel touched her hair, Ruby had almost kissed her. But instead Ruby had squeezed her hand. God, who knew that touching someone's hand could make her so wet.

It was too much for her, so she had to run out. Maybe Hazel was just a flirt. Maybe Ruby had imagined the whole thing. But if she hadn't, they would've left together and caught a cab. Maybe they would've kissed in the backseat.

Then she thought about Nick. Although she had just met Hazel and might never see her again, suddenly it seemed wrong that she was with Nick. He seemed too tall or maybe too pale. Too easy somehow.

But at least she wasn't scared of him. At the party she hadn't thought about him, but now she wanted to see him. He would be sleeping, his long white body curled around the pillow she slept on when she stayed over. How soft and white he was when he was sleeping. Like a worm. Somehow, thinking of him as a worm endeared him to her. He might be a worm, but at least he was her sweet white worm.

When they were fucking he wasn't a worm, though. He was a man in bed and she liked that. She walked faster. Hazel's face would have been soft next to hers. Ruby remembered one night she had complained about Nick's bristles and he had gotten out of bed and shaved.

Then she was turning the key slowly in the lock, stepping carefully over the creaky boards. She climbed into bed next to him. His back was warm. She curled behind him and he turned to her as if he had been expecting her, and pushed his face into her breasts.

"Where you been all my life?" he said. She missed Hazel and kicked herself for leaving. He started kissing her neck, her long, curving neck that was now an asset, but back in junior high they had called her Pipe Neck and she couldn't get a date.

In her ear he told her all the things he wanted to do to her. That got her going and she pressed her legs together so he could push them apart. He held her down and touched her, slipped a finger in her mouth.

But she was angry now and with one shove she got on top of him and kneeled at his head and lowered herself just out of reach. He said please. When she was close to coming, she put her hands against the wall and moved around on his mouth. The blankets slipped to the floor. Then she slid down and put him inside her. She started moving like she would fuck away any regret she had.

He looked up at her face, which seemed intent, but on what, he didn't know, and his uncertainty made him start to lose it. She kept going, touched his nipples matter-of-factly to make him hard again, but there was something he didn't like about her tonight. With her hand she put him back in her. He came too soon, but she didn't let that stop her, she just hurried herself and came again.

It was past midnight. She sat naked in the warm room. The food was on its way. She had just ordered from Hunan Delight. It was her job; she did a better Chinese accent. Nick and she both agreed the food was better when she ordered. From the bathroom, she heard water running in the sink, then Nick slurping and swishing water around his mouth, and it sounded just like her father gargling at the table after dinner to loosen bits of food stuck in his teeth. Ruby reached into his closet for the dark silk robe he had found for her at Goodwill. She put it on. It cost only a dollar but made her feel rich and slutty at the same time. Her mother had never seen the robe; if she had she would worry that Ruby might catch diseases from other people's clothes. But once she stopped worrying, she'd be impressed: only one dollar. You can't even buy half a chicken for that.

Ruby pulled the blanket over her head so she didn't have to listen to Nick's gargling. Hey Nick, it's Ruby, not Adrian. I like the taste. Adrian was his last girlfriend. She wouldn't kiss him until he rinsed the taste of pussy from his mouth.

He came back to bed. His hands were wet and cold. The doorbell rang and she watched him step into his crumpled boxer shorts and pull on his paisley robe. She laid the bedspread on the floor, picnic-style, and set out plates and bowls. Nick came back as she was setting the kettle on the stove. He shed the robe and the boxers and unpacked the familiar tins. The smell of greasy gringo food mixed with the smell of sex.

For the first time, the sight of his soft penis didn't seem to fit with the tins of dumplings, noodles, rice. It had just been in her mouth, but suddenly she didn't want it so near her food. It seemed too exposed, as it did when she stood behind him, holding his dick over the toilet, assisting. She wanted him to put his boxers back on. Not hungry, she sat with her legs folded under her and picked at her beef lo mein.

"Eat. You ordered all this food. Aren't you hungry?" He offered her an egg roll. Grease fell on her robe when she bit into it, leaving a dark circle. It would never come out unless she got up and did something about it right away. On any other day, she would have jumped up and soaked it in soapy water.

"Nick?" She wanted to say something about going to the party and the woman she kept thinking about.

"Yeah?" He barely looked up.

"The broccoli done enough for you?" she said. He took a piece, crunched it a few times, then swallowed it down. Her robe kept falling open and she wished she had a sash to keep it closed.

"I can eat it," he said.

"I went to a party tonight. At Miranda's."

"You should've told me. I would've gone." He didn't really seem mad.

"I just went. At the last minute."

Nick picked up a piece of duck with his fingers. "So how was it?"

"Oh, same old thing. Everyone was drunk, lots of people making out."

"Really?" He had stopped eating and she could see the interest in his eyes. He loved to watch.

"Did you meet anyone?" He looked down at the food.

"I talked to a few people."

"Who? Who'd you talk to?" He was eating again, so she knew he wasn't worried.

She told him about seeing the old crowd, but she was thinking about Hazel.

"Michael was there? Did he chat you up? He always had a crush on you." He kept putting duck in his mouth. She was talking and not eating. He was eating all the good meaty bits and leaving the bony parts for her. This made her quiet, and she felt sad suddenly that she loved a man who took the good bits for himself. She had been taught to give the good bits to the other person and that the other person would give her the good bits, and in this way, they would take care of each other. She watched the duck disappearing into his mouth. She refused to scrabble around in the dish for the last good bits.

"You kiss anyone?" He stopped eating and waited for her answer. He knew how those parties got sometimes.

"Here. Want a dumpling?" She put one on his plate.

"Did you?"

"In the kitchen." She was about to say she was just joking, that she had wanted to but hadn't.

"Goddamn it, Ruby," he said quietly. He wiped his fingers and now he was mad. "What's he got? A bigger dick? How many dicks do you fucking need?"

"Don't yell at me." Then she sat stony and still. The fatty parts of the duck were turning white. Maybe she could sneak a dumpling while he ranted. She was hungry again. Knowing that Nick could go on, she grabbed him by his shoulders and shook him. He didn't fight her but let his head flop around like a rag doll. That made her remember that she loved him. "Sweetheart. Stop now. I love you," she said. He had gone far away and she pummeled his shoulders, trying to get to him. She longed to slap his face but knew he wouldn't let her. She punched his arm until he winced and grabbed her wrists.

"Stop hitting me. What? You love me or something?"

"Yeah. I love you."

"You love me," he said, serious. She loved him but wondered whether she ought to leave him anyway. She thought of the way he ate his noodles, the excess falling to the plate. That was no reason.

"The dumplings are greasy today," he said finally, pushing at the food as if it were to blame. She sat down next to him. He got up and started clearing the dishes.

He stopped at the door. Without turning around, he said in a low voice, "How come I'm not enough?" She wanted to go to him, but her legs felt stuck to the floor.

"It's not you. I don't know. I met a girl. Her name's Hazel." Making up the kiss had started as a joke, but now it was too late. She would probably never even see Hazel again. When she thought about Hazel she felt afraid, as she had been afraid in the sixth grade when she would sleep over at Mary Ann's house. Ruby wore one of Mary Ann's nightgowns that seemed softer than her own and then she would brush her friend's hair. Then they would get under the covers and practice kissing. They became good at it and Ruby became afraid that she would like practicing better than the real thing, so one night when Mary Ann turned to her and said, "Want to practice?" Ruby answered, "No, thanks," as if beautiful Mary Ann in her long flowered gown had just offered her a hot chocolate or a peanut-butter cookie. Ruby stayed up that night and watched Mary Ann's eyes moving back and forth under her lids.

"Hazel? She's a girl?" Nick had a funny look on his face.

"Yeah, she's a girl."

"Why didn't you say so?"

"I just did."

"I thought you meant another guy."

"Why are you so happy all of a sudden?"

"Oh, I don't know. It's different."

As they had been talking, Ruby had gotten angrier and angrier and now she thought of putting all her clothes back on and going home. Nick opened his arms. "Come here," he said. She went ahead and fit her head carefully against his chest.

"No more fighting," he said.

"Okay." She was tired of talking and still a little drunk.

They were quiet for a few minutes and she was starting to fall asleep when he said, "You know, it's funny how people say, 'Oh, isn't she beautiful when she's angry?'" Something in his tone made her stiffen and draw her arms closer to her chest.

He went on. "How can they mean that? They're just saying that. Just before, when you were standing there in your robe, not holding me, not even looking at me—you know it drives me crazy when you do that, when you go so far away—I was thinking, Who is that ugly Chinese woman standing in my room? But now here you are and you're beautiful. I don't even notice your Chineseness. You're just Ruby who I love." His voice was tender and awed.

His arm draped around her back suddenly felt unbearably

heavy. And hairy. She had never noticed it before. Her arms fell away from his body and she got up to brush her teeth. It was incomprehensible to her that he could sleep without brushing his.

In the bathroom, she thought about Mrs. Strain. Behind her wide straight back, the third-grade class had called her Mrs. Strain the Pain on the Brain. That made them crack up laughing. Mondays meant spelling homework and Fridays meant quizzes. On Monday evenings, Ruby sat at the ironing table and she'd ask her father for a pencil even though she had plenty of pencils in her schoolbag. It made him happy when she asked him for one. He made a big show of choosing the nicest one, a tall one with a good eraser. He sharpened it, inspected the tip and blew the dust away until it was just right.

One night she wrote her homework with special care, recalling penmanship lessons, made sure her swoops and dives stayed within the lines. The spelling words were getting longer and she was writing bigger. They didn't fit five across. She wrote three across and then two on the next line.

The next day she stood in line and looked at Mrs. Strain's hand, brown as her wooden desk and decked out in big silver rings, fingers tapering to dark polished nails. She drew big red checks on other kids' homework. Some kids had done five across. They must have written small. Another kid had done five down. Ruby put her notebook on Mrs. Strain's desk and waited for her check mark.

Mrs. Strain looked at Ruby's notebook as if she couldn't understand it. What was the big deal? Ruby wondered. Three across on one line and then two on the next. Mrs. Strain pointed at the notebook and wrinkled her nose as if she smelled some food she didn't like. "What is this? Some kind of crazy Chinese crossword puzzle? I don't have all day to figure this out." Ruby reached out to take her notebook away from her teacher's eyes. Mrs. Strain slapped her hand and wrote a big red X across the page. Ruby took her notebook, holding it close to her chest so she wouldn't drop it. She went back to her desk.

She put the notebook back in her schoolbag and saw that the hole in her bag had gotten a little bigger. Her mother could sew that for her. Ruby kept her head down as if she were looking for something way in the back of her desk, something that wasn't there anymore. They were all waiting and she kept her face in her desk so they couldn't see her. I will not cry, she told herself, I will not.

Maybe if she looked hard enough for that thing at the back of her desk, she would find it. Maybe it was back there behind the pencil case and the broken eraser. She had liked Mrs. Strain.

At lunch when the other kids pulled up the corners of their eyes and chanted "Ching Chong, Ching Chong," she did not cry. She did not cry as she walked home, dragging her schoolbag on the sidewalk. She did not cry at dinner when her mother asked her how was school today or even when she said fine and then shut her mouth real quick.

She cried in Nick's bathroom. She wanted to tell him why her face was twisted shut. Her angry face, her ugly Chinese face. Not you too, Nick, she said to him in her head, not when I trusted you with my face, trusted you not to slap it and twist it out of shape.

She dressed quietly.

Chapter 24

*H*er heart was broken, but in the mornings she still got up and put on her temp clothes and went to work and typed and answered the phone. Some days she stood a long time in front of her closet. When she wore her tight clothes, men looked at her and tried to talk to her. She didn't want that. When she wore her big clothes, she felt that she was flopping around inside them, a little lost.

She and Nick had made plans together. Now they weren't going to cook the steaks in the freezer or take up jogging or go to London for Christmas. It had been a week since they had broken up. He called her every day, but she wouldn't talk to him. She was dying to talk to him. When she knew he wouldn't be home, she called his machine to listen to his voice. One night she was walking home from the train station when she looked up and saw a cognac ad on the side of a bus. Nick liked cognac. First he had made her admire the golden color, but she still hadn't liked it. Remembering the terrible taste almost set her to crying again as she walked home.

Good thing tomorrow was her mother's birthday. Ruby could distract herself with shopping for a present. She called her mother, but instead of asking her what she wanted for her birthday, she said, "Where were you yesterday? Dad said you were out. He said you're always out."

"Look like a nice day, so I take a walk. I go up to the fruit store. The grapes look nice and big, so I buy a pound."

"Dad said you were gone for hours."

"After I go to the store, I walk to Elmwood."

"Elmwood? You walked all the way to Elmwood?"

"They open up a new hamburger joint over there. You know me, I don't eat hamburger, but I go in and order a cup of tea. Seventy cents for a little cup of tea!"

"What kind of hamburger joint? McDonald's?"

"Yeah, McDonald's. People were eating Big Macs."

"You went to McDonald's."

"I sit there, and after a while I feel kind of hungry. So guess what? I got a fish burger."

"A fish burger?"

"It was good." Bell talked quickly so she wouldn't have to mention that in the morning she had stood in front of the closet looking at some shirts that Ruby had left behind, and that she had touched them and taken them out and smelled them. To see if they needed washing, she had told herself. Then she had tried them on. The sleeves were a little long, but otherwise they fit.

"Hey, you left some shirts here," Bell said.

"Ma, what's the matter?"

"One blue one, one white one. You still need them?"

"My shirts? I'll get them tomorrow. What's wrong?"

"You eat yet? You better go get something to eat." There was a strange hitch in Bell's voice.

"I'm not hungry. I just ate. Wait, Ma. Don't go yet."

"Getting late. You must be busy."

"I'm not busy. What're you doing now?"

"I better get ready and cook."

"Me and Nick broke up," Ruby blurted out.

"Nick?" Bell looked up at the ceiling as if she couldn't quite recall the man who had called there every day.

"We broke up. But it's okay. I don't care."

"What happen? He try to go with another woman?" He didn't look like that kind of guy, but you never knew.

"He's not like that." Ruby was tempted to tell her mother

that she had tried to go with another woman and that many of their fights had been about her going with other men.

"He was kind of skinny. Easy to get sick. How he take care of you if he so skinny?"

"Who needs him to take care of me? I can take care of myself."

"I know, I know. If you can do it yourself, do it yourself. But sometime—"

"He's a grown man and he doesn't know how to eat. He takes all the good parts for himself." As soon as she said it, Ruby wished she had kept quiet.

Bell's face was grave. Not knowing how to eat was worse than going with another woman. "You don't need that," Bell said when she finally spoke. Then she said, "I better go cook now." After her mother hung up, Ruby put the phone down quietly and pictured her mother in her new yellow kitchen. It was too bright, Ruby decided, way too bright. She imagined her mother rushing over to the rice barrel and measuring out a cupful. Then she would take the cleaver from the drawer and chop and chop.

On the Saturday her mother turned sixty, Ruby took the Long Island Rail Road home. She had always known that it stopped in Springfield, but it had never occurred to her to take it. The railroad was a train that other people rode on, not people who lived behind a laundry. You had to live in Long Island and have a white sofa. Ruby was a subway kind of girl. But that morning she couldn't stand the idea of going down the stairs and waiting on the platform and being underground for two hours with nothing to look at but grumpy people and, out the window, the long dark tunnels.

So she paid the extra money and took the railroad. The seats were padded and the trainmen wore little caps. They asked her where she was going, not like on the subway, where no one cared. In her lap she carried her mother's present. It was hard to find something that her mother would like; she didn't care for flowers or candy or jewelry or perfume.

The train got to Queens so quickly that Ruby didn't have enough time to get nervous about coming back. The train let her off at the other end of Springfield and she walked past the beef-patty shops and the beauty parlor with a-hundred-percent-human hair, past the tropical ice cream shops and the people sitting on folding chairs on the sidewalk, telling each other their troubles. And what troubles they were!

When she got within a few blocks of the laundry, she saw a small figure moving back and forth in front of the store. She had to get closer before she saw it was her father sweeping the sidewalk. When she was a kid, if she was a little late getting back from school, she would find him outside, sweeping. The whole block would be clean, no candy wrappers or broken glass. When he spotted her, he'd put down his broom and go inside. On the stove would be a bowl of Campbell's keeping warm and he would make fried-egg sandwiches.

Now he was sweeping again. He stooped to pick up a soda bottle.

"Hi, Dad."

"If I don't pick up these bottles, some kid might come by and throw it through my window."

"How's your arm? Still sore?"

"I'm not fifty anymore." He leaned against the broom and looked across the street.

"Hey, I took the railroad today."

"The railroad? How about that? I live here over twenty years and I never took that train. How was it?"

"Fast. Fancy. I liked it." They walked toward the kitchen. Bell was stirring her big soup pot. "Hey, Ma. Happy Birthday." Ruby bent and kissed her mother on the cheek. Bell tilted her face slightly to help her out.

"Nice dress. Kind of fancy. How come you're dressed up?" Bell said.

"I have to do laundry. Everything else was dirty," Ruby said.

"Want some soup?" Bell said to her.

"Hey, that plant out in the store has new flowers. Did you see it?" Franklin said.

"Kind of," Ruby said. Her father stood looking at her. "Well, let's see it," she said. She left the kitchen and stood in the store and looked at the cactus with white flowers all over it. "That's real nice," she said. From the kitchen, she could hear her mother dishing up the soup. She admired the flowers some more, then she said, "I guess I better go eat my soup now."

"Yeah, your soup must be ready."

Ruby went back to the kitchen. She didn't know if she had spent enough time looking at the flowers, but she didn't want the soup to get cold. Her mother watched her as she was eating. Then Lily and Hector came in with a big box wrapped in gold paper. They all kissed hello. They had never done that before, but it seemed the right thing to do. Lily had lipstick on. It made a smudge on Ruby's cheek.

"Hey, did you hear about those bees? Killer bees, swarms of them. They killed a man down in Georgia. He was out in a field," Franklin said. He stopped, as if suddenly too tired to finish his story. Bell had taken out her chopping board and was smashing cloves of garlic. "So the bees . . ." Franklin started again.

Bell put down her cleaver and turned around. "The bees?" she said in a low voice.

"That's right. They got him. Hundreds of bites. He tried to run. But he was a goner."

"Those bees, you think they can fly over here?" Bell said.

"They sure can. But they won't," Franklin said.

Hector pushed the gold box at Bell. He liked his mother-in-law but thought she would feel better if she had faith in God. "Here. Open it," he said.

"Nice paper." Bell pulled off each piece of tape without ruining the wrapping. "Very nice. Just what I need," she said. It was a food processor.

"Chops, minces, blends, grinds," Ruby read from the box.

Bell perked up a little. "Does it make juice? Carrot juice?" she said.

"I didn't know you liked juice. They had one that made juice," Lily said.

"We'll exchange it," Hector said.

"I don't really like juice," Bell said. Then she reached for the box from Ruby. She shook it gently before opening it. "Oh, sneakers. These are great." She took off her slippers and tried on the sneakers. "Look just like shoes." She looked quite sporty, testing them out around the kitchen.

Hector and Lily had set up the food processor and were cutting carrots and apples into smaller and smaller pieces. Franklin went into his room and came out with a card. He handed it to Bell, then sat down. Everyone watched her with unrestrained interest. He had never given her anything before except little good-luck envelopes with money inside which she would deposit back into their joint account.

The card had flowers on it and writing. "To my loving wife." When she opened it, two plane tickets fell out. "What's this?" She picked them up by the edges. "Here, read it."

"Looks like two plane tickets to Florida," Ruby said.

Franklin was quiet, watching his wife's face the whole time. He leaned toward her. She leaned toward him too for just a moment. Then she got up and said, "Who wants cake?"

No one answered at first. Franklin sat back in his chair and held the tickets in his hands. Then Hector said, "Cake. I'll have cake."

Bell took a long time undoing the string around the box. Franklin got up and rummaged in the drawer. "You want a knife?"

"I save the string," said Bell. She kept working on the knots. "Those tickets," she said.

"You always wanted to visit Louie and Sheila. And now that you and Ruby not going right now . . ." He turned the tickets over and over as if he couldn't believe them either. Bell had gotten the box open. It was quiet except for slabs of cake falling onto paper plates. She was cutting the cake into very big pieces. None of them ate that much cake, but they all picked up their forks and started eating, as if, by eating it all, somehow things would work out: Franklin and Bell would go to Florida together and visit their old friends. In the afternoon, they would take a picnic lunch to the beach and look out at the water. They would sit at a table under a tree and maybe they would talk. After the sun went down and it got cool, maybe they wouldn't want to leave right away, so Franklin would take his sweater and wrap it around Bell's shoulders.

There was only the soft sounds of cake being washed down with milky cups of tea when Bell said, "Can you get your money back?" As soon as she said it she was sorry. She really did want to go to Florida. While she had been cutting the cake, she had thought for a minute that they could go (after all, her retired friends went away on trips), but then it hit her that they would be the same husband and wife they were now except they would be in Florida and it would be hot and she wouldn't know where to buy groceries, but otherwise they would be the same.

"Don't you want to go?" Franklin said dully. He put his fork on the table.

"Who wants this last piece of cake?" said Bell. No one wanted it. Franklin took the tickets and tucked them back into the card.

"Did you talk to Louie lately? Maybe they don't have room." Bell put some cake on her fork, raised it to her mouth, then put it down again. Her mouth was too sad and small for cake. On the side of her plate was a blue cream flower. Usually, she saved the flower to eat later on a saltine, but today she didn't know if she could eat it.

"They have room. They always invite you to come down," Ruby said. As impossible as she knew it was, she wanted her mother to look up and take the tickets and say, "Yes, what a nice birthday present. Thank you. We'll go and have a nice time in the sun." Even as she wished for it, she knew it was the same as wishing she had been born into another family.

Bell put a piece of cake in her mouth but pulled her lips back, not letting them touch the fork. Then she got up and cleared the table, piling up the uneaten cake. She dumped the paper plates and cake into the trash. No one had ever seen her throw food away.

Her sneakers were black with a light blue design. She did a few knee bends, then put one foot behind to stretch out her legs. She reached for her toes and almost touched them. "These sneakers sure are comfortable. Who wants more tea?" With the kettle in her hand, she did a little jog around the kitchen.

Ruby watched her mother, but she was thinking about the ride home on the railroad. Her mother would insist on walking her to the station, saying she had to pick up some milk. She would leave Ruby on the platform and say she was going home, but she would linger at the shop windows across from the railroad. She would examine the plants outside Woolworth's and check out the vegetables at the green market. Once in a while she would look up to make sure Ruby was still on the platform. Ruby would look down and catch her mother hanging around. She would wave. They would wave a few more times before the train came and then Ruby would wave from her window, not sure if her mother could see her. As the train picked up speed, she would look out the window and watch for the store.

It was getting late but Ruby sat in her mother's house and watched her moving lightly around the kitchen in her new sneakers. Ruby pictured her training every day, running around the house, from the kitchen out to the store and back again, then out the door and around the block, and after a while, the whole neighborhood. She'd start out slow and steady, run as far as she could, then walk home, swinging her arms. People would start to recognize her and would say hello as she ran past. She'd run around the whole neighborhood, up and down every little side street. But soon even that run would be too small, so she would keep on, past the junior high school, past the library and the supermarket, past the catering place and the hamburger joint and the bar with topless dancers. It would be easy for her to run in her new sneakers. She'd run past Dunkin' Donuts, where she and Ruby used to go for glazed crullers, past all the tambourine-shaking churches, past her old lady friend, who would wave from her window. She'd run past all the familiar streets, Main, Cedarhurst, Hollis, Union. She'd keep running, past streets she had never seen before, past houses with people cooking and eating, talking and yelling, fighting and loving in dark rooms. She'd keep running, the sound of her own breathing in her ears, arms and legs pumping their long easy stride, taking her away to another place.

Chapter 25

It was morning. Her mother's birthday was over and Ruby was back in her own apartment. For weeks now, she had dropped her clothes wherever she happened to take them off. Slowly now, she started to gather her laundry from the floor and the chairs and the bed. She got the towels and the mat from the bathroom and the kitchen cloths. Instead of lifting the laundry bag onto her shoulder and going down to the corner laundromat, she sat down again with the heavy bag in her lap. Looking for quarters, checking pockets for old tissues, deciding whether it would be two big machines or three little ones was too much to handle. She dumped the sack on the floor and pushed it over with her foot. God, she was sick of looking at her own dirt.

The summer she and Nick lived in the same dorm, they would do their laundry together. After the wash cycle started, they would add soap and then go to breakfast at the Silver Spoon Diner. As they ate their eggs and toast, the machines were washing away the week's dirt, spinning the water from their clothes, and as they drank the last of their tea and coffee, the machines were slowing to a stop. If she hadn't been so hungry, she would have liked to sit on the bench and watch Nick's undershirts twisting around her pajamas, her jeans rolling on top of his, until finally the tiny red light would turn off and the machine slow to a stop.

If she called Nick, she could tell him about her mother's birthday and the tickets to Florida and how it had been too late.

No one was going to Florida. Not Ruby and her mother, not her mother and father. Maybe some other time, her mother had said.

Sometimes Ruby told herself that she had never loved Nick at all. She knew he had adored her. He'd been an oaf at times, but he had loved her and she wondered if that wasn't worth something. When she lay in bed at night and looked out the window at the bit of sky there and listened to her neighbors going into and out of their apartments, she thought maybe she would call him and they could be friends. After all, she didn't hate the guy. She ignored the feeling that she was tricking herself, that coffee and talk was only an excuse. It would take her another month to call him and then they would go out to dinner and she would remember how easy it was to be with him and at the end of the night, when he had walked her home and stood outside and asked if he could come in and see her new place (since it was late and no one would know), she would open the door, as later she would open her legs, in welcome. Afterward, she would be sad and would let him comfort her. It would still be over, but because she wanted him for the night, she would end up having him for another year before she would finally leave again. He would never get over the shock of her leaving him for a woman.

But as she sat there with her laundry, she wasn't ready to call yet. She got up and started going through her pockets looking for quarters. And then she realized she didn't have any detergent. The bundle of clothes lay on the floor in front of her. She had never felt quite so alone.

Before she could change her mind, she picked up the bag and dragged it down to the laundromat and, for the first time, really looked at the handwritten sign in the window next to the national flag of Ecuador. The sign read: "Service or Self-Service. Your Choice." She dumped the bag on the counter and stood touching the tightly packed clothes, much as she liked to touch her stomach after eating a big dinner.

The old couple behind the counter looked up from the news

program, which showed people standing next to piles of rubble that just a few hours ago had been their homes. The roof and the ceiling and the walls were gone, but a few things stood upright, like a refrigerator on a front lawn. A woman opened the door of the refrigerator and took something out and ate it. It looked like a pickle. A few people were stooped over, as if suddenly old. Others looked down at the ground, kicking bits of brick and wood, looking up and down the street as if they had misplaced their houses and would remember any minute that they lived across the street, where the buildings were still standing.

"A terrible thing," the woman behind the counter said. She stood up and took off her big square glasses and rubbed her eyes. Her husband started to get up too, but she motioned for him to keep his seat on a milk crate. "For drop-off?"

"For drop-off," Ruby said dumbly. She watched as the woman put the bag on the scale. The needle jumped back and forth before settling on eighteen pounds. Ruby folded the ticket into small squares and tucked it into her pocket. There was no struggle now. She felt such relief that she wanted to climb onto the scale, curl up on top of her laundry and close her eyes.

"When you need it? Tonight?"

Ruby nodded and the woman turned back to the TV set. Bridges buckled and cars slid into the ocean. From outside the store, Ruby watched the woman dragging the bag over to the row of machines, fishing around in her pocket for quarters.

All day, Ruby thought about the woman and her silver husband washing her clothes, talking to each other in Spanish, a little boy (their grandson) doing homework on the bench out front. The woman's shirt had been full of tiny holes from the tickets she pinned to herself as she worked. She would sort Ruby's panties into darks and lights and she might avert her eyes from whatever stains were there. Her hands wouldn't flinch as she turned socks inside out. Maybe she would put the delicate things in a little mesh bag.

At the end of the soak cycle and the beginning of the wash

cycle, she would add bleach to the whites and later she would add fabric softener. The wheels on the cart would stick just a little as she wheeled the clothes from the washer to the dryer, but she would pull it just so and the cart would follow. Another customer might come in and she would take his laundry as casually as she had taken Ruby's.

Then the dryer would stop and she would reach her hand in to see if everything was dry, otherwise she would ask the boy to bring her some change from the box under the counter. When everything was truly dry, she would shake the wrinkles from the sheets hot from the dryer. She would call her husband over, hand him one end, fold the sheet in half the long way, then in half again. They would walk toward each other, the husband handing over his end.

Ruby thought about them as she went about her day, as she swept the hair from the floor and scrubbed out the bathtub and made a shopping list. She put her head down as she passed the laundromat. On Broadway, there were pumpkins at every green market. She patted them and kept walking. She stopped in front of Citarella Fish. There was such a glamorous display in the window that you could almost forget about the blood and the smell and the scales flying across the room. She went in. The sea bass were dark and shiny. She touched one with her finger. It was cold and slippery. She picked it up by its tail. Then she dropped it back onto the ice and walked out of the store.

At home, Ruby took the ticket from her pocket and unfolded it. Then she called home. She wanted to say something to her father about the Florida tickets, but instead she told him she had forgotten to get her mother's recipe for sea bass and would he tell her to call when she got home.

When Ruby went to pick up her laundry, the woman was wiping down the tops of the machines with a cloth and the man was mopping the floor, washing away the powdery soap that crunched underfoot like sugar. She thought the couple looked at each other as she walked in, so she listened to their talk to see if they said *la chinita,* the Chinese girl. The laundromat smelled warm and clean. Ruby wanted to take the washcloth from the woman, dip it into the bucket of soapy water and finish the rest of the machines. "I've washed people's clothes too, it's just this one week; next week I'll wash my own clothes," she wanted to tell them. The woman came over and took the ticket and handed her the bag of freshly washed and folded clothes and smiled as if nothing was wrong, but Ruby knew she couldn't go back there. She would have to go to the other laundromat, which was four blocks away and looked like the kind of place where the dryers didn't get hot enough no matter how many quarters you put in, and if you stepped out to get a cup of tea and didn't come back in time, people would steal your clothes.

The counter was warm and smooth. Ruby stood there and then she reached into her pocket and tried to give the woman a couple of extra dollars. "Please," Ruby said and finally the woman shrugged and took the money. The bag of laundry was small and dense now, easy to carry.

At home, there was a message from her mother. As she listened to the message, she opened her laundry bag slowly, as if afraid of what she would find. Her clothes were stacked neatly and everything seemed cleaner and softer than when she washed them herself. The socks were paired, the fitted sheets tucked neatly into their corners, even her panties were folded into perfect little squares. It seemed a shame to wear any of it and start dirtying it all over again.

On the machine, her mother was speaking slowly. "First, pick a sea bass with clear eyes, not cloudy. When you get home, wash it in cold water, inside and out. Make sure there's no more scales left. Soak the black beans in some warm water. Put the fish in a bowl, chop garlic, scallion and ginger. Pour a little soy sauce on it, not too much. Then steam it until it's done, maybe twenty minutes. Heat some oil in a pan. Make sure it's hot, but not smoky. Pour it over the top. Watch out for small bones."

EATING CHINESE FOOD NAKED

MEI NG

ABOUT THIS GUIDE

The suggested questions are intended to help your reading group find new and interesting angles and topics for discussion for Mei Ng's *Eating Chinese Food Naked*. We hope that these ideas will enrich your discussion and increase your enjoyment of the book.

Many fine books from Washington Square Press include Reading Group Guides. For a complete listing, or to read the Guides on-line, visit
http://www.simonsays.com/reading/guides

DISCUSSION QUESTIONS

1. What does Franklin's fixation on bad news reveal about his character?

2. Bell, the mother, is constantly preparing and touching food, particularly when she is nervous. How is this relevant to the title of the novel?

3. How did the lack of affection in Ruby's household affect her behavior as an adult?

4. Why is the trip to Florida such an important, yet volatile plan? Why does Bell cancel it?

5. Franklin does not allow Bell to attend English language classes. Why not? How does this further isolate Bell?

6. Why is Franklin so interested in the squirrel trap? If the squirrel was destroying Bell's garden, why wasn't she more concerned?

7. Ruby had been vehemently opposed to her boyfriend taking his laundry to be done, yet she does that herself later in the novel. What had changed that allowed her to do that?

8. Bell saved the money that she earned while working overtime surreptitiously. Was she planning on leaving her husband? Why or why not?

9. What is the source of Bell's shyness and shame?

10. Why is Ruby's meeting with Hazel at the party significant? How had the importance of this meeting been foreshadowed?

11. Bell hoards things in the basement, such as the dresses she makes for her grandchild Sylvie. What does this tell the reader about the other objects stashed away in the basement?

12. What was Ruby looking for when she went home with strangers?

13. Why do Nick and Ruby break up?

14. Why do the three siblings cry at Van's Bar-B-Que?

15. Food is constantly prevalent in this novel. What does food mean to the different characters? How do they communicate through it?